SNAGGLE TOOTH (A PATRICK FLINT NOVEL)

PAMELA FAGAN HUTCHINS

ABOUT SNAGGLE TOOTH

When a plane crashes at the base of Black Tooth Mountain in a wicked summer storm, Patrick Flint's moral compass leads him away from a trail ride with his family and to the wreckage in a search for survivors. But what he finds may teach him that not everything is what it seems, and not every life is worth saving.

FREE PFH EBOOKS

BEFORE YOU BEGIN READING, you can snag a free Pamela Fagan Hutchins ebook starter library—including an exclusive Patrick Flint short story, *Spark*—by joining her mailing list at https://www.subscribepage.com/PFHSuperstars.

CHAPTER ONE: FLY

Patrick

THE JAGGED OUTLINE of Black Tooth Mountain loomed outside the Piper Tri-Pacer, so close that Patrick Flint felt like if he opened the window and reached out, he'd be able to touch the cold, unforgiving rock with his fingertips. His pulse accelerated. The peaks exuded a powerful magic. If Wyoming's Bighorn Mountains were his church, the place he felt his strongest connection to God, then Black Tooth was its steeple. If he weren't flying the airplane, he would have closed his eyes for a moment of reverence.

A hideous sound inside the plane broke the spell, loud enough that he heard it through his headphones. He banked into a turn that would align the plane to skirt the peaks, on course for a landing strip at the Dubois Municipal Airport, one hundred and fifty miles away. When the Tri-Pacer had leveled out, he looked over at his sixteen-year-old daughter and unwilling co-pilot for the day. Her face was buried in a brown paper bag with only her blonde hair showing. A book lay face down in her lap. *Julie of the Wolves.*

"Mind over matter, Trish."

Her blue eyes lifted and met his. "I've never even understood what that means."

Patrick had been dealing with Trish's motion sickness since she was a small child. She used to throw up before he even put the car in gear. He knew the fluid in her inner ear was not her friend, but she made it far worse for herself by looking down at a book. "Eyes on the horizon. You know better than to read in a plane. It makes it worse."

"Can we just go home? I have plans." She retched again, but it only resulted in dry heaves.

"Drink some water." He gestured at the canteen he'd brought with them. It was wedged between the seats. "We'll go home after we fuel up in Dubois and drop off the supplies for the Fort Washakie Medical Center." While the Riverton Regional Airport was closer to the Shoshone and Northern Arapaho Wind River Reservation clinic, he didn't like competing with the commercial airliners, and Fort Washakie nurse Constance Teton had agreed to meet him at the smaller airfield in Dubois.

"How much longer until we land?"

"An hour."

She rolled the top of her sloshing bag. It looked dangerously close to bursting, and he was relieved when she set it on the floor. She picked up the canteen and gulped.

"Little sips. Come on, you know this."

She rolled her big eyes. He remembered wistfully the days before she'd mastered the eye roll. Those eyes had gazed at him like he was her hero. It had been a while since he'd seen that expression on her face, at least directed at him. But she took a smaller sip and capped the water. "Next time bring Perry. He loves to fly."

"I never get any time with my best girl anymore. And you'll be leaving us soon."

"Dad, it's 1977. I haven't even started my junior year of high school. I'm not leaving until August of 1979. That's like *forever*, you know?"

"Two years. A blink." She wouldn't understand how fast time flew until she was a parent herself.

She sighed and stared out the window.

He admired the heavily treed terrain as it flashed beneath them. He'd had a dual purpose for this flight today. The first was to log hours in the Tri-Pacer while doing something useful—delivering an old portable x-ray machine that the hospital in Buffalo was retiring and donating to the Indian Health Service clinic. He'd finalized the purchase of the Tri-Pacer only a week ago, after leasing it for the last two years. He needed to know the aircraft like he knew the human anatomy. It had taken him four years of medical school, several of residency, and nearly three of practicing medicine to get to that level of expertise. He'd been a licensed pilot for only four years, and he wanted to move on to studying for his instrument rating, as soon as he felt he was an expert on everything about his machine.

The other reason for the flight was to get a bird's eye view of Highland Park. In mountain parlance, a park was basically a meadow, although usually a large one. In this case, it was an immense treeless expanse, a last gasp of breath before the ebony rocks of Black Tooth jutted toward the sky in dramatic angles and jumbles. He planned to trail ride up to the park that weekend for a campout with his kids and his buddy Henry Sibley.

The timing was right. His family had just concluded their highly stressful testimony in the trial of Barbara Lamkin, Trish's former basketball coach. The woman had murdered the rival for her affections, Jeannie Renkin, the wife of her lover, the *then*-sitting District Court Judge in Johnson County, Wyoming, Harold Renkin. Unfortunately, the Flints' son, Perry, had been the sole witness to Lamkin's crime, and Lamkin had tried to snuff him out, along with Trish and Patrick's wife Susanne. A truck wreck on the way to Lamkin's hideaway, combined with Perry's heroism, had saved their lives. The trial had been delayed until Lamkin delivered the judge's son. Johnson

County Deputy Ronnie Harcourt and her husband Jeff were fostering the infant boy, and they would be allowed to adopt if Lamkin was convicted. Patrick couldn't see any scenario under which a jury wouldn't put Lamkin in jail for life, at a minimum. She was eligible for the death penalty, which had been reinstated the year before, but he didn't hold out hope that a jury would impose it. For a hang 'em high Western state, Wyoming was notoriously averse to the death penalty.

The trial wasn't over yet, but the last Flint to testify had been Patrick the day before, and now he had a three-day weekend away from it and from work. A trail ride and campout on Highland Park would be the second-best thing to climbing Black Tooth itself. He'd have to save that climb for another time. It required technical rock-and-ice climbing skills his teenagers didn't have. That *he* didn't have. To do that, he'd hitch his wagon to someone who'd already made the climb successfully.

Susanne hadn't even pretended to be disappointed to miss out on the excursion. She did have a good excuse, though. Two in fact. Patrick's sister Patricia was in town, and Susanne had committed to throwing a party-not-to-be-called-a-baby-shower for Ronnie Harcourt. He didn't quite get it. The Harcourts' adoption of little Will wasn't official yet. He'd always thought it best not to jinx things by counting chickens before they hatched. But Susanne assured him that optimism didn't hurt and that the Harcourts were in sore need of all-things-baby and a heaping dose of encouragement. Just as long as they didn't call it a shower. He'd miss his wife, but her absence was for the best. She wasn't a big fan of horses, and, after their June canoeing trip into the Gros Ventre Wilderness had gone wildly off track, it would be wise to give her some space before he roped her into another mountain adventure.

He glanced at his daughter's wan face and sour expression. Maybe talking about the weekend would distract her from how she felt. He pointed out her window. "See that park?"

He snuck a quick look over his shoulder, trying for a last look at the ten Sawtooth lakes that stairstepped between the sheer western wall and the monolithic sawtooth ridge on the east side at the peak. The lakes were just a glint in the distance more than a thousand feet above him. But even from that distance, he was stunned to see a crumbling wall of rock, falling in slow motion. He could almost imagine he felt the debris cutting into his face, that he could smell the dust, that he could hear its roar, but of course, he couldn't.

He shouldn't have been that surprised to see a rockslide, though. People liked to imagine mountains were stable. Solid as a rock. Not so. From avalanches to rockslides to mud slides, gravity had its impressive way. Even the inception of the mountains themselves was about brutal movement. Volcanos. Earthquakes. Plates of the Earth's crust smashing against each other and buckling up like the hood of a car in a head-on collision. In the case of the Bighorn Mountains, thousands of feet of sedimentary rocks on top of an even older base layer of igneous and metamorphic rocks were uplifted by these tectonic shifts to form the range. The granite in that base was what was now exposed on its crest. And the lakes, U-shaped valleys, and cirques—like the steep-sided hollow he could see at the base of Black Tooth and its adjacent peak, Penrose? They were the remnants of huge, powerful, moving glaciers, long since gone.

The mountains provided a harsh and constant reminder that nature was all powerful and ever mercurial, and Patrick loved it. *Maybe I should have been a geologist instead of a doctor.*

Trish grunted, and he tore his attention away from the rockslide.

He tried again to lure her into conversation. "Highland Park is at ten-thousand five-hundred feet, at the base of Black Tooth Mountain. That's where we're taking the horses."

"Yeah. Cool. But about that . . ."

Patrick's chest tightened. He knew where that tone was taking them. "Yes?"

"I was thinking you should make this a guys' trip. You know, just you, Perry, and Henry."

"I thought you wanted to spend time with Goldie." Goldie was her Palomino horse, a beautiful mare who hadn't gotten much attention since Trish had discovered boys.

"I could still ride her. And if I stayed in town, I could help Mom and Aunt Patricia with Ronnie's party."

Not that he was dumb enough to say it to his daughter, but the reason Trish was in the plane today and would be going on the ride that weekend was her mother. With the kids home for the summer, Susanne needed a break from Trish's mouth and attitude. Perry at thirteen was still sweet and not afraid to show his mother that he loved her. Not so, Trish. In Susanne's opinion, it was past time for Patrick to take a turn bearing the brunt of their daughter's teenage ways.

Patrick rubbed his temple. "Nice try. But we're going to have a great time."

A gust of wind tipped the wings of the plane. He tightened his grip on the stick and scanned his instrument panel. Patrick left nothing to chance, from his pre-flight check to constantly monitoring the health of the aircraft, the weather, and his surroundings. All was well, so he relaxed and glanced at Trish.

Her bottom lip jutted out like it had been busted. "Marcy's dad is taking a group of kids out to the lake on his boat on Saturday."

"And it won't be the last time he does it." To cut off further debate, he dipped the left wing. "Look at that. A herd of elk." Twenty or more of the majestic creatures were loping across a high mountain ridge.

"Dad!" Trish's voice was a screech. She clutched his arm, which jerked the stick to the right. The plane wobbled in the air. Her screech gave way to a full scream.

He righted the plane with his left foot pedal and gentle left pressure on the stick. "If you don't like the excitement, don't be pulling on my arm. It's attached to the steering."

"Fine."

He pushed the stick forward a bit, causing the plane to lose some altitude. The elk sped up. For a few seconds, he followed them with the nose of the plane, watching them flow like a school of fish, parting around a rock outcropping, then rejoining on the other side. Then he leveled out for his descent down the western side of the mountains. No use stressing the animals out. They had enough to worry about with predators on the ground and bow hunting season opening soon.

***

AN HOUR LATER, give or take, Patrick dropped in for a landing in Dubois. The airstrip was at 7,300 feet elevation, with spectacular views of red rock formations and the rocky spires of the Wind River Range. The Flints had driven through this area the month before on their way to the Gros Ventre Wilderness, and, despite how poorly their canoe trip had gone, Patrick was glad to be back.

He tore his eyes away from the natural wonders and forced himself to focus on the landing.

He keyed his transmitter. "Dubois, this is Tri-Pacer Niner-Seven-Eight-Charlie-Papa, requesting permission to land."

A few seconds passed, then he heard a staticky reply. "Tri-Pacer Niner-Seven-Eight-Charlie-Papa, this is Dubois. Cleared to land." The voice read off the altimeter setting. "See you on the ground."

"Roger that."

Patrick lined up the plane. When he was parallel with the end of the runway, he cut the throttle all the way back, pushed the stick slightly forward, turned on the carburetor heat, and started his glide. He made a ninety-degree banking turn to the left, recovered, then made another to line the Tri-Pacer up with the runway. *Airspeed looking good.* He kept his neck loose, checking for other aircraft and birds. When he was fifteen feet off the ground, he applied slow back pressure on the stick to break the glide, until, when the plane was about two feet off the runway, the stick was all the way back. The aircraft settled onto its tricycle wheels, and he moved the stick forward. Slowly, he began to bleed off speed. *Perfect.*

A few hundred feet ahead, he saw a dark splotch on the asphalt. At first, he thought it was a shadow, but as he drew closer, he could tell it was three dimensional. An animal? He couldn't choose a course around it until he knew whether it would move, and in what direction. The propeller on the Tri-Pacer's nose was lethal, of course, but impact with a critter could result in a dangerous broken windshield, or, worse, flip the small aircraft. He stepped on the brakes as hard as he dared, not wanting to send the plane cartwheeling from its own momentum. The Tri-Pacer shuddered and shimmied, and he fought to maintain control. *Dear God, don't let me wreck this thing. It's not even paid for yet, and I've got precious cargo.*

Trish had been sleeping, thankfully, but she woke up with a start, her voice panicked. "What's going on?"

"Hold on," Patrick said through gritted teeth.

Ahead, the figure loomed closer. It was low to the ground and completely stationary. Had another plane already hit it? A dead bison? Or moose? A small bear, perhaps? What had seemed dark from hundreds of feet away now revealed itself as blue, red, and black. The blue perplexed him. It wasn't the color of an animal, except for maybe a blue roan horse. Maybe the blue was a tarp or bag? He gauged the distance on either side. There was no room to pass without veering one wheel off the pavement. *Too dangerous at this speed.* He considered opening the throttle, pulling back on the stick, and hopping over it, but decided not to risk it. He was out of room. There was no longer any reason to focus on whether it was moving. He had to double down on stopping.

Thank God he was piloting a Tri-Pacer. The little plane was the next best thing to a helicopter when it came to short strips. And this strip had suddenly become very, very short. With only feet to spare, the Tri-Pacer jerked to a standstill, nose tilted down. Patrick wiped sweat from his brow and exhaled. He had been so focused on stopping that he had almost forgotten about the figure that had made it necessary. Now he couldn't see it.

"Dad . . ." Trish's voice was taut.

Patrick glanced over at her. Her eyes were huge. "What is it? Are you okay?"

"You saw that, right? You saw the man in the runway?"

"The man?"

She nodded. "He looked . . . dead."

A dead man—on a runway? It was hard to believe. Maybe she thought she saw a man, but it was probably a deer. But he had to check it out. "Stay in the plane."

Patrick turned off the switch, advanced the throttle to full forward, then closed it. He opened the lightweight door, not waiting for the propeller to stop spinning, something he would not normally ever have done. He climbed out and jumped to the ground, peering through the distortion caused by the blades. He still couldn't identify the figure. Giving the propeller a wide berth, he ran around his aircraft until he could see the figure in front of it.

And, to his surprise, he saw that Trish was right. It was a man, with an emphasis on "was." An American Indian. And what was left of him wasn't a pretty sight.

CHAPTER TWO: TOSS

Buffalo, Wyoming
Thursday, August 11, 1977, 10:00 a.m.

Perry

"THROW ME THE BALL!" Perry shouted to John Pantis.

John didn't react. What was wrong with him? Perry's best friend was usually completely focused during their personal practice time. Today he'd spent half his time staring off into the distance.

Perry waved his arms. "Hey, John. I'm over here." His voice was a little sarcastic. But then he was a little irritated.

John finally pulled his gaze away from a group of girls who were practicing cheers in the end zone, fifty yards away. "Huh?"

John had grown four inches since last season, which Perry, at five foot three, could forgive him for, but just barely. John was a shoo-in for starting quarterback on their eighth-grade team. But what he'd gained on Perry in height, he'd lost in strength, because Perry had been lifting weights like a mad man for a whole year.

Perry flexed a bicep and admired his muscle. "Dude. Throw. Me. The ball. I'll never make wide receiver if I don't get in some catches."

John's face was flushed. He pulled his arm back and released a wobbly spiral that sailed over Perry's head. Really, what was wrong with him? Perry ran after the ball and tossed it back to his friend. The ball careened off John's chest. This time, Perry followed John's gaze and really zeroed in on the girls. Kelsey Jones was staring back at John, her head cocked, one hand over her mouth as she giggled into the ear of one of the other cheerleaders.

Oh, no. Kelsey? Not John. *He couldn't. He wouldn't.* They didn't have time for girls. Football season was about to start. Not that Perry could fault John on his taste. Kelsey was maybe the cutest girl in their class. Long, straight brown hair. Big, dark eyes. And a wide smile that made Perry smile back at her even when he didn't feel like it. Perry didn't stand a chance with a girl like her. She was taller than him, for starters. And she was popular. Perry was . . . he didn't know what he was. He had friends. He was involved in sports. He wasn't an outcast. He just wasn't the guy most likely to be voted homecoming king their senior year.

But John had a chance. John was pretty much a stud. Perry's mom said his family was Greek. They'd moved to Buffalo the same year the Flints did, from somewhere on the east coast. John had a permanent tan and curly dark hair. And, of course, he was tall. If Perry was as tall as John, he figured girls would be looking at him, too. But that wouldn't mean he'd slack off during football season because of it.

Perry's mind rushed through his options. He could ignore this disturbing development. He could confront John and bring him to his senses. Or he could separate John from the problem. John had gotten a new horse earlier in the summer, and he and Perry had taken some cool rides around their houses, but John had never gone on a real mountain trail ride. Perry knew it was something his friend was dying to do. He could invite him.

It was worth a try.

"Nimrod," he said.

John picked up the ball and shot Perry a funny look. "Sorry."

"My dad is taking us on a trail ride into the mountains tomorrow. We're going to camp out. Want to come with?"

John's vision cleared and his eyes lit up. "That sounds cool. But what about practice?"

"Practice with the team doesn't start until next week. It's our last weekend of freedom."

"But you've been obsessed about our practices."

"Sure, because it's the only way we're going to make starting quarterback and wide receiver. But I guess it's okay for us to take a few days off. As long as we bring a ball with us. We can get in some work on the mountain."

"Far out." John lifted his hand for a high five, and Perry slapped his palm against his friend's.

From way off the field, a man shouted, "Perry Flint, is that you?"

Perry looked over and saw a guy with white-blond hair, the mountains behind him. It was mid-August, and there was barely any snow left on the peaks. It was so far into August, in fact, that it barely smelled like summer anymore. In early summer, he could smell the funny blue trees that his dad called Russian olive out here on the field.

Perry squinted at the guy. He had told his mom he was getting a ride home with John's dad, who had dark curly hair. It couldn't be him. And Perry's dad was flying somewhere with Trish. Anyway, it didn't look like him either.

The guy waved, heading Perry's way. Perry waved back and walked toward the man, with John right behind him. Then Perry got a funny feeling. The trial. He'd testified the day before, in the morning. It had brought back a lot of bad memories of the night Coach Lamkin had tried to kill him—and his mom and his sister—but some good ones, too. He had pulled his mom and Trish from a truck before it blew up, after a mountain lion ran in front of them and the coach drove it off the side of a cliff. People had made a really big deal about that. He'd been kind of a hero, he guessed. There had been a lot of reporters in town for the trial wanting to know all the gritty details. They'd camped out at the courthouse and even showed up at the Flints' front door.

Perry's dad had been polite but firm with them. "No interviews. We all just want it behind us." Privately, he'd told Perry and Trish that he didn't want to contribute to Coach Lamkin getting any more press or glorification.

If this was a reporter, would it be okay with Perry's dad if Perry told the story of how he'd rescued his family? Nothing about the coach, of course.

The guy shouted, "It's George. George Nichols. I'm the electrician. I've been working at your house."

Not a reporter. Perry moved even closer. The guy had killer sideburns, which Perry was definitely going to grow himself, as soon as his facial hair came in. If his facial hair ever came in. His dad had grown a beard last winter, and it was so patchy that his mom used to shake her head and say, "He looks like a mangy dog," when his dad left the room. Then Perry finally recognized the man as George. For a moment, he was disappointed, but then he grinned. Perry's dad had met George at the hospital when George had been working on a job there. He said George was the most handy and practical young man he'd met in a long time, and his dad didn't toss praise around lightly, so Perry knew he liked the electrician.

When George had been working at their house, he had showed Perry how to make sparks by touching two wires together. Then George had told Perry about the time he'd lit a trash can on fire to set off the alarms at his high school so he wouldn't have to take a test. Perry had confessed to George that he'd pulled a fire alarm to get out of school early to go skiing the previous March. George had gotten suspended. Perry had, too, and grounded. They'd talked about football some. George had played safety for the Sheridan Broncs in high school. But what was he doing at the field here in Buffalo?

"Hey, George! What are you up to?"

"I was just doing some work at the school. I decided to come out to the field when I saw people tossing the ball around." George closed the rest of the distance between them.

"It's just me and my friend John. John, this is George."

"Nice to meet you, sir." John shook George's hand.

"Sir? I'm not that old." George guffawed. "But nice to meet you, too, kid."

Perry had an idea. "John's helping me learn to play wide receiver. Do you wanna line up against me while I run some routes?"

George flipped his blond bangs from his forehead. "Sure. Why not?" He started jogging in place, then stretched side to side.

Perry settled into his stance with George in front of him.

George winked. "Don't worry. I'll go easy on you, kid."

Perry laughed.

"Hike," John yelled.

Perry took off running, with George sticking to him like glue. John threw the ball, and Perry leaped for it. As he was coming down, George collided with him, and Perry hit the ground like a sack of potatoes, mouth full of grass and dirt. All the air whooshed from his lungs, and the sky turned black with blinking stars for a few seconds. Then a hand grasped his and George pulled Perry to his feet.

"Man, are you okay?"

Perry nodded. He wasn't, not completely, but he wouldn't have admitted that for anything. Some smelling salts would have been nice, though.

"Are you sure you want to play wide receiver, kid? You're kind of on the small side for it."

Perry would have answered in the negative, if he'd had enough breath to form any words. He made an okay sign and got back down into his stance.

CHAPTER THREE: LAND

Patrick

HOURS AFTER THE DRAMATIC LANDING, Patrick wrapped up his statement to an officer from the Dubois Police Department. Trish had given hers first and was waiting for him at the tiny pilot's shelter with Constance Teton. All in all, the process had been much quicker than Patrick would have imagined. The cops had shown up darn fast for law enforcement in this area, where small cadres of officers had to cover incredible square mileage.

Just as the officer released Patrick, the man's radio squawked. "Be advised that the FBI is on the way to the Dubois Airport crime scene."

Patrick's eyebrows rose. He'd expected Federal Bureau of Investigation involvement with the murder of an American Indian so close to the Wind River Reservation, where they had concurrent jurisdiction with the tribal police. But talk about fast—same day, when they were based out of Billings, over three hundred miles away? Either they were running low on things to do or someone thought this was a big case. It was all the hint Patrick needed to get out of Dubois before someone decided it was essential that he stick around to talk with the Feds as well.

He wiped sweat from his forehead as he walked over to Trish and Constance. It was already nearly eighty degrees out. The women were in the shade of the building. Constance—a tall, pretty Shoshone nurse in her twenties—was standing. She gave off a strong odor of perfume. Without the wind to disperse it, it was the kind of scent that would have given Patrick a headache. Trish was sitting on the ground cross-legged with her chin in her hands, elbows on her knees.

His daughter had met Constance a few months before, on the heels of the murder of Big Mike Teton, Constance's husband. Constance had been in a tailspin at the time. She had convinced herself she had feelings for Patrick, then made a pass at him in front of Susanne and the kids. The incident hadn't created a favorable impression on his family. Now Constance was wearing a diamond on her ring finger, which Patrick suspected meant she was engaged to her boyfriend of several months, Tribal Police Officer Justin Dann. But with their history and with Trish watching and listening, Patrick didn't dare inquire about the woman's romantic life.

An ambulance sounded its siren twice, then slowly drove the remains of the man they'd found in the runway away from the airstrip.

"Hello, ladies. I just have to fuel up, Trish, and we can be on our way. Constance, I hope the clinic can put that x-ray machine to good use."

"We will." Constance was staring after the ambulance. "You know who that was, don't you?"

Patrick cocked his head. "No." Other than a height of about five foot eleven, weight of maybe one hundred seventy-five pounds, probable age in his early thirties, and race—American Indian—Patrick hadn't been able to determine much about the man. His skull had literally been flattened on one side and half his face had been scraped off.

"It was Jimmy Beartusk."

Patrick shrugged. The name didn't ring a bell.

"He was one of Elvin Cross's cousins. Grew up with all of us on the reservation, although his father is Crow."

Patrick hadn't ever met Beartusk, but Elvin was *not* okay. Far from it. He ran with Eddie Blackhawk, Constance's brother, and the two of them dabbled in illegal poker games and thuggish behavior. "Speaking of Elvin, how is your brother?"

Constance and Big Mike had given Eddie a home on their ranch, and he'd repaid them by hosting secret games there that could have landed them all in prison. And, after Big Mike had died and Patrick had been pushing the tribal police to classify his death as a murder, Eddie had threatened Patrick. At the time, Patrick had suspected Eddie had a hand in his brother-in-law's death, although it turned out that the threat was nothing more than Eddie's usual attitude toward outsiders he believed were meddling in reservation business.

Constance sighed. "He's all right. Busy. He's been staying out of trouble."

Patrick wasn't sure he believed that, but he responded to be polite. "Good."

Her eyes looked hopeful. "He and Elvin have gone legit. They've started running tours on the res for big money types out of Jackson Hole."

"What kind of tours?"

"Nature, mostly. To see the area, the wild horses, migrating animals. But also some cultural experiences, like our pow wow and sweat lodges."

Patrick couldn't picture Eddie and Elvin willingly bringing outsiders onto the reservation and into their culture, but stranger things had happened. "I hope that's a success for them. Did Beartusk work with them?"

"I'm not sure. Maybe." Constance frowned. "Do the police know what happened to him?"

"They don't. But I could hazard a guess." He glanced at his daughter.

She sighed and made his name into a two-syllable word. "Dad, I saw him. You can't make it any worse than I've already imagined."

She was right. He rubbed his forehead. "It looked like he fell from a plane."

But not from that great a height. His head was flattened, but intact otherwise. While a human body falling has a terminal velocity—a top speed—based on weight and wind resistance, the height for someone to achieve their max before hitting the ground was pretty substantial. Like Empire State Building substantial. From that height, he would have expected to see more severe damage than Beartusk sustained.

Constance nodded. "Or was tossed. Otherwise, why didn't someone stick around and report it?"

She wasn't saying anything Patrick hadn't thought of himself—the damage to Beartusk's head was greater than that to the rest of his body, for instance, which told Patrick that the man probably fell headfirst. But that wasn't conclusive to being pushed, and Patrick tried to stick to facts instead of speculating. Besides, if he were to speculate, pushing someone from a plane wasn't an easy task. Quarters would have been cramped. Beartusk wouldn't have gone willingly unless he was incapacitated first. That close to the ground, the pilot couldn't have given up controls to muscle Beartusk out. A third person would have probably been on board to do the tossing. If a tossing is what had occurred. Unless Beartusk had been unconscious, high, extremely drunk, drugged, or dead already, he'd known what was coming. There would be an autopsy ordered in a case like this one, and the police would be able to determine whether he'd been drugged. Probably even whether he'd been pushed.

No matter how it happened, it was horrible to contemplate. Patrick pictured a plane lifting off the runway, quickly climbing to an unsurvivable height. A door opening. Strong arms pushing a man out.

His body tumbling in the air. The wet crunch as he hit the ground. Patrick couldn't think of anything much worse than falling from a plane and anticipating the moment of impact when the ground would rip off your skin, break your bones, and crush your brain and internal organs. He'd been the doctor on the scene a few years before in Dallas when a woman was pushed off a penthouse balcony to a ground-level concrete walkway. Her bloody, contorted form still haunted his dreams. Now, it would be replaced by Beartusk's.

Patrick winced and put an end to his grim musings. "Whatever happened, it didn't occur long before we landed. His body was still warm."

Constance pushed her hair back, agitated. "What kind of animal would do something like that?"

"Someone who was really upset with Beartusk, I'd say. Hopefully, if he was pushed, it won't be too hard for the police to figure out who did it and bring them in."

Constance snorted. "Yeah, right. You obviously don't remember much about justice around here. At least on the reservation."

And this from a woman dating a tribal cop. There was a reason the Wind River Reservation and its residents had a reputation for violence and lawlessness, and he remembered it well. "Well, if you hear anything about it, let me know. I've got a vested interest."

She nodded. "Thanks again for the x-ray machine."

He shook her hand. "No problem."

"Will we see you at the clinic soon?"

Trish's head popped up. Whatever he said now was being catalogued and would be reported back to her mom.

"I'll have a few days off next month and come in with Wes then."

"I may be gone. Justin and I, we're—um—we're getting married. Taking a little honeymoon time in Vegas. I never had that with Big Mike."

"Congratulations." Patrick didn't bother to try to hide his relief.

***

TWO HOURS LATER, their landing at the Johnson County Airport was blessedly anticlimactic. The wheels of the Tri-Pacer gripped the tarmac and slowed gradually. The runway had never been in better shape since Patrick had been flying there. He and other pilots had Mountain West Airlines to thank for it, as one of their planes had put down there by mistake a few months before, thinking they were landing at the nearby—and larger—Sheridan County Airport. No one had been injured, but the damage from the Boeing 737-200 had resulted in a fresh layer of asphalt, as well as a suspension for the pilot who had landed without air traffic control clearance. His case was still pending in federal court. As a pilot, Patrick prayed he never committed the kind of boneheaded mistake that made national news, or, God forbid, harmed any living creature.

He turned off the runway and taxied to his tie-downs, where he shut the plane down. In the sudden silence, the acrid smell in the cabin seemed stronger. Trish climbed out like a sloth, clutching a sloshy bag of what had been her lunch in Dubois, before she'd succumbed to another bout of air sickness on the way back to Buffalo. Her face was a pale greenish-gray.

After he'd secured the plane and completed his post-flight ritual, he and Trish walked in silence toward the office in the hangar. The wind blew jet fuel fumes straight into their faces. Trish put her hand over her nose.

"Would you look at that?" Patrick whistled as they passed a new-looking Cessna 421 with red and green stripes. *Like Christmas.* A low-wing twin engine, it would seat from six to seven depending on the configuration. And it was pressurized. An expensive plane. Nicer than any he'd ever seen locally.

"Whoop-de-doo," Trish muttered.

It was certainly nicer than the red-bellied 210 Centurion beside it, a plane so old that it had the vintage strut-braced wing design. Centurions were great planes, though, and if this one's owner would have invested the time and money to take care of it, it would have stood up well next to the 421. The owner in question was tinkering with the skin of the fuselage at that very moment. Bruce Folske, a legend at the airport, both for his heroic exploits as a pilot in Vietnam and for his daredevil tendencies in civil aviation. His latest renovation to the plane had been to install a jump door on the passenger side so he could take up skydivers.

Patrick shouted, "Bruce."

The compact man turned and waved, then rubbed his shiny bald head. "Greetings, Dr. Flint. And little Flint."

Patrick could feel Trish's eye roll. "Fixing her up?"

"Oh, ya know. A little spit and polish."

"Don't I know it. I bought that Tri-Pacer I've been leasing. Lot of that for me from now on."

"That old flying milk stool? Took you long enough." Bruce laughed, then spat tobacco. The wind carried it dangerously close to Trish, who shrunk back. "Let's grab bad coffee in the office sometime and you can tell me how much it set you back."

Patrick tried not to react defensively to the comment about his new plane. It had earned the nickname honestly because of how close together its wheels were. He just considered it part of the family now, and, as such, felt a need to protect its honor and reputation. "Sounds good. Be seeing you."

Bruce saluted.

Patrick pulled open the office door, entering after his grumpy daughter. From the far side of the room, a man in military-style boots and work coveralls with the sleeves cut off at the shoulder raised a hand in greeting. He had crewcut gray hair, deep dimples in each weathered cheek, and sparkling blue eyes.

"Want some, Flint?" He was pouring coffee into a Styrofoam cup from the electric percolator on the counter. He grinned at Trish.

"From the looks of you, young lady, I'd say your father was doing loop-de-loops again."

Trish groaned. "Practically."

Patrick shook his head. "Thanks for the offer, Ernie, but I'm good."

"Nice day for a flight." Ernie dumped half a jar of Coffee Mate into his cup and stirred it with a finger discolored by airplane grease.

"Gorgeous up there."

"I heard you had an incident in Dubois."

Of course he'd heard. By now the news had reached every airport in the state. "Yeah. It was something else." Ernie waited for details, but Patrick didn't have the energy to give them. He was mentally worn down from the ordeal and long day of flying.

"Everything all right with your bird?"

"Running like a top. Could you fill her up when you get a chance?"

"As soon as the morning rush lets up, I'll get right on it."

Patrick smiled. The Johnson County airport did a decent business, but it wasn't exactly a hub of frenetic activity. "You good here?"

Ernie turned, blowing on his coffee. The airport was his one-man show. Air traffic control, maintenance, mechanics, fuel, flight instruction, help with tie-downs, leasing of hangar space, directions, and maintaining the runway, which largely meant plowing snow and shooing wildlife away. All Ernie, all the time. "Good enough. Strange-talking characters been fueling up here lately, then taking off again. Little more than touch-and-gos in their fancy Golden Eagle. Foreigners." He spat out the last word like chewing tobacco.

The Golden Eagle—another name for the 421 Patrick had seen tied down outside. "From another country?"

"No, Chicago or some such."

Patrick laughed. "I hope you're using your diplomatic skills." Ernie was a Marine with four divorces to his name. There was no one Patrick knew with less diplomacy.

"Who, me?" Ernie winked. "But, honestly, I was, until they went and hired Bruce for a short haul job. He's taking up his Centurion. I told them he ain't got no business flying it until I get that fuel leak fixed, but would they listen to me?" He shook his head, the answer obvious.

Patrick would never fly a plane with a fuel leak. Bruce was a risk-taker, though, which Eddie knew well. They'd served together, in the same squadron. It was how they ended up in the same small town at the same small airport. Brothers for life.

"How bad is the leak?"

"Oh, it's a slow one, at least for now. But Bruce is dead broke. He can't pay for the job until after they pay him, and I can't order the parts without Bruce's dough. We're all in a pickle." His phone rang, and he waved goodbye as he answered it. "Bronx Zoo House of Primates. Can I help you?"

Patrick waved back and put a hand on Trish's shoulder. The two of them made their way out to his truck without any more conversation. With every step, the weariness Patrick had been fighting since Dubois grew heavier. Even with Ernie's levity, the pall of finding the dead man on the runway hung over him. They got in the truck, and Trish put her head on the door and went to sleep, or at least feigned it. Patrick swallowed back a sigh. Sometimes being the adult wasn't fun. The staying awake and driving while others slept, the putting on a brave front for everyone else, the soldiering on when you didn't feel like it.

He put the truck in gear. He couldn't wait to get home, hug his wife, and take a long, hot shower.

CHAPTER FOUR: GULP

Susanne

PATRICIA SAND—PATRICK'S baby sister—stood at the breakfast bar. She adjusted her flowered, round-necked top and poured two water glasses of rosé wine to the rim, without asking Susanne whether she wanted any. Which Susanne did, but, at the same time, did not. The part of her that was bone weary after a week of reliving the Barb Lamkin ordeal wanted the whole bottle anyway. But the part of her that had miles to go before she slept did not. It was so early, unseemingly early, not even happy hour, and she had so much to do to prepare for Ronnie's party the next day. Her stress was compounding. She hadn't heard from Patrick and Trish, and they were late getting back from their flight to Dubois. Perry hadn't been home all day and as mischievous as he was, she was always waiting for the other shoe to drop or the phone to ring. George Nichols, the electrician, was a no-show. How was she going to make dinner with no electricity in half the house—the half that included the kitchen—much less throw a party for fifteen women? And it had been out for two days already. Two long, long days shuttling food into coolers and cooking on the grill out back.

Susanne glanced at the clock, again. Four p.m. Where were Patrick and the kids? She noticed a small hole of light in her vision. *Oh, no.* A migraine was coming. Patrick had taken her to a neurologist in Denver the month before about her headaches. The doctor had given her a prescription, warning her that it would only work if she took it at the first sign of a migraine. The pills knocked her out, and she hated them, but she couldn't afford to be in bed sick, especially tomorrow. She went to the kitchen cabinet. She kept her medicine there so she could take one fast with a glass of water. She pulled out the bottle and dumped a pill in her hand.

"You never age a bit, Susanne, and you get prettier every year. Do you color your hair?"

Susanne put a hand to her long brown locks. They were naturally wavy and matched her eyes. Her mother's hair was darker and had gone salt-and-pepper when she was Susanne's age, but her own hair wasn't showing signs of it yet. Her thighs, on the other hand, were criss crossed with veins, and she wasn't crazy about the lines around her eyes. *As long as Patrick likes how you look. And he seems to like it quite a bit.* She smiled. "No. And thanks."

"You're welcome." Patricia took a dining chair close to the open window, then set down her wine on the checkered cloth placemat. She sipped daintily, her Patrick-blue eyes sparkling over the rim, and her center-parted Dorothy Hamill-cut hair swinging forward on her pretty, round cheekbones. "Mom won't quit talking about the canoe trip."

Originally, Patricia had planned for a long weekend visit, which Susanne had been elated about. As the youngest in her own family, she loved being the adored big sister. But then the visit had extended into ten days. Ten days, each growing longer than the last, with the dual pressure of the trial and being the hostess with the mostest to her sister-in-law. Not that Patricia had come with expectations of being entertained. Susanne just couldn't help herself. But, taking her own shortcomings out of the equation, she still ascribed to the Benjamin Franklin adage that guests, like fish, started to smell after three days.

And the visit might extend even longer. Patricia didn't have to be back in Austin to teach her kindergarteners for another week. Susanne was starting classes at Sheridan College then anyway, resuming her quest to obtain a degree in education. With the hours she'd accrued at colleges in Austin and Dallas, she only had three semesters to go until she'd be student teaching. It seemed so close and yet so far. She'd hoped to have a little break between Patricia's visit and her own return to academia, to mentally prepare herself, but it didn't appear she'd be getting it.

Ferdinand, the family's Irish wolfhound, flopped down beside Patricia. The two had become best buds, thanks to Patricia ignoring her brother's admonitions not to feed the beggar from the dinner table. He'd finally given up. Susanne had a feeling this was a big hairy genie that wouldn't go easily back into a bottle when Patricia left.

She filled a glass of water from the tap and swallowed her pill, hoping she was in time to stop the migraine. Patricia's comment still rang in her ears. She just bet her mother-in-law Lana was still talking about the Gros Ventre Wilderness canoe trip. They'd all nearly died at the hands of the horrible men they'd run into there. Trish and her cousin Bunny had gotten lost, then been kidnapped. Perry had sustained a life-threatening head injury. Patrick had twisted his ankle, and Lana had sprained her wrist. If Susanne never went on another outdoor adventure with her husband, it would be too soon.

A breeze wafted through the window, lifting Patricia's bangs and ruffling the sides of her hair. "Does this view ever get old?"

Susanne looked out the window above the sink. "No, it really doesn't. Especially in the spring and early summer when the wild-flowers are out. Although a lot of the year it's nothing but ice and snow." She could hear the meadowlarks singing and the water burbling as Clear Creek tumbled past the back of the house. A smooth, grassy lawn rolled down from the deck to the towering cottonwoods that lined the banks. Far beyond the creek, the foothills of the Bighorn Mountains muscled their way out of the plains up toward bright afternoon sunlight.

"Do you think you're ever moving back to Texas?"

Susanne paced the kitchen. It was shadowy without electric light. Her mind had wandered to what she was going to feed her family for dinner. To say Patrick wasn't big on eating out was an epic understatement. The man was allergic to spending money. But they'd cooked and consumed their freezer reserves, and, without power and refrigerated food, peanut butter and honey sandwiches were about all she could throw together. *Well, so be it, then.* She assembled the ingredients on the counter, vaguely aware that Patricia had said something to her from her seat at the table, ten feet away. She opened the peanut butter jar and recoiled. The smell. The oily, peanut-y smell of it was overpowering.

Uh oh. Sensitivity to light and smell were . . .

A sudden wave of nausea nearly bowled her over. She gripped the edge of the countertop, trying to keep the migraine at bay through sheer force of will. The hole in the light grew larger, and then, inside it, she saw a series of images flit through. Patrick and an American Indian man she didn't know. Trish and Perry, kneeling on the ground by a stack of felled timber. Henry and Ben—the young man the Sibleys had taken in a few months before—riding horses at full speed through a forest, dodging tree limbs. And Barbara Lamkin, holding a baby in a dark parking lot.

"Susanne, I said do you think you'll ever move back to Texas?" Patricia repeated.

Susanne's visions faded. She drew in a deep breath. "I don't know how to answer that." Continuing to breathe through her mouth, she laid out slices of soft wheat bread on plates. The strange images were coming more frequently with the aura recently, and she didn't understand it. She hadn't told Patrick about them. She didn't want to scare him. *Come on, drugs.* She cleared her throat. "Patrick loves it here. So do the kids. We've made good friends."

"But don't you miss being close to family?"

"I do. Terribly. We'll see." When Patrick had agreed they'd buy their dream house on the creek, she had committed they could stay in Wyoming indefinitely. Susanne was a good sport, and she wouldn't go back on her word. As long as family kept visiting them, she'd be all right. But she could do with a good, long trip back to Texas, and soon.

The front door opened. "Mom, I'm home!" It was Perry.

"Where have you been?" She wheeled with her hands on her hips. *Too fast.* The room tilted, her stomach lurched. But it wasn't just her son. Perry's best friend John was with him, as was their electrician, George. And Perry had a black eye and blood all over his face and shirt. "Oh, my!" She put a hand on her chest. "What happened to you?"

George raised his hand. "I'm sorry, Mrs. Flint. He begged me not to go easy on him."

"What?" This grown man, this virtual stranger, had done this to her son? He was twice Perry's weight. Seven or eight inches taller.

Perry grinned. "It's okay, Mom. We were playing football. George was a safety in high school, so I was running routes on him."

George nodded vigorously, his blond curls bouncing. The man looked a little bit like that rakish singer, Rod Stewart. She wasn't sure that was a good thing. "He did really well, too, Mrs. Flint."

So, George was playing football while her freezer continued its unscheduled defrost? She forgot all about her son's injuries. "I thought you were going to be here today, George. I was counting on you. I have out-of-town company, and tomorrow I'm throwing a party. I need electricity in my kitchen."

He put his hand over his heart, a horrified look on his face. "I had you on the schedule for tomorrow afternoon."

Susanne fought to keep her voice under control. *Catch more flies with honey than vinegar.* That was easier to do when her head wasn't hurting. Well, she'd just have to settle with catching a few less flies.

"Tomorrow afternoon is when this house will be full of ladies expecting to be fed and entertained. Tomorrow afternoon is too late."

George frowned, his forehead folding up like a pleated shirt, his ice-blue eyes meeting hers with a direct, steady gaze. "I'm sorry. I don't know how I got that mixed up. I'll be here first thing in the morning. I'd start now, but your parts are back at my place, out near Big Horn."

"How long will it take you to get things working once you start?"

"A coupla three hours, I'd guess."

"The party is at three-thirty."

"No problem, ma'am."

"You promise?"

He held up two fingers, one of which bore a long, jagged scar. "Scout's honor." Then he grinned. "Does that count if I was never in Boy Scouts?"

The front door opened again.

Susanne turned. Trish led the way in. Patrick followed her. Her eyes rested on her husband. Six feet in his socks, beautiful blue eyes, skin tanned from the outdoors, a trim physique, and light brown hair, thinning on top and receding a little bit in front. In her mind, perfect.

"Finally," she said. "I've been worried about you two."

"Honey, we're home. And so is our front yard badger. Cute little booger," Patrick said. "Have I ever told you how special he is to American Indian culture? Not just because he never surrenders, but also because he digs deep for knowledge, insight, and healing powers. As a loner he is . . ."

"Self-reliant. Yes, you have. Quite a few times, actually." So many that she could recite his litany. But the badger had been digging up her grass and flowers all summer. Patrick, claiming a lifelong love of the tough little creatures—and an appreciation for their control of rodents—had refused to trap it. They were pretty cute, actually. Those black badges on their cheeks, the white stripe down their faces. But the digging claws! They could burrow underground in the time between when she spotted one out the window and before she came out with a broom. She thought she'd finally chased it off, but apparently not. "I know you've got a lot to do if you're going to be leaving for Highland Park in the morning."

"Out the door by five a.m." Patrick walked toward Susanne, arms open.

Something in his eyes and posture looked off, but she couldn't put her finger on what it was. She fell into his hug.

Patricia stood, her culotte pants swinging below her knees. She crossed her arms. "Fine. Just run off and leave your only sister on the last weekend of her visit. I know where I rank." Her voice was light and teasing.

Patrick laughed into Susanne's hair. "You're welcome to saddle a horse and come with us, sis."

"Uh, no thanks. I had my fill with Nightmare."

"Midnight."

They both laughed with the easy jocularity of family. It was an old joke between the two of them. When Patricia had been a young girl, the Flint family had gone on a trail ride. Patrick and Pete, their brother, had ridden off and left Patricia. Her horse, Midnight, had turned around and run for the barn. She'd started screaming, "Whoa, Nightmare, whoa," and had refused to get on a horse since. She wasn't a big fan of planes either and had declined Patrick's offers to take her up in his new toy.

"Hey, Dad, can John go with us? We've got room in the trailer for his horse, right?" Perry's voice seemed less high pitched than it had even that morning at breakfast. Susanne's little boy was growing up.

Patrick released her. "Sure, buddy. But that means we have to leave by four."

John said, "My dad can bring Plug over later, Dr. Flint, and I can spend the night, if you want me to."

"That will work."

Perry grinned. "And can I bring a gun?"

"Not a chance."

"But when?"

"When you're sixteen. And then only in the mountains." His father clapped him on the back. Then he noticed George for the first time. "George." The two men shook hands, and Patrick clapped George on the elbow. "Great to see you."

"Likewise," George said.

"If John's going, does that mean I don't have to?" Susanne decided that Trish looked worse than Patrick. She was always green around the gills after flying, but this was different.

"Nice try," Patrick said.

"What happened today?" she asked her daughter.

Trish feigned nonchalance. "Dad nearly ran over a dead guy on the runway in Dubois. Now, I have to go take a shower. I'm supposed to pick Marcy up at five."

Susanne felt heat seeping over her face. *The drugs. Finally.* "What?"

"I'll tell you all about it, Susanne." Patrick was using his soothing-the-patient's-family voice— a very bad sign. "

"Are you kidding me? You ran over a dead guy?" Patricia knocked her wine over. Red liquid flowed onto the floor.

"I'll take that as a yes, Mom. Thanks." Trish disappeared up the stairs before Susanne could form a response.

She dashed into the kitchen for a towel. Her fingers felt numb, and so did her lips. More signs the medicine was working. She headed back into the living room. Ferdinand was lapping up the spilled rosé. Everyone was talking at once. Susanne stared at the mess for a moment, then set the towel down, picked up her wine, and drank it down in one long series of gulps.

CHAPTER FIVE: SNEAK

Trish

"I WISH I didn't have to go this weekend." Trish leaned her head into Ben's shoulder, her bottom lip in what she hoped was a pretty pout. Her parents thought she was with Marcy. She felt a little bit guilty about that. They didn't know about Ben. Couldn't know about him. They wouldn't approve. But what they didn't know wouldn't exactly kill them or anything.

She gazed out over Lake Desmet from the bench seat of the ancient pickup truck her parents had helped her buy with her babysitting money. White foam edged the waves that stretched across the lake's surface to lap against the foot of the red cliffs on the other side. The wind had picked up like mad in the last hour. Just in time for a mountain trail ride in the morning. Wind made horses crazy. *Great.* After the day she'd had today, with the awful plane ride and then nearly crashing into a dead man when they landed in, like, California—not really, but they were so far away from Buffalo that it felt like it—she thought she'd earned the right to stay home that weekend. But no. Her dad was *so* unreasonable. Which reminded her that she had to tell Ben all about her day. She would. In a minute.

"I wish I was going with you." Ben wrapped a strand of Trish's hair around his finger.

She loved it when he did that. She loved everything about him. His thick black hair, the little scar on his forehead, his broad shoulders, his kind eyes, his gentle hands. How he smelled like outside—dirt, sunshine, and clean sweat, with a hint of plain old soap. The way he looked at her. Especially the way he looked at her, like she was something precious.

Six months before, she had *thought* she loved Ben's cousin, Brandon Lewis. That was before Brandon had turned out to be a big fat meanie. Then, he'd broken up with Trish because she wouldn't have sex with him, about the time she'd found out he two-timed her with a *teacher*. If she'd known about the teacher, she would have broken up with him first.

Of course, she also used to think she hated Ben. His awful father and uncle had kidnapped Trish and forced Ben to go along with it. Now his father was dead—killed by hers during her rescue—and his Uncle Billy Kemecke was in jail, for life. Ben had done a stint in juvie because of the whole thing. But, after he'd been released, when she'd gotten to know him, she'd realized he was a good person and had been a victim, like her. If he hadn't done what he was told, worse things could have happened to her, and his family would have made him pay. Maybe even killed him, like they'd killed their cousin, right before Trish's eyes.

Still, even when she'd realized Ben liked her, she'd resisted her own feelings. But then she'd gotten lost with her cousin Bunny in the Gros Ventre Wilderness the month before and nearly died. She'd had a major change of heart. Ever since she'd gotten back, she and Ben had been together. Completely, totally together.

And it was amazing.

She rubbed her cheek against his shoulder. As she did, her chin brushed against the silk collar of her shirt. It was just a little bit disco, and she couldn't believe her parents had let her buy it. "You know you can't come to Highland Park with me. No one knows about us."

"I don't see why we can't tell people. It's been nearly two months."

"Because my parents would freak out." And that was putting it mildly. Not only because Ben had been part of her kidnapping, however unwillingly, but because he was two years older than her. Brandon had been, too, and they'd let her date him, but they regretted it. She should never have confessed to her mom that Brandon had pressured her to have sex. Now her parents were all like *no older boys*. Hadn't she proved herself when she'd refused Brandon?

Ben slipped his fingers under her hair and onto her neck. She shivered. She loved it when he did that, too. He leaned down and kissed her. *Oh, God.* She loved that most of all. She had a feeling that it was going to be a lot harder to say no to Ben, not that he'd asked. But the way he made her feel, all tingly and gooey. This was the way it was meant to be. He was the one. She just knew it.

When they came up for air, Trish buried her face in his chest. "I'm so glad you're going to stay here and work on the Piney Bottoms Ranch until I graduate. I think I'd just die if you left."

Ben stiffened and didn't reply.

"What is it?" Trish sat back.

He huffed out a big breath. "Henry and Vangie have offered to help me pay for the University of Wyoming after I get out in December."

Trish bit her tongue. After his dad had died the year before, Ben's life had been in turmoil. First, juvie. Then when he got out, he'd moved in with Brandon and his mother, Donna Lewis. They'd kicked him out when Ben had provided evidence against her for conspiracy to commit murder. Donna had pled guilty and gone to jail, as she should have. Luckily for Ben, Henry and Vangie Sibley had given him a place to live, and they'd given him a job on their ranch, too. He was a semester behind at Buffalo High, but was on track to graduate mid-year, which was pretty good, considering everything.

So, she should be happy for Ben about the college thing. He'd been planning to save up the money to pay for college himself. But Laramie was four long hours away. She'd never get to see him. He'd get lonely. What if some college girl dug her claws in him, and he forget all about her?

She forced herself to say, "That's, um, great, Ben."

He relaxed. "Yeah, they've been really good to me. But I'll miss you bad."

Trish chewed her lip, thinking. Last year, one of the girls on her basketball team had graduated early by taking extra classes and going to summer school. Trish could do that, if she could talk her parents into it. She had the highest GPA in her class. How could they say no when she was doing so well? Her dad was already bummed that she was leaving in two years, but her mom would probably throw a party. She was constantly telling people how Trish drove her crazy.

"What are you thinking?" Ben narrowed his eyes at her. "You've got that look you get."

"What look?"

"The one that says you're about to throw me a curve ball."

"Who, me?" She batted her eyes.

He laughed. "You, definitely."

"Well, I have this idea . . ."

His eyes sparkled. "Me, too. I was thinking we could take a blanket down by the lake and watch the sun set."

"That would be nice. But my idea is even better."

He waggled his eyebrows at her. "I like the sound of that."

She put her hand on his chest, but suddenly felt shy and couldn't look him in the eye. "How about I graduate early and join you in Laramie next fall? Then we'll only be apart for a few months."

He frowned. "Would you still be valedictorian?"

Why didn't he sound excited? Her hand fell from his chest. "I don't know."

"What about the cross country team? You're just getting started, and you're really good." Trish had started training that spring, after she'd quit basketball. She'd loved basketball, but having a coach who tried to kill her had kind of ruined it for her. It turned out that she loved to run even more. She wasn't fast, but she could go a long, long way. "I'll bet by the time you're a senior you'll qualify for the state meet."

Trish jerked herself over to the passenger side of the truck. "What are you saying? Don't you want to be together?"

"Of course I do. But a year isn't that long. Not if we really love each other."

Her voice was a wail. "It's forever to me! But apparently it doesn't bother you."

He reached for her hand, and she let him take it. "It does."

"Then you want me to do it?"

"No, I mean, I don't know."

Trish jerked her hand away. Heat crept up her neck, into her face and then her ears. When it had crawled into her scalp, she screamed, "Out."

"What?"

"Get out of my truck. I'm going home."

"Trish, you're my ride."

"Out!"

"Come on, Trish. There's no one else around out here. Don't do this."

"Don't do this? What—don't make you walk? Or don't graduate early so we can be together?"

"You're acting nuts. Can you just calm down?"

"Get. Out. Now."

Ben stared at her with wide eyes for long seconds, then he shook his head and snorted. "Fine. It's only ten miles back to the ranch from here, in cowboy boots. Maybe more. No problem." He got out, slamming the door.

Tears in her eyes, Trish hit the gas, which wasn't easy in her bell bottom flare jeans and high-heeled faux Dingo boots. She sprayed gravel as she headed for the interstate. Then she remembered she hadn't even told Ben about what had happened in Dubois. Not that it mattered anymore. He obviously didn't love her like she loved him. He probably wouldn't have even cared.

Why was she so unlucky with boys?

CHAPTER SIX: RIDE

Park Reservoir, Bighorn National Forest, Bighorn
Mountains, Wyoming
Friday, August 12, 1977, 8:00 a.m.

Patrick

PATRICK BREATHED in the fresh forest scent as he tightened Duke's cinch strap one last time. The horse was a notorious stomach puffer, and he didn't want Perry ending up underneath the animal's belly. Then he looked over the sparkling water. They had parked the trucks and trailers under towering pines in a campsite at Park Reservoir, and the waterline was only twenty feet away. He turned toward Henry, a lanky rancher with a perpetual twinkle in his eye. Henry was walking from horse to horse, pushing on the saddle bags to make sure they were properly secured. Patrick continued checking gear on the rest of the horses, ending with Plug, John's horse, a nice-looking sorrel with sleepy eyes that widened when Patrick gave the strap a pull.

Henry sidled up to Patrick. "Pretty grim book you packed for the trip."

For a second, Patrick was confused, then he realized Hank must have seen him pack *Horseman, Pass By* in his saddle bag. "I haven't started it. I picked it up since it's a western."

"Not light reading. But that Larry McMurtry can write. Anyway, decide for yourself." He nodded. "Last chance to back out of this ride."

"Why would I do that? I've been looking forward to it all month."

"Didn't you hear what happened up on Black Tooth last week?"

"No. I've been a little distracted with the Lamkin trial."

Henry shook his head. "Rocky Perritt, one of the Sheridan County deputies, died making the climb."

"A novice?"

"Hardly. He'd summitted Black Tooth twelve times before, and he had a lot of experience rock climbing in the Tetons, too, but he fell anyway. They brought him down a few days ago. Still had on his Denver Broncos baseball cap when Search & Rescue found him, they said."

Patrick couldn't help thinking that a helmet was more suitable headgear for a rock climber, but he kept it to himself. "Unlucky number thirteen. That's terrible. But it doesn't change my mind. We're not rock climbing. Just trail riding and camping."

"Yeah. But some people are superstitious."

"Has it rattled you?"

Henry grinned. "Nah. Some people doesn't include me. But in case it comes up, I wanted you to know."

Patrick slapped him on the back. "Thanks." Then he turned back to the kids and raised his voice. "Time to go. Everyone been to the bathroom? Have everything you need?"

Patrick had packed the saddlebags himself, so he knew they all had bedrolls, rain gear, and their equal shares of camping equipment and supplies. He'd stashed the food and water on his big mount, Reno. The Percheron-Quarter horse cross had been improving steadily since breaking his splint bone a year before. The vet, Joe Crumpton, had declared the animal fit for the journey earlier that week—after Reno had performed well on a series of shorter rides over the last few months—shaking his head and smiling as he did so. At one point, everyone involved had been convinced Reno would be nothing more than a pasture pet for the rest of his life. The horse had proved he was made of sturdy stuff.

Trish stood from her perch on the trailer wheel well. She hadn't said a word since she'd gotten up that morning. Something was wrong, but Patrick would rather wrestle a mountain lion than ask her what it was. He hoped if he ignored it, she'd come around. Perry and John were skipping rocks into the reservoir, to the chagrin of several old timers fishing from the shore. The water was fifteen feet below its early-summer peak depth, due to the use of its contents for irrigation down Sheridan-way. That didn't stop the fishermen, though.

The two boys raced back to the trailer, galloping like colts and startling poor Plug fully awake.

"We're ready," Perry said.

"Next stop, Bighorn Reservoir, then," Patrick said.

"We could have just ridden up the Penrose Trail and saved an hour and a half of driving, you know," Henry said.

"You're still jawing about that?" Patrick grinned. "Too many people. Not as scenic."

"We'd be halfway there already."

"Everyone's a critic." Patrick turned to the teenagers. "You guys have jackets, right?"

Perry said, "Yes, sir."

Trish's head moved. He took it as a nod.

John frowned. "I didn't bring a coat. I like it cold." He made a muscle and laughed. The boy was wearing a short-sleeved t-shirt that said Buffalo Bison Football on it.

Patrick had an extra flannel shirt packed away. If worse came to worst, he'd give the boy his own coat and tough it out in the flannel.

"It can get mighty cold up there, even in August. You can borrow mine, if you need it."

John shrugged. "I won't, but thanks."

Ah, youth. "Okay. Here's how it's going to go. Henry will be riding in front. He knows the way. I'll take the sweeper position in back. The rest of you space out between us. Let's mount up and head out."

"Yee ha," Perry shouted.

Trish gave her brother a withering glare, but John laughed.

A few minutes later, the group left the forested perimeter of Park Reservoir, heading single file through a park toward a cluster of rustic cabins known as Spear-O Wigwam. Patrick tilted his head back and drew in a deep breath. This was the life. A mule deer doe and fawn sprinted across the meadow away from them. Magpies cawed as they flew overhead, examining and complaining about the interlopers. The air was crisp and fresh, smelling of pine and loam. Above the trees, snow still clung to the tops of the peaks of the massif. He half closed his eyes, savoring the moment. There was just something about the way late summer sunlight bathed the world in a yellow glow that made him feel at peace. This was the way to do it. And it beat a week of work, trial testimony, and giving statements to police about dead bodies on airstrips—not to mention worrying about keeping his little sister happy when the family was so distracted—six ways to Sunday. It was good, too, to be venturing into Cloud Peak Wilderness with Henry. Henry was born and raised at the foot of the Bighorns, and there wasn't a more capable man on the planet, unless maybe it was Patrick's friend and co-worker Wes Braten.

Patrick was so happy, in fact, that he started singing. Mac Davis's "Hard to Be Humble." He thought it was a good fit for him.

"Dad, no," Perry said. His son sounded horrified.

Patrick remembered fondly the recent days when Perry would sing along with him. He ignored his son and kept singing, until he ran out of words that he knew. Then he started over at the beginning.

After they passed Spear-O Wigwam, the group re-entered the

forest and turned left up the winding road toward Bighorn Reservoir, with Trish in front of her brother and John following Perry. Henry's three-year-old Appaloosa gelding Spot was still in training, and he was jumpy compared to the other horses, but he had a nice, ground-covering walk. Trish and John were keeping up well, but Perry was having to trot his stout Paint every few minutes. Reno was steady and even. Happy seeming, although Patrick was hypervigilant about the horse's stride and ready to give him a break or even turn around if he showed the slightest problem.

For a while, there was no sound except the clatter of horse hooves on the steep, rocky road. Then, the boys started discussing their upcoming football season. Loudly.

"We aren't going to see a single animal today if you boys keep up that racket." Patrick wanted them to have fun, but he also wanted to spot some big game. Moose. Maybe a few elk. A bighorn sheep if they were very, very lucky.

Perry didn't take the hint. He shouted back to Patrick. "Do you think I have a chance at playing wide receiver, Dad?"

It was a sensitive subject. Perry wasn't blessed with height. Or with a vertical leap that would help him beat a cornerback or safety to the ball. But he did have heart and desire. "If you keep working at it, you've got a shot."

John said, "We just can't get hurt this year." He'd suffered from a concussion the previous season. Perry had broken his ankle, once during the season and once after it.

Perry's voice exuded enthusiasm. "I think when the coach sees our chemistry, he'll have to put me in with you."

Patrick smiled. Besides heart and desire, Perry was dogged, which was a great trait on the field, and less so in a conversation when he wouldn't drop whatever subject he was currently obsessed with.

The boys kept talking, the horses kept walking, and the group reached Bighorn Reservoir, where the wind was tossing up whitecaps on the water.

"Where'd that come from?" Patrick called to Henry.

Trish spoke. *Finally.* "It was like that last night, too."

"Where were you that you were in the wind? Didn't you and Marcy go to a movie?"

Trish mumbled something—Patrick wasn't sure what.

Before he could ask her to repeat herself, Henry reined Spot around to face the group. "The almanac says it's going to be clear."

Patrick scanned the skies. There were only a few wispy white clouds breaking up an otherwise endless blue. "If it stays nice, maybe we can take the Cross Creek trail to catch the Solitude trail further along."

Henry laughed. "And have to navigate through the woods cross country? Let's live to die another day, cowboy. We're sticking with the marked trails the whole way."

"Never hurts to ask." Patrick gave in with a smile. "All right. The horses should be warm now. Let's speed up and make some time."

Henry clucked, and Spot spun around on his back hooves, heading out in slow, bouncy trot. The other horses followed at the same speed, but with less energy expenditure. Reno sighed, a commentary on the folly of youth. Patrick relaxed and looked around them. The trail ringed the east side of the reservoir on a finger ridge. Below it, a wide strip of sand abutted the water. He'd hiked part of this trail with Wes in July, and, back then, the water had lapped almost to the tree line. As with Park Reservoir, the low August waterline at Bighorn was due to irrigation of the ranch and farmland at lower elevations. Arid Wyoming made the most of the water resources from its mountains.

Fifteen yards ahead, Spot suddenly snorted, threw his head down, and started bucking. His gymnastics caused a chain reaction down the line of horses. Goldie did a one-hundred-and-eighty-degree rollback with Trish sticking to her saddle like she was glued to it. Plug jumped backwards so far that he crashed into Duke. Duke crow hopped away from him, all four feet coming off the ground, if only by an inch or two. Both boys hung on.

Patrick expected a mild reaction from his normally calm horse, but Reno went bananas. He reared, wheeled, and tried to bolt. He wasn't as nimble as the youngster, Spot, but he was all muscle, and when he decided on a course of action, it was hard to dissuade him. By the time Patrick had him back under control and returned to the group, a bull moose was crossing the trail and crashing through the trees, heading away from the reservoir and toward a smaller pond on the other side of the ridge. How the massive animal made it through the trees without catching his wide span of antlers was a mystery, but he did it without so much as knocking one against a branch.

Patrick murmured soothing sounds to his horse, holding him tight and patting his neck, which was frothed with sweat. Now he understood the animal's panic. Reno hated moose more than anything in the world.

"Everyone all right?" Henry called.

"I'm fine," Trish said.

Perry shot him a thumb's up.

"I-I-I'm good." John's voice was shaky. *He doesn't sound good.*

Patrick walked Reno in a circle, testing the horse's gait to see if he'd injured himself in his dramatic flight. He seemed fine. "We're good, too."

"Sorry about that. Spot is still a bit of an overreactor, but he's learning. This ride will be good for him." Henry lowered his reins and urged Spot forward.

Patrick squeezed Reno with his heels, and they fell in line behind the group. Patrick blew out a forceful breath to expel the lingering stress from the moose encounter. A jumpy young gelding and a nervous teenage boy. Patrick was still in his happy place, but the dynamic was something to keep an eye on.

CHAPTER SEVEN: SHOCK

Susanne

BALANCING grocery bags on both hips, Susanne looked out the back door to the deck. Patricia was enjoying a hot mug of something, thanks to the kettle of water Susanne had boiled on a Coleman stove earlier. Ferdinand was stretched full-length in the sun beside Patricia. With Patrick at work and the kids at school and in activities, he was usually Susanne's dog. *Fickle beast.*

She called, "I'm back from the store."

Patricia's voice carried through the screen door and open windows. "I thought that electrician was coming this morning?"

Susanne winced at the mention of the electrician. She was painfully aware of the passing time and continued absence of George. Luckily, her migraine medicine had worked last night. She'd woken up this morning a little lethargic, but with only a mild headache and no aura.

She started unloading the bags onto her beautiful dining room table, her most prized piece of furniture, and the first one she and Patrick had ever bought new. "I hope he'll be here soon. But I'm going with things that don't have to be refrigerated or cooked for the party, just in case."

Patricia leaned her head on the seat back and closed her eyes. She looked completely relaxed, without a care in the world. "That's smart."

"It's either that or cancel, and I can't do that. Vangie and I mailed the invitations a month ago." Of course, at the time, they hadn't expected Barb's trial to be happening this week. It had been scheduled to start three weeks earlier but was postponed when the new judge had an emergency appendectomy.

"Sorry to ask again, but what time does it start?"

"3:30."

"Could I borrow your Suburban until then? I've been dying to explore the Main Street shops in Sheridan."

Susanne gritted her teeth. Patricia's role as the significantly younger baby sister in the Flint family meant that her every need had been attended to since birth. She was sweet. Loving. Kind. Lots of fun. And completely oblivious to the amount of work that went on around her. But, on the bright side, with Patricia in Sheridan, she wouldn't be underfoot, slowing Susanne down. And, to be fair, Patricia didn't even know Ronnie. It wasn't her responsibility to prep for the party. Even if her help would have been nice.

She said, "The keys are hanging on the hook by the door to the garage."

The screen door opened and thwacked shut. If one of Susanne's kids had let it slam like that, she'd have reminded them how to shut the door properly. But Patricia wasn't one of her kids.

"Thanks. I think I'll do my nails first. Only one more week of vacation!" Patricia set her coffee cup down by the sink and walked out of the kitchen, Ferdinand on her heels.

Susanne set to cutting and chopping and didn't bother answering her sister-in-law. Soon, she started making decent progress. Salami slices and cheese cubes tooth-picked to green pimento olives, with Ritz crackers to be arranged in a wheel around them. Sweet-smelling strawberries and cantaloupe for a fruit tray with some store-bought poppy seed dressing. Carrots, celery, and radishes for a colorful veggie platter. She'd whip up some buttermilk ranch dressing right before the guests arrived, never mind that the rest of the quart of buttermilk would probably go to waste. A platter of Vienna sausages, which she hated. A bakery cake—chocolate with cream cheese icing —she cut into dainty squares, stopping a few times to scrape excess icing off the knife and lick her fingers. Vangie was bringing punch, coffee, and ice cream. The menu wasn't as elaborate as Susanne had envisioned, but no one would miss the barbecue smokies and cheesy tuna casserole with crumbled crackers on top, except for her.

About the time she'd finished, Patricia walked through the kitchen toward the garage. "See you at 3:30."

Susanne waved. "Have fun."

The door closed behind Patricia. Ferdinand made a mournful sound and joined Susanne in the kitchen. Susanne covered her creations to protect them from the late summer flies, then went outside to arrange the tables and chairs on the deck. With his new best friend gone, Ferdinand wouldn't leave her side, and she tripped over him more than once.

"I don't know why I thought I needed you around," she told him, but she patted his rump.

He wagged his tail.

When she was satisfied with how the furniture looked, she decorated the deck railing and tables with blue and white crepe streamers and balloons. She rubbed her nose. She'd always hated the rubbery taste and smell of balloons, and she usually left it to Patrick to blow them up, but today it was her job. She cocked her head, evaluating the colors. Vangie had promised to bring daisies, which would add a needed punch of yellow. Then she brought out her enormous baby gift—a rolling walker, its seat covered in cheerful ducks with big orange beaks—and placed it on top of one of the tables. It was too big to wrap, but she'd taped on a card and tied a pair of baby-sized cowboy boots to the tray with a jaunty red bow.

Back in the kitchen, she looked at the clock and was aghast. Nearly noon already. She still had to shower and beautify herself before Vangie arrived at two-thirty. She headed to her bathroom, turned on the shower, and undressed. She loved the room with its claw foot tub and dark green and brown curtains. She and Patrick had redecorated it to match the forest-themed bedroom. Ferdinand flopped down on the mat with a weary sigh. He thought shower time was boring. But before she could step under the water, the phone rang.

One foot in the shower stall, she paused. *It could be Vangie. Or Ronnie.*

She wrapped herself in a towel and ran to the extension on Patrick's bedside table, a necessity for a doctor on call at all hours. Clutching the towel with one hand, she lifted the receiver to her ear with the other. "Hello?"

"Susanne?" a male voice asked.

"Yes. Who's speaking?"

"This is Max Alexandrov."

Susanne tensed. Max Alexandrov was the young county attorney prosecuting the Lamkin case. A verdict. He had to be calling about a jury verdict. She crossed the fingers holding up the towel. "Hello, Max."

He cleared his throat. "We've had a development this morning, and I wanted to let you know about it before you heard it from someone else. Or on the news."

She put her hand on her chest. "Oh, no. Did the jury find her not guilty?"

Ferdinand walked to the door into the bedroom, his eyes intent on her, his head tilted to the side.

"It hasn't gone to the jury yet. But, uh, well, Barb disappeared."

Susanne frowned. "What do you mean disappeared? Like she was taken by a UFO?"

"Uh, no."

"Prisoners don't just disappear in the middle of a trial." Her voice was strident.

"A guard took her to the ladies room, and she never came out."

A hole of light shimmered in Susanne's vision. *No.* "I don't understand."

Ferdinand sidled up to her, pressing into her legs.

"We don't either. We're not sure if she went out the window, or if the guard helped her escape, or if she traded identities with someone and snuck out under his nose, or—"

"No. I mean I don't *understand*. Where is she?"

"We don't know."

"So, she escaped. She didn't disappear. She escaped."

"I'm afraid so."

"Perry saw her murder Mrs. Renkin. She tried to kill us. My family. And we testified against her. She was in jail because of us."

"I know. I'm very sorry."

Susanne's brain spun in circles. *Barb, out. Barb, out. Barb, out.* She moved to the window between the bed and the bathroom. Part of her expected to see Barb staring back in at her, murder in her eyes. But no one was there. "She's coming for us, isn't she?"

"No. She's long gone by now, Susanne. It's a small town, and we were searching for her within minutes. But we did put a patrol in your neighborhood."

"Wait. When did this happen?"

"On a break from the trial this morning."

"Which was when?"

"About an hour and a half ago."

"And you're just now warning us."

"We've been handling it, I promise."

"Then how did she get away in the first place?"

"Could I speak to Patrick?"

Susanne went silent, trying to form rational thoughts. She was scared. Barb was dangerous. But Max was right. It was a small town. If Barb had been headed to the Flints, she'd have already come and gone. Susanne jammed her fingers into the lid of her left eye. Sometimes it helped stave off the pain, if she could find exactly the right pressure point.

"Susanne, are you there? I'd like to speak to Patrick, please."

"Patrick and the kids are up in the mountains."

"Do you have anyone there with you? I know this is upsetting."

Susanne slumped onto the edge of the bed. Ferdinand put his jaw on it and laid his head against her thigh. *My dog.* "My sister-in-law." Sort of. Just not right at that moment. "Later today I'm having friends over for a . . . get-together."

"Can I do anything for you?"

"Catch her. Catch her now. And put her away for good."

"We've got every law enforcement officer in the state on the lookout. We'll find her."

Susanne thought about Wyoming. Four hundred thousand people, give or take, in a wild and rugged state covering more than sixty million acres. Barb had the advantage. "She's from Laramie."

"Yes. We're going to be looking there. And everywhere."

An intense longing for Patrick made Susanne feel weak in the knees. But if he were home, he and the kids would have to learn about Barb's escape, too. Patrick would be furious. Perry would be worried. Trish's sense of betrayal would flare back up. Feelings they had all thought they were past. Feelings they *deserved* to be past.

She took a long, slow breath. "Okay."

"I'll let you go then."

"Wait. The guard. What happened to the guard? Is he okay?"

"He's fine. Embarrassed. In a lot of trouble."

Susanne said goodbye and hung up the phone. She slid her hand across Ferdinand's wiry coat. Her head was crashing fast now. She needed to go take her pill, but she couldn't make herself get up. Her family's testimony had done no good. Reliving the memories of

Barb terrorizing them had been for nothing. The woman had escaped.

And then another awful thought hit her. Barb Lamkin was the mother of the baby Ronnie had been caring for since birth and was hoping to adopt. Susanne didn't want to have to be the one to tell Ronnie. She hoped someone was calling her. Had already called her.

For once, she wished she were in the mountains with her family. She was actually envious of their disconnect from what was going on. They'd be so upset when they heard the news. All Susanne could hope for was that Johnson County would have their escapee back in custody by the time Patrick and the kids returned.

CHAPTER EIGHT: SULK

Solitude Trail, Cloud Peak Wilderness, Bighorn
Mountains, Wyoming
Friday, August 12, 1977, Noon

Trish

WIND BUFFETED Trish as she reined Goldie to a stop on a rocky
saddle overlooking a deep basin. Her butt was killing her, and she
hoped they were finally stopping for lunch. She eased weight off her
tush and looked around. Above them, fields of boulders covered a
half-ring of low summits. In the distance, she spied Black Tooth
Mountain for the first time since they'd started riding. Only yesterday
she'd seen it from the air—whenever she'd had her head out of a
paper bag, anyway. The view was amazing, and she wished Ben were
with her. He'd love it.

She regretted forcing him out of the truck the night before. At the
time, she'd been so upset with him. He was probably really mad at
her. As soon as they got back, she would make it up to him. But their
fight hadn't changed anything for her. She loved him. She was more

determined than ever to graduate early and follow him to Laramie. She couldn't lose him.

"Looks like a snaggle tooth." Perry pointed at Black Tooth. "That mountain needs to see a dentist."

Trish thought it was mildly humorous, but she kept her lips in a straight line. Her dad, of course, laughed like Perry's comment was the funniest thing anyone had ever said. John barely glanced at Perry, and he didn't make a sound.

Henry chuckled, then he shouted to be heard over the wind. "That's our last descent, up ahead. Down in the basin is the east fork of Little Goose Creek." Of course, Henry said it as "crick," like everybody in Wyoming did. "Highland Park's just over the next ridge."

"Let's get out of this wind and eat lunch," her dad shouted back. "Would there be a good spot in the basin?"

Henry nodded. "Shelter would be good. I don't like the looks of those clouds coming in from the north."

Rats. No lunch yet. Trish looked back in the direction they'd come from. John had dropped his reins over his saddle horn and wrapped his arms around himself. The clouds behind him were dark and angry looking. *So much for Henry's almanac forecast.* But she had enough mountain experience to know weather could turn on a dime up here. She sighed. At least she'd brought a heavy coat and rain slicker. Goldie heaved a big sigh, too.

Henry clucked to Spot, and the two of them led off down the trail.

Within a few minutes, the incline became very steep. Trees closed in on either side of the trail, and big boulders in the center made things even more treacherous.

"I don't think Plug can do this." John's voice was scared.

Plug was crowding Goldie. He was picking up on John's mood and it was making him less careful with his feet and spacing. Rocks started sliding into the back of Goldie's legs. The mare snorted and flinched.

Patrick said, "Loosen his reins." Trish's dad sounded like he was right above her. She snuck a look back and had to look up. The trail was so steep, it was almost like they were in a pyramid, with Goldie at the base, Plug on her, Duke on Plug, and Reno on Duke. The sensation made her feel unbalanced, and she whipped her head around to face forward down the trail.

"He might run off."

"He won't. He knows what he's doing. You've just got to let him."

"But he keeps sliding. He's going to fall."

Perry said, "If Plug slides, Goldie will catch him."

Not a comforting thought.

"Bad idea, Perry," her dad said. "He's got four-wheel drive, John. I've been watching him, and he's had three feet on the ground the whole way down. Trust him. But you also need to stay a little further from the horse in front of you. That goes for all of you. We don't need them sliding into each other or a hiker coming up the trail."

Trish hoped John did what her dad had told him and gave her and Goldie some more space.

But the mention of hikers brought another discomforting thought to her mind. "Should we be worried that we haven't seen another human since we left Park Reservoir?"

Her dad laughed. "Trish, nice to have you join us."

"Huh?"

"You haven't spoken all day."

"Whatever," she mumbled, pitching backward in the saddle as Goldie picked her way down a practically vertical section. At its base, the ground leveled out, and she joined Henry on a grassy area beside the trail where a creek trickled by.

"We're at the bottom of the drainage," Henry said. "This is a good lunch spot."

John practically vaulted off his horse as soon as it stopped. His legs were shaking so hard that he nearly fell when he hit the ground. He looked over at Trish, and she pretended she hadn't noticed anything. Perry and her dad joined the group.

"Trish and Perry, hobble the horses, please." Her dad dismounted.

Trish didn't bother grumbling. Someone had to do it so the horses could graze without running off. "You hold them. I'll hobble them," she said to Perry.

He nodded, gathering up the reins of the five animals. Her dad stood beside Reno rummaging in his saddle bag. Trish fished hobbles out of the horses' saddle bags and started with Goldie, fastening the straps around first one front leg, then the other. When she was done, she took off the mare's bridle and replaced it with a halter, then set the bridle aside and turned her loose. She started on Duke next.

"John, put this on." Her dad tossed his jacket to Perry's friend.

John didn't argue.

"I should have checked that he'd brought one before we left the house," her dad said, low under his breath so John couldn't hear.

Trish couldn't believe anyone would come up into the mountains for a weekend without bringing a coat. But then Perry had said John was from the east coast somewhere. Maybe his parents weren't outdoorsy like hers were. She moved on to hobble Spot.

"How's Hank doing?" her dad asked Henry, still rooting around in Reno's bag.

Henry grunted, "Oh, great. Vangie and I don't get any sleep. You know how it goes."

"That I do." Her dad closed Reno's bag and started passing out peanut butter and jelly sandwiches. Trish stuck hers in her pocket and got back to hobbling. "And Ben?"

Trish paused mid-hobble on Spot.

That question got a sigh. "Good overall, but last night he walked home from Lake Desmet. Said his friends left him there. I don't know what to make of it."

Trish hated hearing the story from Henry. She felt even more guilty about leaving Ben. She hoped he didn't hate her. He had to forgive her. He just had to. She moved her hair away from her ear to hear better, then started Reno's hobbles.

"Even the best of teenagers can be tough to raise." Her dad raised his eyebrows at Trish. She didn't react. "You're doing good by him. It can't be easy for the kid after what he's been through."

Trish wanted to stick up for Ben. To tell them all what a great person he was, but she restrained herself. No one else could know about their relationship yet, and if she said any of the things she wanted to, she'd give herself away. Finished with Plug, she settled on the ground by John and unwrapped her sandwich. The boys were quiet as they wolfed down their food.

Henry said, "Speaking of things that aren't easy, how was the trial?"

The two men copped a squat and continued talking about Coach Lamkin between bites. Trish listened to their conversation and watched the horses. They'd grazed their way over to the stream. Goldie had hopped her hobbled front feet into it and was standing there with water cascading out the sides of her mouth.

Perry stuffed his empty sandwich bag in his pocket. "Coach Lamkin could get the death penalty."

Her dad said, "Unlikely, son. She's a woman who's had a baby in prison. I can't see a jury sentencing her to death."

"Life in prison at least?"

"I sure hope so."

Trish hated thinking about Coach Lamkin. She'd trusted her. She'd *liked* her. And the coach had just been using her to keep tabs on Perry and the Flint family, plus she'd tried to kill her and Perry and her mom. Testifying against her old coach, with the woman sitting there staring daggers at her the whole time, had been awful. But Trish had held her head high and told her story, even though it was humiliating to admit she'd been totally fooled by her. If it meant Coach Lamkin would get life in prison, it was more than worth it.

When they'd all finished their sandwiches, they caught their horses, re-bridled them, removed the hobbles, and got back on the trail. This time, Trish hung back behind John and Perry, in front of her dad. She slowed Goldie down to create some distance between her and Duke. Goldie didn't like it and pulled at the reins. The mare was happiest tightly packed in the middle of a group. But Trish needed to talk to her dad, and she knew he'd never be more receptive than when he was out doing what he loved.

"Dad, can I talk to you?" she said.

His voice sounded amused. "You can, and I'm glad you finally want to."

Luckily, her back was to him and he couldn't see her roll her eyes. "I've made a decision about school."

"Oh, yeah? What's that?"

"I'm going to take extra classes this year and next summer."

"That's ambitious. Why?"

"To graduate early. I'm so done with high school and this town."

She braced herself for his response. It was swift and decisive.

"I don't think that's a good idea."

"Dad, I'm at the top of my class, I'm mature, I'm responsible, and I don't have anything to stick around for. Marcy and I aren't even friends anymore." Marcy had been her best friend until Coach Lamkin was arrested and fired. For some crazy reason, Marcy had felt more loyalty to the basketball coach who killed people than to her best friend. She and Marcy weren't enemies, but they would never be the same. "And I hate being in the same town as Brandon. It's embarrassing. People are mean to me now that his mom is in jail, too." Some people in town blamed Trish, when she was the one Donna's brothers had kidnapped, which made zero sense. And it had been Donna who'd tried to get revenge on the Flints for Patrick killing one of her brothers and the other one going to prison. The fact that Ben had known she'd hired a hit man and had told the cops was no one's fault but Donna's.

"I thought you were with Marcy just last night."

Trish ground her teeth. That lie had been the wrong one to tell. "Um, I was. But, like, with a big group of people. It's not the same thing."

"Well, those aren't good reasons to run away."

"I wouldn't be running away. I'd be going off to college."

"Seventeen is too young to leave home."

"Dad, lots of people do."

"You're not lots of people."

She clenched her fist on her saddle horn, opening and closing it, opening and closing it. "I can't believe you won't even consider it."

"I did. Consider it considered, and now let's enjoy our time in the wilderness."

Trish squeezed her heels into Goldie's ribs. The horse shot forward, eager to close the gap between herself and Duke. The narrow trail passed through fields of boulders on either side, and, as Goldie loped, Trish fumed. Her dad never said yes to anything. But she wasn't giving up so easily.

CHAPTER NINE: CRASH

Perry

"I CAN'T WAIT to throw the ball around when we get there." Perry had insisted that his dad make room for his football in Duke's saddle bags.

But despite Perry dangling out the lure of football, John didn't respond. It was like Perry was talking to a wall. He hadn't been able to get John to talk for the last hour.

Perry tried again. "The air is thinner up here. We'll be able to really sail that thing."

Still, no response from John.

He was beginning to regret inviting his friend. John wasn't very good on a horse, and he was kind of a fraidy cat. Perry would never have believed it if he hadn't seen it with his own eyes, but John had been terrified coming down the last hill. He was shivering, too, even wearing Perry's dad's heavy jacket. Perry was barely even cold.

He leaned forward as Duke lunged up a steep section. Ahead of him, he heard John say, "Whoa," and saw him pull back on Plug's reins. Even Perry knew that was exactly the wrong thing to do when a horse was climbing, and he wasn't much of a horseman. Not like his dad and sister were.

A gust of wind caught the inside of his jacket and made it into a sail. He batted it flat again. The higher they rode, the harder the wind was blowing. It was mostly coming from behind them, which should have made the climbing easier, but that didn't seem to make the horses any less unhappy about it. They all had their tails tucked and heads down.

A sharp thunk got his attention. Something had hit his saddle. There was another thunk, but this time whatever it was pelted him in the head. And then there was no distinguishing between the millions of thunks that all sounded at once, because hail was falling from the sky like someone had dumped a truck load of marbles down from heaven.

John screamed so loud that Perry heard him over the hail. He dropped Plug's reins and pulled the coat over his head.

"Get in the trees," his dad yelled.

But there really wasn't much in the way of trees nearby. Just little scrubby ones way off the trail. Perry rode Duke over there anyway, putting the trees between himself and the direction the hail was falling from. It helped. Soon the horses and riders were clustered together so tightly that Perry felt the steam coming off of Reno's flanks beside him.

His dad leaned down from Reno and patted Perry on the shoulder. "Are we having fun yet?"

Perry groaned. "Not hardly."

Henry said, "You all need your rain gear."

But it was already too late for slickers. The hail was mixed with rain. They were all sopping wet, except for Trish, who had managed to get her rain jacket on before the worst of the storm started. Of course—Trish always did everything right.

The pounding went on for a long time, maybe ten minutes. When it stopped, the sun came out immediately. It was straight overhead and brilliant, but the skies in front of and behind them were black. Deep black. Perry was afraid they weren't through with the storm yet.

"That was intense," he said.

Trish said, "Dad, we still have time to get back so I can go to the lake with Marcy."

His dad frowned. "I thought you said she wasn't your friend anymore."

"I would really like to go home." John's quivering voice sounded strained.

Perry's dad and Henry shared a long look.

His dad said, "Well, I guess—"

But whatever was going to come out of his dad's mouth next, Perry would never know, because all of a sudden, a plane buzzed right over their heads, too low. Its engine was making a weird sputtering noise. They all stared at each other. Duke started pawing the ground. A few seconds later, there was a loud sound, almost like a boom, then screeching metal, and a banging and rumbling.

Perry knew it could only be one thing. The plane had crashed, just out of sight over the rise.

CHAPTER TEN: STEADY

FLINT RESIDENCE, BUFFALO, WYOMING
FRIDAY, AUGUST 12, 1977, 2:00 P.M.

Susanne

VANGIE BUSTLED IN, shaking her dark pixie hair, her eyes lively. She was balancing baby Hank on one hip, which was pulling down the waist band of her polka-dotted blue skirt. A bag of ice hung from her other hand. She was so tiny that it made Hank seem bigger than he was. "I'm sorry I'm early." Her Tennessee accent was even stronger than usual. "But I hated that you were here by yourself when the news about Barb came in." The two of them had discussed Barb's getaway on the phone earlier, as well as the fact that the party would be held without electrical power.

Ferdinand shoved his nose into the back of Hank's diaper.

"No, Ferdie." Susanne pulled the dog away. "It's okay. I'm bouncing back."

And she was. She'd shed some tears in the shower—after she'd fetched the shotgun, loaded it, and put it beside the shower door—but after she'd gotten out, she'd steeled herself. Barb was not coming for her family. It was silly to think she would have wanted revenge more than her freedom. She was trying to escape. But one woman alone wouldn't be able to evade law enforcement forever. They would catch up with her soon and put her back in jail where she belonged.

In the meantime, the person Susanne should be worrying about was Ronnie, not herself. Barb's escape would rock her friend. Ronnie and Jeff were not childless by choice. Susanne knew they were on tenterhooks waiting for the chance to finalize the adoption. This setback, even if it was just a delay, wouldn't be easy for them.

But it didn't change things now. They had baby Will. This party would celebrate that and help them provide for him. Lord knows that child needed a good home. She couldn't imagine what it would be like for him, the birth child of two incarcerated felons. Would they have called him Will Renkin or Will Lamkin? Either would have been a horrible cross to bear. Will had landed with the best parents she could have imagined, though. With the Harcourts, he would overcome his birth parents. The sky would be the limit for Will Harcourt.

But had she and Vangie jinxed the adoption by throwing this party? Never mind that they hadn't called it a shower. *A rose by any other name, right?* She gave her head a tiny shake. *Don't be ridiculous.* No. The party was a blessing and a gift to the Harcourts and Will. It was Susanne's job—and Vangie's—to keep the mood upbeat and optimistic. To give Ronnie the support she deserved, not just for her friendship, but in return for the support she willingly and selflessly gave to everyone in the community as a deputy and a darn good person. And to distract her from thinking about Barb Lamkin and whether her escape would be a monkey wrench in Will's adoption.

Susanne could do this. She *would* do this.

Vangie had carried the ice into the kitchen, where she put it in a cooler Susanne had gotten out earlier. "This child is going to be the death of me." She walked back toward Susanne.

"Hand him over to me." Susanne released Ferdinand and held

out her arms. "Hank misses his Auntie Susanne." Babies were the ultimate in good distractions. He was just what she needed.

"Gladly." Vangie transferred her son to Susanne. "This is going to take me a few trips."

Ferdinand followed the diaper.

"Just set everything out on the deck. We're having the party in natural light. Isn't that right, Hank?" Susanne cooed.

"Got it." Vangie went out the front door and was back in a few moments, lugging a big pump thermos. "Coffee."

Susanne danced around the living room in the semi-dark, humming the tune to "Kiss An Angel Good Morning," her current favorite song, and only tripping over Ferdinand once.

"Ferdie likes to dance, too, Hank," she crooned.

Was there anything as wonderful as a warm baby? Hank was chewing on his fist and laughing, watching her with his mother's intense brown eyes. Vangie had dressed him up for the shower in denim pants, a tiny t-shirt that read YEE HA, a red bandana around his neck, and miniature cowboy boots like the ones Susanne had attached to her gift. If she'd gotten her way, she and Patrick would have had at least two more babies. Now that her kids were in their challenging teenage years, she was beginning to see the wisdom of the decision to stop, but she missed this.

She smiled at Hank. "You look so handsome, Hank. Are you going to be a big rodeo star someday?"

Vangie traipsed back through the room, this time with a sloshing punch bowl covered in plastic wrap. That was all it took for Ferdinand to change allegiances. He trotted after her, sniffing the floor for spillage. "I was tempted to spike it, but we have too many ladies from church coming."

"I have a bottle of champagne if you change your mind."

"Let's save it for the after party."

"Oh, goodie." Hank cooed as Susanne rocked him on her hip. "Also, I bought paper plates and cups and plastic cutlery. We're going upscale today."

Vangie was already back at the front door, where Ferdinand deserted her to return to his dancing partners. "I love it when we go classy. Last trip. What time will Ronnie be here with Will?"

"Now. Or soon. But I don't expect guests until 3:30."

"You're dreaming. Our Sunday school class is always five minutes early."

Susanne laughed. The phone rang. She danced Hank and Ferdinand into the kitchen to answer it. "Hello?"

"Uh, Mrs. Flint?"

"Speaking."

"This is George."

She let a long beat pass. She was very upset with George Nichols. "Hello, George."

"I'm sorry I didn't make it this morning. I had something come up." He paused.

Susanne didn't fill the silence. Hank babbled at her, but her mood had soured. She bounced him robotically, her earlier enthusiasm gone.

"I won't be able to come today after all. I'm very sorry, Mrs. Flint."

"I hope it's something *really* important, since my party guests are very important to me."

His voice sounded strangely excited. "It is. I hate having to reschedule, but it really is. I've been hired to take some clients up into the wilderness. How about I come Monday?"

If I don't find someone else in the meantime. The lure of the darn wilderness. What was it with the men in Wyoming? "That will have to do. Thank goodness it's summer and we don't need to run the pumps for the boiler."

"Yes, ma'am. That is a lucky thing. Well, I have to go, but I'll see you Monday."

"If you run into my family, I don't recommend you tell Patrick you stood me up." In over a million acres, there was almost no chance he'd run into them, but it made her feel a little better to say it.

"Yes, ma'am. I'm sorry again."

Susanne hung up the phone. She had to shake this off for Ronnie's sake. Ferdinand pawed at her foot. The dog was ever attuned to her moods, and she stroked his head. Then she gave little Hank a serious look. "It's hard to find good help anymore, young man. But we're not going to let that stop us from having fun, are we?" He chortled and punched a hand in the air. She nodded. "That's what I thought. Now, let's go help your mommy."

CHAPTER ELEVEN: AID

HIGHLAND PARK, CLOUD PEAK WILDERNESS, BIGHORN
MOUNTAINS, WYOMING
FRIDAY, AUGUST 12, 1977, 2:00 P.M.

Patrick

LIGHTNING STREAKED ACROSS THE SKY, lighting up the
black clouds re-gathering over Highland Park like a disco ball. Patrick
caught sight of Black Tooth. He couldn't help but marvel at the
peak's majestic outline, before it disappeared into the dark again.
Thunder boomed as he caught the lingering scent of ozone. John
screamed and Plug reared. Patrick had been worried the boy's
anxiety would impact the horse, and rightly so, it appeared.

He was closer to the two than Henry, so he hurried over, grabbing
Plug's reins and urging Reno in close. Plug continued rearing. Each
time was less high, but the antics were getting to Reno, who began
tossing his head and snorting. Another bolt lit up the sky. Thunder
shook the ground. The hail and rain restarted with a vengeance.

As Plug rose up on his back legs again, Patrick leaned in and grabbed John around the waist. "Hold onto me." He dragged one hundred and thirty pounds of frightened teenager off Plug.

John clasped his hands around Patrick's shoulder and neck like he was drowning. He scrabbled against Reno's side, kicking and flailing, panting and close to hyperventilating. Reno whinnied and shuffled his feet. John's hands were choking Patrick. He dropped Plug's reins to pry the boy's fingers off. Plug took quick advantage of his freedom, galloping away across gloomy Highland Park like the demons of hell were on his heels.

"I'll get him," Henry yelled. "Yah."

Spot took off after the other horse, a blurry streak in the hail and rain. John continued struggling against Patrick.

Patrick used his calmest voice, but it came out strangled from the grip John had on his throat. "You're all right, son. I'm going to set you on the ground now. You're choking me, and I need you to let go of me while I put you on your feet."

John didn't release him. The hail sounded like a drum roll, the lightning like a cymbal crash.

"I'll help." Perry dismounted from Duke and led his horse over to them.

Patrick appreciated Perry's help. It would make this go faster, so that he could turn his attention to getting them all under shelter. The hail wasn't too big so far, but that didn't mean there weren't some monster ones up in the clouds waiting to smash a skull. He was far more concerned about a lightning strike than hail, though. Right now, he was the tallest thing around for hundreds of yards atop his draft cross horse.

"Can you put an arm around his waist, Perry? I need to lower him to the ground."

"Sure, Dad. John, I've got you." With Duke's reins in one hand, Perry reached for his friend's torso.

When Perry touched him, John kicked out wildly.

Perry shouted, "Ow," and backed away, one hand over his mouth.

"Are you okay, son?" Patrick had finally managed to work his fingers under John's. The boy was going to leave a wicked bruise on his neck, but at least Patrick could breathe more easily now. He looked over at his son. Blood was running from under Perry's fingers. He hated not being able to get to him.

Perry grimaced. "I think he knocked out my toot'."

Trish guided Goldie closer to her brother. She shouted to be heard over the storm. "Are you okay, shrimp?"

Perry moaned. "Not really." His Ls sounded more like Ws.

Yep. A tooth out.

Patrick said, "Take Duke, Trish, before we lose another horse." Not that docile Duke was showing any signs of bolting, but stranger things had happened.

She nodded and scooped up Duke's reins, leading the horse a few feet away.

Patrick felt his lips moving with no sound coming out as he plotted how to take care of everyone at once, and he didn't even care. He had wanted to be gentle with John, but the kid was in shock, and he had to get him to snap out of it so he could help Perry and get the group into the trees.

"John." Patrick's voice was loud, sharp, and jarring. "You're fine. I'm putting you down, now. If you don't help me, it's going to be a rough landing."

John answered, but his voice was high-pitched and brittle. "Don't! No!"

"John," Patrick said in his deepest dog training voice, "On the count of three, you're letting go, and I'm setting you down. If you don't let go, I'll have to drop you. You don't want that, do you?"

"N-n-no, sir."

"Good. Here we go. One, two," Patrick wrenched the boy's fingers away from his neck and caught him by the wrist, "three." When John didn't release his shoulder, Patrick twisted and yanked the boy's other arm away by its wrist, lowering him to the ground at the same time.

John landed on his feet but then fell on his bottom and slid backwards. He caught himself on his elbows and didn't get up. His bottom had dug a short trench through the sparse vegetation, mud, and small rocks. The landing had knocked the silence out of him, and now Patrick could hear the boy's sobs.

Patrick felt terrible for him, but John wasn't injured, and Perry was. "Trish, can you help John, please?"

"Yes, sir." She dismounted and led the horses with her to John. One thing about his daughter, she might put on a sulky teenage girl act more often than he liked, but when the chips were down, she was someone he could count on. Steadfast. No nonsense, no arguments. Helpful. He was grateful for it right now, with everything breaking down.

Patrick moved his horse beside Perry. Behind him, he could hear Trish talking softly to John, but not her words.

He dug his field medical kit out of his saddle bag and pulled Reno's reins through a belt loop on his jeans. Kneeling by Perry, he said, "Let me see."

Perry moved his bloody hand away from his mouth. One of his upper teeth was missing.

Patrick nodded. "Ouch."

"Should I put it in my pocket?" Perry's voice whistled through the new hole in the front of his mouth.

"Might as well." Patrick got out his flashlight and searched the undergrowth for the tooth. It was a futile exercise, and, after a few minutes, he gave up and turned his attention back to his son. "Now, say 'ah'."

"Ahhhhhhh."

Patrick shined the light at and into his son's mouth. It barely penetrated the darkness, and Patrick had the sensation that the sky— hail, dark, and all—was falling into the beam. But he could see Perry's lip at the end of the tunnel of meager light. It was split, but not too badly. Gently, he lifted Perry's upper lip.

"Ow."

"Sorry." Patrick nodded. The tooth appeared to have come out cleanly, and Perry's gum didn't look like it needed stitches. There were butterfly bandages in the medical kit, but they wouldn't stick inside Perry's wet mouth. Nor would they do much better on his lips. Patrick pondered his options. The best course of action was just to stop the bleeding and give Perry something for the pain.

He fished for Tylenol and handed two to Perry along with the canteen. "Take these."

Perry did, wincing when the canteen touched his lip.

"Good." Patrick smiled at him. "We'll be calling you Snaggle Tooth from now on."

Perry moaned and shook his head.

Patrick gave him a wad of gauze. "Does anything else hurt?"

"No, suh."

"Okay, then. Apply as much pressure as you can with the gauze. It's going to take a while to get it to stop bleeding."

"Yes, suh."

"You'll have to do it even when we're walking. We're heading for those trees over there now." Patrick pointed.

"What trees?"

"You'll see them when the sky lights up. They're there. I promise. But I have to check on John first."

Perry nodded and lowered his voice. "What's wrong with him?" Wrong came out as "wong."

"He just panicked. We'll help him to the trees and get him settled down and warmed up. He'll be fine." Patrick was being optimistic for Perry's sake. He was already planning an emergency descent, leading Plug with John safely on the ground, hiking.

But then he remembered what they'd seen just before the lightning storm. A crashing plane. Not something easy to forget, but given the circumstances, it wasn't at the forefront of his mind. *Son of a biscuit.* They couldn't go anywhere. That plane had gone down nearby, and there might be injured survivors. Time and weather weren't on their side, if so.

Patrick might be their only chance.

CHAPTER TWELVE: EXCITE

Big Horn, Wyoming
Friday, August 12, 1977, 2:00 p.m.

George

GEORGE NICHOLS SHOOK off the last of his hangover as he saddled the third horse. Something smelled stale and funky, and, judging by the taste in his mouth, he was afraid it wasn't the animals. He finger-combed his sideburns, then rubbed his eyes. He had to get himself together.

He smacked the horse on the side to get it to release its breath. "Quit your puffing, you old nag."

The animal exhaled, and George pulled the cinch tighter.

The day hadn't started off well. He did feel terrible that he'd forgotten to set his alarm and stayed in bed with the pretty tourist he'd picked up the night before in The Mint Bar in Sheridan. He thought the world of the Flints, and he wanted to do a good job for them. Life had a way of ruining his best intentions sometimes. Women liked him, and he liked them, especially after a few shots of whiskey. He'd make up for it by doing a great job for Mrs. Flint on Monday. And he wouldn't even charge a penny for it.

But things were looking up. Orion Cardinale, a city slicker with a funny accent, had booked George for a cool job. Orion needed an ASAP guide, complete with riding and pack horses, to take him and two other men up onto Highland Park in Cloud Peak Wilderness. Orion, along with two buddies named Luke and Juice, would be looking for a friend who was overdue returning from camping with a girlfriend who wasn't his—now very suspicious—wife. Orion figured his friend was just enjoying himself a little too much in the mountains, but said that if they didn't find him, the wife would be sending someone else to do it. And if she discovered the girlfriend, it would be bad for everyone involved. George came highly recommended, according to Orion, and he'd offered to pay double George's going rate. George didn't even have a going rate, so he'd made up a number on the fly, then immediately wished he'd quoted it higher.

The job would be an odd one, for sure. George had worked for an outfitter for a few seasons and still pitched in occasionally when they were shorthanded. He knew the mountains as well as anybody, he expected, so that part was straightforward. But Orion had said they needed someone who could keep his mouth shut, because of the girlfriend.

George had assured him he was their guy.

It had been a mad scramble to get ready. George had promised the manager from the ranch he called home a big payday in exchange for letting him borrow a few of their horses. It was no sweat off the manager's back. They didn't need them that weekend anyway.

So, now George was getting the four saddle and two pack horses ready.

He brushed the glossy black coat of his own Shire draft before strapping the pack saddle to his back. "You think I'm crazy to take this job?"

The horse snorted and seemed to nod.

"Easy for you to say. You get all the grass you want to eat, free. Me, I've got bills to pay." And more than a few overdue. This job would move his finances from red to black. Even without charging the Flints for his work at their house. He'd had no choice but to take this job and leave Mrs. Flint in the lurch, as bad as it made him feel.

When George had the horses ready, he assembled enough gear to keep his clients warm, dry, and alive for a few days, and packed it into the back of the truck. Finally, he loaded the horses into the trailer and pointed the rig up Red Grade Road. Orion and his buddies were stopping for food and supplies on the way and meeting George at their rendezvous point: the snowmobile lots above Big Horn.

It was only after he was driving, as his head cleared and he had time to think, that he wondered just who his clients were. They hadn't sounded like they lived around the area, even though there were plenty of people from all over the world that gave the Bighorns a try. Most of them didn't last the first winter, of course. George knew just about everybody there was to know in Sheridan, Johnson, and Big Horn counties, short timers or locals, and he'd never heard of Orion, Luke, or Juice.

He guessed he'd find out more about them soon enough.

CHAPTER THIRTEEN: RESOLVE

PINEY BOTTOMS RANCH, STORY, WYOMING
FRIDAY, AUGUST 12, 1977, 2:00 P.M.

Ben

BEN TOSSED the basketball against the side of the Piney Bottoms ranch house. The house bounced it back at him. He did it again. And again. And again. The pounding of the ball was helping him, somehow, but not enough to make everything better.

He was still upset about the night before. He'd messed up. When Trish had said she was going to graduate early to enroll in the University of Wyoming, it had scared him, and he hadn't handled it well. She'd been really upset. He didn't even blame her for making him walk home. Not much, anyway. He hadn't explained himself well, or at all.

But he hadn't known what to say.

He loved her. Had loved her from the first time he'd seen her at Buffalo High School. He'd loved her all through the horrible night when his father and Uncle Billy had forced him to help kidnap her in retaliation for the death of his grandmother. They'd blamed Trish's dad for it. Ben hadn't known what to think. He'd just known that if he didn't help them, it would be even worse for her, and ultimately for him, too. It didn't justify things, but it was the truth. Then and now, he just wanted to be a better person. One who would deserve an amazing girl like her.

He'd had all night and all day to think about what to say to her. He wrapped his arms around the ball and hugged it to his chest. He dropped his chin, the smell of rubber basketball clearing his head like it always had, since he'd first picked up a ball as a young kid. He'd been good from the start. And, until he'd moved to Buffalo, he'd been a star on his team back home, playing forward for his high school. That was part of the past though. In the present, he was just lucky to have a roof over his head and be dating the prettiest girl in town.

He was ready now. He knew what he needed to tell her. But Trish wouldn't be back until tomorrow afternoon at the earliest. It felt like an eternity to wait to make things right.

She'd been going up to Highland Park with her dad and Henry. And Ben knew a short cut up there, from Henry. Henry had been grumbling good naturedly about meeting the Flints at Park Reservoir that morning when Ben had gotten up to help load the horse in the trailer.

"It's a shorter drive to Hazel Park off Little Goose Creek and a shorter ride to Highland Park from there as well," he'd said. "Park Reservoir. I don't get it."

Henry and Vangie kept a beat-up truck with an old single horse trailer parked behind the barn for emergencies. The truck didn't run all that great, but the keys were under the mat. And when Ben had moved in, they'd told him to pick a ranch horse and consider it his. He'd gotten to know Jackalope pretty good. Nobody would ever accuse him of being a rodeo cowboy, but he could stay on him well enough to ride up a trail. He could be ready to leave in two minutes, which would mean he'd be unloading Jackalope at Hazel Park in less than two hours. The horse was in tip top shape. If he rode hard, he could find their camp before dark.

There was only one problem. Trish didn't want anyone to know about their relationship.

As if in agreement with Trish, a raindrop smacked him in the forehead. Bad idea, it seemed to say. Then two, three, ten, three dozen, all of them shouting at him. Bad idea. Bad idea. Bad idea. He froze for a moment, fighting the doubts creeping into his mind. If Trish was going to graduate early to follow him to Laramie, her parents were going to find out about them anyway. She had set them on a course to make their relationship public. Rain or no rain, it didn't matter. He had to find her and talk to her, and nothing would convince her how important she was to him better than a big gesture. Riding after her in a storm would do the trick.

He threw the ball into the grass and ran for the house.

CHAPTER FOURTEEN: ENCOUNTER

Trish

TRISH HUNKERED with Goldie and Duke on the south side of the stunted trees. Her dad had found the little stand of pines on the edge of Highland Park. It wasn't much protection, but since the wind was blowing hard from the north and the hail and rain were falling in an almost horizontal line, it helped some.

She shielded her eyes with her slicker.

Beside her, John was shivering and talking to himself. "So cold. Just w-w-w-w-wanna go home. Not on my dumb horse."

It was nonsense that didn't require an answer. No one was going anywhere in hail and lightning. It was cold—she agreed with him about that—but not freezing. She kicked at the white stuff on the ground. It mushed under her boot. No ice anymore. The hail was melting. And at least John was calm, finally.

She patted Duke on the neck. The Flint horses had done really well, despite all the excitement. Plug hadn't, but in her opinion that was more John's fault than Plug's. Horses were empathic. They soaked up and reflected whatever emotions were going on around them. It happened with her all the time. If she was in a bad mood, it made Goldie act nervous, like she was afraid Trish was going to take it out on her or something. If Trish was relaxed and happy, Goldie was almost playful, like she felt safe. Once, back when she'd been dating Brandon and they'd had a big fight, she had run down to see Goldie, thinking the horse would make her feel better. Goldie had run from Trish and wouldn't come back to her even after Trish got a bucket of sweet feed for her.

John had been scared, so Plug had gotten scared. It was only natural for a horse.

She tried again to coax John into talking to her about something besides how miserable he was. "Hey, John, do you know what teachers you have for your classes this year, yet?"

"Never been so cold. Never. Never."

Trish gave up. He'd totally lost it. Honestly, Perry was a lot worse off than John was. Her brother's jacket was covered with his own blood. His face was pale, too, like he was really hurting. Poor kid. Not only was he a shrimp, but now he also looked like a toothless redneck. The thought made her smile. She couldn't wait to tell him that, but he was on the other side of John and her dad, and the storm was too loud for him to hear her. Maybe she'd wait until he felt a little better anyway.

She peered out at the storm. The hail and rain fell in a sheet. Between the precipitation and the dark skies, it felt like the world had collapsed in around her. This ride had been even worse than she'd expected. She was tired. It had been six hours and ten miles since they'd left Park Reservoir. There was no sign of the weather letting up yet. Even when it did, her clothes and saddle wouldn't dry for hours. And the smell. Ugh. She didn't mind the smell of wet horses, but the nervous animals had decided they all needed to relieve themselves, right where they were standing. It wasn't pleasant. She was wasting her time up here babysitting John and freezing to death when she could be working things out with Ben. She pictured his face, in a warm, dry place. They could have met up at the library. Or at the lake again.

But no—her dad had to drag them up onto Highland Park during a hailstorm. It was so like him.

Ben. She wondered what he was doing right now and whether he was mad at her for making him walk home. She would have been mad if the tables were turned. She sighed and wiped water from her face. It hadn't been her best moment. Her emotions just got so *big* when it came to Ben. And the thought of being apart and him finding someone else had made her, well, *crazy*. That was no excuse, though. She knew better. Knew it firsthand, unfortunately, because last spring during a snowstorm, Brandon had left her to walk home alone on a deserted road outside of town. She'd been scared and angry, even after he'd come back to get her. And despite how that had made her feel, she'd gone and done the same thing to Ben. It made her stomach clench. She didn't deserve Ben to forgive her, but she needed him to. He had to. She couldn't lose him.

"Trish, a word, please." Her dad shouted to be heard over the storm. He motioned her to move away from John.

She tugged on the lead ropes, and the horses resisted. Clearly, they were worried she'd lead them back out into the storm. They didn't want to give up their sheltered spot. She wasn't going to make them, though, because she didn't want to give up hers either. She pulled hard and steady until they relented. Still, their steps were slow motion. When she'd finally moved them about six feet, she squeezed behind Goldie and turned toward her dad, who had followed her. It was close quarters. "Yeah?"

He lifted his eyebrows. "You mean 'yes, sir?'"

She swallowed back a smart reply. It would take energy she didn't have to fight with him right now. All she wanted was off the mountain. "Yes, sir?"

"You heard that plane a little while ago?"

She nodded. "Yes, sir." She hadn't thought about it at all since then, what with John going nuts and Plug running off and the storm and all. Crazy that it had slipped her mind. It had been right over their heads. "Do you think it crashed?"

"I do. There might be survivors with injuries. I have to go see."

Her chest constricted. "And leave us here alone?"

"No, no, I wouldn't do that. I won't go anywhere until Henry gets back. I just wanted to tell you, because I'll need to move out fast when he does."

His answer still made Trish uneasy. Henry was great—better than her dad in some ways—but her dad was her dad. She didn't like the thought of him being gone while she and Perry were up on a mountain in a storm with John acting all weird. But of course her dad would want to help the survivors. It was his job. More than that. It was who he was. But how could he do it all by himself? She wondered what people would look like after a plane crash. Smushy? Bloody? Gory? She shivered. She used to think that because she loved animals she wanted to be a veterinarian, but between dissecting a frog in biology class and her dad cutting open an antelope in front of her, she'd changed her mind. And people were way worse than animals. She was the wrong person for a crash scene, but it's not like Henry could go. John and Perry were in bad shape. That left only her.

"Do you need me to come along and . . . help?" *Please let him say no.*

"Thank you, but no. I want you to keep an eye on John. I'm worried he'll do something dumb that gets himself or somebody else hurt again. He's calmer with you than the rest of us"

A little bit of the tension that had been building up in her released. "Okay. I will. And Perry, too." A new sound caught her attention, different from the relentless hail and rain. Hoofbeats. "Henry," she said. "He's coming."

Her dad nodded and put his hands around his mouth like a megaphone. "Henry. We're over here."

Lightning flashed, revealing Henry, Spot, and Plug, plus a surprise. There was a man on Plug's back. Trish gasped. Henry saw them and nodded. He reined Spot toward the trees, dragging Plug and his new rider behind him.

Henry vaulted off Spot before the animal came to a complete stop. He helped the other man down. The guy moved stiffly, like he was hurt or something. Together, they stumbled to the cover of the trees, with Henry pulling the horses behind him. Goldie chuffed and shifted her feet. Henry stopped beside Trish and her dad. Spot and Plug shoved their way in beside the other horses. Young Spot bumped into Goldie, and she showed him her teeth. Perry and John sidled between the trees and horses and joined the group.

"Be nice," Trish warned her horse.

A long roll of thunder boomed. Spot moved out of Goldie's range, and the mare relaxed. Plug seemed totally fine now, even though he'd just brought a stranger across the park in a storm. Trish wasn't surprised. It was John, not Plug, that was Plug's problem.

Henry shouted to be heard, motioning his thumb toward the man with him. "I found him out on the park. He's from the crash."

Between the darkness and the rain, Trish couldn't see the newcomer's face. He had long, dark hair, and he definitely wasn't dressed for the weather. He had nothing on but a t-shirt and baggy jeans. She pressed a hand to her mouth. There was blood and other stuff on them that she didn't want to think about, and he was standing funny, with one shoulder lower than the other. It was hard not to stare. Her dad saw stuff like this all the time, and he didn't bat an eyelash. She didn't know how he did it. She tore her eyes away and looked at Henry's face instead. He was still talking, loudly.

"He said there are no other survivors, Patrick." Trish felt a rush of relief, then guilt. No survivors meant her dad didn't have to go to the crash site, but it also meant people had died, which was sad. "His name is—"

Her dad shook his head, cutting Henry off. "I know who he is. Eddie Blackhawk."

The man nodded. "Dr. Flint."

From the tightness around her dad's mouth, Trish didn't think he liked Eddie very much. "How do you know him, Dad?"

"He's Constance Teton's brother."

"Constance? The woman we saw in Dubois?"

"Yes."

Henry turned to the boys. "Your horse is all right, John." Then his eyes widened. "What happened to you, Perry?"

Perry bared his teeth. "John kicked my tooth out." Blood dripped down his chin, like he was a vampire taking a break from a feast.

"You need to press harder with that gauze." Her dad's eyes never seemed to leave Eddie's face, though.

"Yes, sir." Perry shoved the wad of bloody gauze back into his mouth.

Her dad moved close to Eddie. His voice was hard. "How many others were with you?"

Eddie stared back at her dad. Trish got a better look at his face. He was an Indian, and his eyes were black and hard. "The pilot and one other guy. They didn't make it."

"How do you know they were dead?"

"I've seen dead before. People, animals. I know what it looks like, man."

"Did you check their pulses?"

Eddie's voice sounded annoyed. Not scared or freaked out, like Trish would have been if people had just died before her eyes and left her alone in a crashed plane in the wilderness. "Yes. They were dead."

Trish said, "So, you don't need to go to the plane, Dad."

Eddie shook his head. "Nothing there now."

Her dad frowned. "You got pretty lucky then."

"I guess. If you can call it that."

"Where were you headed?"

"Buffalo. I hitched a ride to come visit some family."

After a long silence, her dad pointed to the ground at the base of a pine. "Sit there, Eddie. I need to take a look at you."

Eddie shook his head and stepped back, slipping in the mud and catching himself with one hand on Plug. "Nah, man, I'm fine. I just want to get out of here."

"Does your head hurt?" Her dad closed the gap between himself and Eddie. He lifted the man's chin.

Eddie ducked away. "What? No. I didn't hit my head."

"Your abdomen, neck, or back?"

"No. The only thing that hurts is my arm." He tapped it with one hand. "I've been hurt worse falling off a horse."

Her dad's lips started moving. Talking to himself, Trish knew. He wouldn't let someone walk away from a plane crash without a thorough examination. He was so into being a doctor that he sometimes went overboard.

Eddie put a hand over his heart. "I swear. All I want is a warm bed. Some painkillers would be nice, too, if you've got any."

Trish could have been knocked over with a feather when her dad said, "Fine. Let's get off this mountain."

CHAPTER FIFTEEN: SEIZE

George

HAIL AND WIND pelted the trailer as George unloaded Yeti, the big, black and white Shire draft he'd bought from the last outfitter he'd worked for. The horse stuck out his nose and whinnied, calling for the other horses, who were already out. One of them answered. George knew the animals weren't happy about the weather. He'd edged the truck as close as he could get to the tree line on the northeast side of Hazel Park, hoping it would break the wind and wetness. It had worked, somewhat.

His new client Orion Cardinale and the man's buddies, Luke and Juice, were standing under the trees out of the weather. George's impression of the three men wasn't favorable so far. They were dressed wrong, for starters. Orion—the shortest of the three but just as heavy as the others due to a belly that looked like a full-term pregnancy—was in zip up black leather boots. Water was beading off his black, wavy hair, which was slicked up and back with some kind of pomade. Luke and Juice both had smooth, bald heads and were obviously identical twin brothers. They at least had rubber soles on their boots, but the heels were flat, not like cowboy boots. George hoped none of them ended up sliding a foot through a stirrup and getting it stuck there. It was a good way to get dragged to death. Their pants weren't made for the wilderness either. All three men were wearing slick leisure slacks and unlined leather jackets under the rain slickers George had brought for them. And he could smell them from twenty feet away. Give him a bar of soap any day, not the after shave or cologne or whatever these guys had doused themselves in. Perfume was for women, and even on them it had no place in the wilderness.

George eyed the men and guesstimated their sizes. The three of them all together had to weigh nearly seven hundred pounds. The horses had already endured a rough ride in the trailer since the turn-off from Red Grade Road and especially once they'd crossed over Little Goose Creek. Now they had to carry these behemoths up into the mountains. George would owe them a rest and extra rations when this was over.

George secured Yeti to the outside of the trailer with the other horses. Then he walked into the trees where the men were huddled together. He motioned for Orion to join him a few feet away from the others. Orion slipped and slid his way over the wet pine needles toward George, but Luke and Juice followed him. George frowned. He'd wanted a word with his client alone. It wasn't worth making a big deal over, though.

George leaned close to be heard. "Are you sure you don't want to wait for the weather to break? This is going to make for miserable riding."

"Negative. We want to find our, um, friend." Orion's voice sounded even more foreign in these surroundings, and his skin was darker than most of the people George knew in Wyoming. So was Luke and Juice's, for that matter. "Do you got a map or something to show us the road to this Highland Park?"

"Nope. That's what I'm for." George smiled.

"No offense, but I'm a man who likes to see the lay of the land."

"I'm sorry. There aren't really any good maps of that area, so I didn't bring one." Maps of trails in Cloud Peak Wilderness were notoriously unreliable. Most of the guides and outfitters just learned the mountain and passed on what they knew to each by word of mouth.

"Draw me a picture with words, then."

George frowned. "I don't follow you."

"Explain the route to me in English. *Capisce?*" Orion sounded irritated.

George had watched *The Godfather*. He might not know what *capisce* meant, but he didn't need to speak Italian to understand what Orion meant. He cleared his throat and pointed back out at the road they'd driven in on. "We'll follow this road to its end, where it turns into the Little Goose Trail. After about three miles, Little Goose merges with Solitude Trail. You take Solitude another mile or two up and you'll end up on Highland Park."

"Easy enough." He nodded. "Now, what kind of park is Highland?"

George was a smart enough guy, he usually thought, but half the stuff Orion said made no sense to him. "What do you mean?"

"Just what I said. What kind of park? Is it for kids, is it like Central Park, you know, big and for everybody, or is it more of an empty space?"

George would have laughed if his client wasn't deadly serious. "More of an empty space."

"Is there a sign or a landmark or something, so we'll know when we get there?"

Again, George kept a straight face. But he was beginning to wonder if Orion had any sense. Any at all. "No. But you can't miss it. It's a big, flat, grassy area at the base of the peaks."

"Sounds really memorable." Orion raised his eyebrows at Luke and Juice.

The two men laughed.

"Trust me. After all the boulder fields we'll pass in the area, you'll recognize it when we get there. As for finding your friend, from the park, there are trails heading off in a couple directions, but there's also a lot of visibility. If he's out in the open, we'll see him. If not, I know some popular camping spots we could check out first, before we go too crazy."

"If you say so." Orion nodded. "Little Goose to Solitude to the grassy meadow. Got it. Now, how do you cowboys say it?" He made a goofy face and deepened his voice. "Head 'em down and move 'em out?"

Again, Orion looked at his buddies, and, again, as if on command, Luke and Juice laughed.

It was the worst imitation of John Wayne George had ever heard. "Something like that." He felt ridiculed. And it was clear these men had no experience with the West except for the movies and very little in the outdoors. He got a bad feeling about their experience level with horses. When Orion had called to book George to take them on horseback into the mountains, he'd assumed they could ride. "Have you guys ridden before?"

"You mean a horse?" It was the first time Luke had spoken in front of George. His accent was similar to Orion's but sounded flatter. He brushed water off his face, and George saw a crude tattoo of a clock face with no hands on the back of his hand. George had never seen anything like it in Wyoming.

What did he think George meant if not a horse? "Yes. A horse."

"Nah. But how hard can it be?"

Juice shook his head. "Speak for yourself. One of those beasts already tried to bite me. I don't like them."

While Juice and Luke were disconcertingly similar in appearance, George could now tell them apart, and not just because of Luke's clock tattoo. Something was wrong with one of Juice's eyes. It was red, and the iris seemed to float. Like he'd been hit in the eye, hard, or too many times.

"Don't be a wimp, Juice." Orion held up a hand. "Mr. Nichols, give us a quick lesson. Very quick."

George took five minutes to show the men how to mount and dismount, stop and go, turn and back up. "The most important things are to keep your weight on the balls of your feet in the stirrups and to stay calm. Horses pick up on anxiety, and a scared horse is a dangerous one."

Juice's eyes cut to the horses. His breathing had grown shallow during George's demonstration.

"Piece'a cake. I'm more concerned about bears," Orion said.

"Predators aren't usually a problem out here. We have black bears and mountain lions, but they don't want to see you any more than you want to see them. The most dangerous animals out here are the moose. They can be aggressive, so if you see one, hold your horse back."

"What's a moose?" Juice's voice squeaked.

"Think 'giant deer,'" Orion said. "Bambi, ya know?"

Not exactly. More like long legged grizzlies. But George didn't correct him. "I'm going to ride in front. We'll ride single file."

"That's fine as long as you keep up the pace."

George nodded. He'd go as fast as the men and horses were capable of, and no faster. "Highland Park is about ten miles from here. It should take us two hours to get there."

Luke sneered. "We could walk it faster than that."

"Your horse would probably appreciate it. Feel free to jump off and lead yours any time you want." George crossed his arms. Juice laughed, but then coughed into his hand when Luke and Orion didn't join him. "The terrain is steep and rough. We have to give the horses and ourselves enough time to adjust to the altitude. Altitude affects people differently. For some it can be fatal." George couldn't remember the medical jargon for the high-altitude conditions that killed people, so he moved on quickly, before the men could ask him about it. "And the horses need to stay fresh enough that they'll be able to do whatever we need them to once we're up there. Like haul out your friends."

"Or haul out something." Luke guffawed.

Orion frowned and held up a hand. "Luke apologizes for his bad attitude. We'll be fine. And, Mr. Nichols, here's the first half of your fee." He counted out five one-hundred-dollar bills and put the damp paper into George's hand. "I'll give you the other half when we get back. And, if we finish, our, um, rescue in twenty-four hours, there's another five hundred in it for you. A little, ya know, incentive pay."

George perked up. Fifteen hundred was more than he'd made in the entire summer so far, and it would be his pay day for one weekend in August? He could put up with a few demanding, inexperienced city slickers with smart mouths for that. He could push the horses for that. He stuffed the bills into his wallet. "Thank you, Orion. Now, did you put the supplies in the saddle bags?"

"Beef jerky, Slim Jims, candy, and bug spray into the bags. Check."

"I've got the sleeping rolls, a large tent, and plenty of canteens of water." George nodded. "Time to mount up then."

"Yee haw," Luke said.

This time, George thought about his fifteen hundred dollars and felt a lot less ridiculed.

He shut the trailer gate and pointed the men to their horses, patting his pocket to make sure he had put the truck keys in them. Then he helped the men onto their horses and adjusted stirrups and reins. Scooping up the pony lines for Yeti and another big lunker he'd borrowed from the ranch and whose name he didn't know, he mounted a buckskin named Junior, his own ride. The pack horses were loaded down with most of the supplies and food they'd be carrying in, plus extra empty bags, at Orion's request for his lost friend's things. The other horses were snorting and dancing, unhappy with the strange riders and excessive weight. The men looked just as unhappy with them, and were even more vocal, with more than a few shouts and curses. There was nothing George could do about it. They would all have to work it out on the trail. Or not.

But he was more motivated than before to make sure that they did.

He gave the signal to move out, lifting his arm and gesturing with an open, sideways palm in the direction they were to go. Three pairs of blank eyes stared back at him. He swallowed a sigh. This group of greenhorns was going to be a handful. He clucked to Junior and gave the animal a little rib pressure. The horse took off at a brisk trot, tugging Yeti and the lunker behind him. *The Lunker. That's what I'll call him.*

Hail and rain pelted George in the face. Junior reached the road. His hooves splashed up mud with every step. It was going to be a long, hard ride in these conditions. George decided he needed to put a positive spin on things. There'd be no bonus for him if the men gave up.

George rotated in the saddle to face the other men. "With our head start and at the pace we'll be going, we'll beat Search & Rescue up to your friends."

Orion snorted. "There won't be any Search & Rescue. We're keeping this a private matter. For the sake of a marriage, ya know."

George started to argue the folly of that decision. Search & Rescue had helicopters, stretchers, and trained personnel—the equipment and manpower for real emergencies. But one look into Orion's cool, black eyes changed his mind. Besides, this might not be an emergency. It might just be a case of two people who weren't ready to get back to reality yet.

Still, for a moment, doubt washed over him. What was he getting himself into? It would be a miracle if he got these three all the way up to Highland Park. And if they ran into trouble there, what would he do then?

He tried to think of a good reason to back out and forget Orion had ever called him, but his thinking didn't last long. Not with fifteen hundred good reasons to keep going.

CHAPTER SIXTEEN: FRIEND

East Fork of the Little Goose, Cloud Peak Wilderness,
Bighorn Mountains, Wyoming
Friday, August 12, 1977, 2:45 p.m.

Perry

THE ONLY THING worse than riding in wet clothes on a wet saddle down a steep mountain in a storm was doing it after his best friend had kicked his face in, or at least that was Perry's opinion. His mouth wouldn't stop bleeding. He sounded weird when he talked. His whole face hurt, as his dad would have said, like a son of a gun. Honestly, it was taking all he had not to be mad at John, and John wasn't making it any easier. He hadn't said he was sorry, for one thing. For another, the guy had lost his marbles. He'd screamed and kicked like a little kid up at the park. And he was giving Perry the cold shoulder now. None of it was Perry's fault. So why wouldn't John speak to him? Or even look at him?

Perry ground his teeth. He wanted to chew John out so bad, but he held it in. He kept his eyes forward, over John's head, which wasn't hard, since he was on the ground, leading Plug behind Trish and Henry.

Perry was glad he was on a horse. Behind him, his dad was leading the crash survivor guy—Eddie—on Reno. He understood his dad had to let Eddie ride because the man's arm was hurt, but Perry thought John was crazy not to ride Plug. It was a long walk. In wet boots. His dad and John would have a ton of blisters before long.

John slid a few feet down the trail, screaming until he regained traction. The mountainside was so muddy, it was like it was flowing. Perry had thought it would be easy to find the trail out of Highland Park, but the storm had changed things. If Perry had been the navigator, they would be lost right now. He was glad Henry was in charge.

Plug pulled back from John, backing his rump into Duke's nose. Duke had been following too close. Normally a slow walker on the way out, he picked up the pace when he knew he was heading home. Plug snorted and shimmied sideways. The horse seemed nervous. Perry didn't blame him. After John had gone nuts, Perry was a little nervous around him, too.

"Everyone okay?" Henry shouted.

Duke tossed his head. Perry patted him on the neck. "I'm good."

"Me, too," Trish said.

"We're all right," Patrick called.

John didn't answer. Henry glanced back at him. Perry saw a flash of annoyance in Henry's eyes before he turned back around.

The ground leveled out and Perry detected a loamy odor. They were by the creek where they had eaten lunch. The trail stayed flat for about a minute, then the uphill started again. Duke made funny hub-bub-a-bub sounds with his lips and slowed down, his way of protesting. Perry leaned forward to stay perpendicular to the horizon.

"You're going to be all right, boy," he said.

After about fifteen yards of climbing, Duke stopped for a few deep breaths. Perry felt sorry for him. It was a tough trail, and he was smaller than the other horses and carrying Perry the whole way.

"Dad, Duke is really tired. Do we need to stop for a rest or to give him something to eat?"

His dad said, "They're fine. They could do twice this if they had to."

Perry decided Duke was going to get extra oats and back scratching when they got home. He felt sorry for him, and for his dad and the other horses. Not for John, though. Maybe when his mouth quit hurting, he'd feel differently. "Hey, Dad. Do you think my tooth will grow back in?"

His dad laughed. "Sorry, but, no, it won't. We'll be paying for the dentist's first kid to go to college."

Perry thought about being toothless and funny-looking. Just because he wasn't thrilled that John was making eyes at Kelsey right before football season started, that didn't mean Perry didn't like girls. He had been hoping to find a girlfriend after football was over. But who would like a short guy with missing teeth? "What will they do?"

"They'll give you an artificial one. It will be all right."

"It'll be all right." Trish turned to him and grinned. "You already look like a dork anyway."

Perry gave her a dirty look. "How long will that take, Dad?"

"Well, you'll be singing "All I Want for Christmas Is My One Front Tooth" this year."

Henry and Trish laughed.

Great. Finding a girlfriend would be out of the question. He'd be the shortest guy on the football team and the last one to kiss a girl.

Ahead of him, he heard Henry say, "Whoa, there. Hold up, everyone."

Perry sat back in the saddle, and Duke stopped.

Around a bend in the trail, Perry heard a man talking to Henry. Perry couldn't understand him, but his tone of voice sounded rude.

Henry said, "Sorry. Rules of the trail, mister. Hikers move aside for horses. We won't be but a second."

The man's voice got louder. Then a second person joined in, not rude or nearly as loud. A woman, it sounded like.

Henry kept his tone calm. "I don't make the rules. They're just good sense when you mix people with a bunch of one-thousand-pound animals who don't know them. As you can see, we can't move them into the trees to let you by. But, hey, if you want to make your way through us with your bear bells and your big packs, we can't stop you and good luck to you."

Duke let his head droop, making the most of the rest break. A man with long brown hair in a low ponytail came into view. He was wiry and short, with a pack that towered over his head. In his hands were two metal walking sticks that looked like ski poles. He was swinging them with every step. Goldie snorted and jumped back-wards down the trail when one came within inches of her nose. Rocks tumbled down the trail. The horse couldn't get traction and slid a few more feet. Trish kept her balance, and Goldie came to a stop with her legs splayed. Moaning, John scrambled to the side so she wouldn't land on him. He was breathing fast and heavy, too, and his shoulders were shaking. Plug sat back and pulled against his lead rope. Duke's head popped back up.

"Control your animals," the man shouted. "We have to get out of this weather."

"Like we don't," Perry said under his breath.

Henry now sounded stern. "Keep your sticks down, mister. You're scaring the horses."

"I need them for balance in this mud." The man turned. "Hurry, Alicia. We need to get far away from these rubes."

A pretty black woman appeared behind him on the trail. Her hair was so short it was almost shaved. She whispered, "I'm sorry," to Trish and John as she passed them and kept her walking sticks clutched to her body.

The man's pack bumped into Duke's shoulder as he went by. "Make some room," he snarled at Perry. "This trail is dangerous enough in this weather without you guys blocking the way."

Perry made wide eyes back at his dad. There was nowhere to go to get away from the hiker. What did the guy expect he could do?

His dad shrugged and smiled at him. He mouthed, "It will be okay."

Perry smiled back. But then his smile turned to a frown. Reno was riderless. "Where's Eddie?" he said.

His dad's brows furrowed, and he looked up at Reno's back. "Son of a buzzard bait."

The male hiker stopped short in front of Reno. "Is that animal vicious?" He stabbed a hiking stick toward Reno.

Reno swished his tail and cocked a hoof.

"Yes," Patrick said without looking at him. He was too busy scanning the forest for Eddie.

"How am I supposed to get past him?"

Perry was starting to get angry. Did this man not understand that if he scared the horses, all of them could get hurt? "You weren't supposed to. You were supposed to yield the trail. It's a safety rule. So, I guess you're just going to have to take your chances. Reno doesn't usually kick until you get past him, though, so you may be fine."

Perry heard the lisp through his missing tooth, but he was too mad to care. Then he realized he might be in trouble with his dad for talking that way to a grown-up. He bit his lip, then released it. It hurt where he'd split it. Luckily, his dad was distracted. Perry glanced up at Henry, who gave him an approving nod.

Alicia was standing by Duke's head. "Is your horse friendly?"

Perry nodded at her. It wasn't her fault the other guy was being a jerk. "Hold your hand out to his nose, palm down, to say hi."

She did, and Duke bumped her hand with his muzzle. She smiled up at Perry. "He's cute. Hey, we're supposed to be meeting some friends at Highland Park, but we're running behind because of the storm. Did you happen to see three guys up there?"

Perry started to say no. Then he remembered Eddie had been with two other guys who had died in the crash. They weren't hikers, though. And, technically, he hadn't seen the other two anyway. He shook his head. "No."

Perry's dad had reappeared. He eased Reno up the trail next to Duke. "Excuse me, ma'am."

Alicia moved to the side. "No problem."

The male hiker sneered. "Don't pander to them, Alicia. They don't own the trail."

She turned on him and snarled, "Shut up, Walt. They're nice people."

Perry's dad handed him the reins. "I'll be back." He turned to the hikers. "The longer you stand here, the longer we're all out in this weather. My son was kidding. My horse isn't going to hurt you or anybody. Move on by."

Walt grumbled, but he started down the trail again, swinging his sticks.

Alicia whispered, "Thank you. It's been a hard day. He's not always like this."

The two hikers disappeared around a curve in the trail. As soon as they were gone, Eddie scrambled out of the trees and up the trail to Reno.

"What in Hades made you go running off?" Perry's dad's cheeks were flushed. He stepped close to Eddie with a finger in the man's face.

Eddie wasn't tall, but he had a menacing look that made Perry want to stay far away from him. "I had to take a leak, man. Not that it's any of your business."

"Without telling anyone?"

"Again, none of your business."

Perry's dad scowled. He took Reno back from Perry. "Mount up. We need to get going."

His dad made a step with his hand and gave Eddie a push from behind. Eddie struggled, wincing, back into the saddle, then cradled one of his arms by the elbow. Perry's dad turned to Henry and gave the go-ahead hand signal. The horses and walkers started climbing again. The trees thinned back out, exposing the fields of boulders.

Now that they were wet, they looked darker than they had earlier. The incline got steeper.

"So, what really happened up there, Eddie?" Perry's dad didn't even sound out of breath, but he kept his voice low.

Perry turned his head slightly to the side so he could hear his dad better.

Eddie answered in a nasty tone of voice. "I don't know. I'm no pilot."

"Did lightning strike the plane?"

"I said I don't know."

"You might know more than you think you do. Did the pilot say anything?"

"No."

"Did he radio anyone?"

Slight hesitation. "No."

"Where was the plane going?"

"I told you. Buffalo."

"Coming from where?"

Another hesitation. This one longer. "The res."

"Do I know either of the guys who died?"

"Nah, man. They were just Indians. Dead Indians, now."

If Perry had to guess, Eddie didn't have many friends. He was almost as disagreeable as Walt the hiker.

A wall of wind hit the line of riders and walkers as they crested the ridge out of the basin. Perry lowered his face to keep it out of the hail and rain that was mostly sleet now. Water ran down rain slickers and horse flanks. The horses pushed into the wind for a few yards, then Henry stopped the group at a convergence of trails marked by a large rock cairn beside a grove of pine trees barely taller than their horses. Wooden arrows pointed from a post that was listing over so far that one of the arrows pointed nearly straight up. With Highland Park out of sight in the clouds, there was nothing Perry could see at their elevation and higher but rocks, rocks, and more rocks. Perry was almost disappointed that his dad was too distracted to utter his usual corny line.

Perry whispered it to himself. "They don't call these the Rocky Mountains for nothing." It was good, but not as good as when his dad said it. Perry wrapped his arms around himself.

Henry rode back to Patrick.

"This is taking us too long." Patrick spoke first, in a low voice that sounded agitated. "I think John's in shock. His pupils aren't dilating. He's starting to get the shakes, and he's almost hyperventilating. I need to get him to the ER. Perry could do with some attention, too. And Eddie, of course."

Perry straightened his shoulders. He'd thought John was breathing too hard and quivering. He started to feel guilty for being mad at him. Maybe something was really wrong with him. But John was tough. He'd be fine. He had to be.

"What do you say we take a faster way down?" Henry said.

Patrick squinted and wiped his eyes. "There's a shortcut back to Park Reservoir?"

"No. But this trail—" Henry pointed to the right, "—will get us down to Little Goose Campground. From there it's a short ride into Sheridan and a hospital."

"Not short if there's no one there to give us that ride."

"There will be. Little Goose is a popular campground. And if there's not anyone there, TP Ranch is just a few miles further down the road."

Patrick pulled at his chin and stared over the ridge back toward Park Reservoir. His lips started moving fast, which Perry knew meant he was in a spirited debate with himself. In some ways, his dad was the coolest guy he knew. A doctor. A hunter. An outdoorsman. In other ways, he was a *total* geek. Talking to himself definitely fell in the geek category.

Henry said, "I could ride ahead and get help. Spot is young. He's got a lot left in the tank."

When Patrick didn't answer, Perry couldn't restrain himself. "But we don't know the way down."

"It's just one trail the whole way, son. It empties onto a road that will take you all the way to the campground."

"But what if you're not at the campground when we get there?"

"Then you keep going to TP Ranch. You'll only need to make one turn, a right at a dead end. After that, the road will take you all the way to the ranch entrance. It has a big sign over the gate. You can't miss it."

Perry snuck a glance at John, who looked like he was talking to Trish. "Even John?"

"Even John. It's downhill the whole way from here."

Patrick roused himself from his thoughts. "How long will it take you to get to TP?"

"An hour and a half, maybe two," Henry said.

"And us?"

"Twice that, with walkers. But you won't have to go all the way there. I'll be bringing you back a ride."

Patrick nodded. "You're sure you're okay alone?"

Henry scoffed. "I ride alone most days on our ranch and up into the mountains there. I trained for Search & Rescue when I was younger. I know how to keep myself safe."

Patrick shook his head no, but what he said was, "Okay, then. You'd best move on out. Be careful."

Henry saluted Perry and Patrick with two fingers. "See you down the mountain."

He wheeled Spot and loped the horse onto the trail on the right, past the rock pile and out of sight.

Perry looked back at his dad. His lips were moving again.

CHAPTER SEVENTEEN: VISIT

Susanne

SUSANNE, Vangie, and Ferdinand surveyed the deck.

"Thank the good Lord the weather is cooperating. I'm pleasantly surprised with how it looks," Susanne said.

"I think it turned out really nice." Vangie held out her arms for her baby.

Susanne kissed Hank's forehead. It was warm and soft and smelled sweetly of baby shampoo. "Give me one more minute with him."

"Take all the time you want."

The migraine that had been threatening her earlier after she learned about Barb Lamkin's escape had mostly gone away, which was also a pleasant surprise. The medicine she'd taken before her shower might actually be working. It only hurt a little around the edges now, and her vision had cleared. Enough that she could admire their handiwork.

The deck *did* look nice, and the weather was gorgeous. Blue skies and fluffy white clouds echoed the blue and white crepe paper wound around the top railing of the deck while the yellow sunlight matched the cheerful daisies Vangie had arranged. Balloons in the same colors were tied close to bricks holding tablecloths onto tables. The weather might be mild, but it was still Wyoming after all, which meant breezy bordering on hurricane force winds. The tablecloths had been a find on the remnant table at the fabric store. Brown with cowboys in denim, yellow shirts, and red kerchiefs, their Paint horses rearing with hooves pawing the sky. Susanne had bought the last of the bolt. She'd give the fabric to Ronnie after the party, in case she wanted to make something cute for Will from it. Beyond the deck, the creek burbled, the cottonwoods rustled, and the birds sang. The yard was clear of badger holes. Even her purple, red, and yellow pansies still looked pretty in the flower beds shaded by the deck. And she'd only had to scold Ferdinand one hundred and twenty times, give or take, to stop him from ripping down all the crepe paper. Speaking of which, it was time to put him in the garage, which wasn't going to make him very happy.

Susanne heard a vehicle pull up out front.

"Do you think it's Ronnie already?" Vangie said.

"Maybe. Or it could be my sister-in-law."

"Oh. I'd forgotten she was visiting. Where has she been?"

"She was exploring Main Street in Sheridan today."

Vangie gave Susanne a significant look. The two women had become best friends, and they thought so much alike that Patrick said it scared him sometimes. No surprise that Vangie understood how Susanne felt about Patricia's absence. The door to the house opened and shut. Ferdinand started barking.

"Hush, dog." Susanne called through the screen door, "Patricia?"

When there was no answer, Vangie said, "Ronnie?"

The two women frowned at each other. Susanne handed Hank back to Vangie, shrugged, and headed into the house to see who it was.

CHAPTER EIGHTEEN: INTERCHANGE

Lower Little Goose Trail, Cloud Peak Wilderness,
Bighorn Mountains, Wyoming
Friday, August 12, 1977, 3:15 p.m.

George

"EASY, BOY," George said.

Junior slowed as the trail transitioned from the forest road they'd been following to the Little Goose Trail into the wilderness. The scenery didn't change, however. Pine trees stretching skyward, rain and hail falling down. The normally hard, dry earth sloppy, with mud and water splashing up from Junior's hooves. But the scent of pine needles, fresh and clean, was as head-clearing as it always was in the mountains, and, truth be told, George didn't mind the wet. He'd guided clients through it plenty of times. He preferred the snow, but the outdoors was his preferred location in almost any weather. He'd always believed enjoying the wilderness was about being prepared for anything, and he was warm and mostly dry in a slicker over oil cloth.

After a mile or two on the trail, he looked back at his client. "What brings you to the area?"

Orion's tone was condescending, as it had been the other times George had tried to converse with him on the trail. "The opera and theater."

George was a little miffed. He was just trying to be nice. The guy didn't have to be such a jerk. He tried again, anyway. He was curious about the men. "Where are you guys from?"

"Chicago. Best city on earth."

Finally, a response without sarcasm. But George would have to take Orion's word for it. He had no interest in cities, except for maybe Denver. It might be fun to see the Broncos play once. But Chicago? Why in the world would anyone want to live there? No mountains. Too many people. Just a bunch of big buildings, concrete, and cars.

They passed a wooden sign beside the trail that read CLOUD PEAK WILDERNESS.

George decided their fifteen hundred dollar payment merited a little bit of information. Feeling like a tour guide, he said, "We've just entered Cloud Peak Wilderness. It's a sportsman's paradise, and no wheeled vehicles are allowed anywhere back here. It's nearly as pristine as God made it."

His announcement was met by silence.

"We're basically following the East Fork of Little Goose Creek the whole way. If you took it in the other direction, Little Goose runs right through the towns of Big Horn and into Sheridan."

Silence again

"You guys just let me know if you need a break, something to drink, or have a problem, okay?"

More silence. Apparently, Orion's comment about Chicago was the only conversation George was going to get from him. He stopped trying. The trail was treacherous and deserved their full attention anyway. It was growing more narrow, rocky, and steep. As they climbed, the temperature was falling, too, and instead of mud now, the hail and sleet were leaving a slick layer almost like black ice on the rocks. Several times, Junior had stumbled, and George heard the sounds of the other horses tripping and sliding behind him, too.

He concentrated on keeping himself balanced in the saddle to help Junior. Truth be told, George wasn't much of a horseman, not by Wyoming standards. He'd grown up in town, without horses. Riding friends' horses at sleepovers, he'd only become proficient enough by his teens to keep his dignity when invited to brandings, which were mostly parties on horseback anyway. When he'd taken the outfitter job, he'd been relegated to working with the horses that packed for the hunters. While strength was important, the defining trait of a good pack animal was calmness, so working with them hadn't stretched his skills. That's where Yeti had come from—George had developed a soft spot for the two-thousand-pound draft horse. He'd bought him for a good price at the end of last season, when the animal was deemed too old for any more hard-core seasons of heavy work. But Yeti was as solid as ever for the occasional job, like today, even in the mud and the ice. The Lunker was holding his own with a level head, too. It was Junior that made George nervous. He'd never ridden the Quarter horse in conditions like these, and he wasn't turning out to be as surefooted as George would have liked.

George pulled up at a creek. It was an idyllic spot—at least, it was when the weather was nice—with a tumble of big mossy boulders up and downstream. Only a short section near the trail was suitable for crossing. It was still strewn with rocks, but they were small enough for the horses to navigate, and the crossing wasn't too deep or diffi-cult, except for the daunting climb out on the far side.

After taking a moment to examine the creek bed to make sure things hadn't changed too much since the last time he'd come this way, George urged Junior into the water. Junior acted like it was scalding him, even though he was already sopping wet, and he hotfooted through it on shaking legs, dragging the pack horses with him. When he reached the other side, he jumped up the three-foot incline. George managed to hang on, just, no thanks to Yeti and The Lunker. The bigger horses had made it through the creek fine, but when Junior made his leap, they nearly pulled him over backwards by the pony lines. Junior yielded to the pressure on the saddle horn, landing sideways in a wide stance.

George took a few deep breaths then plastered a stoic expression on his face and turned to encourage the others. He wasn't going to give away how close he'd just come to breaking his neck. "This is a good spot to cross, but only one at a time. Give your horse a loose rein. They know how to find their way through. Your job is to stay on and not get in their way."

Orion and Luke looked skeptical, but Juice was flat out terrified.

"Whoa, Boss. I didn't sign up for this." His voice squeaked.

Orion grasped the saddle horn. "If you don't cross, you're looking for a new job." He kicked his horse's sides with more force than necessary. The animal tucked its hindquarters and jumped forward. It slowed at the water and picked its way through the rocks, making a lot of racket and lunging up the other side but less violently than Junior had. Orion tipped, swayed, and lurched, but he stayed in the saddle, keeping his eyes straight ahead.

"Good job, sir," George told him.

Orion scowled. "This is costing us time."

Luke took a deep breath. "Yah, horse." He smacked it on the rear.

His horse took the creek in three splay-legged leaps then vaulted up the bank, ramming Luke's forehead into the limb of a tree on the other side. George winced. The man fell backward, screaming expletives. He kept his seat, although George wasn't sure how. When he pulled up beside Orion and George, blood was dripping into his eye, and he wiped it away, shaking it off his hand.

Orion raised an eyebrow at him.

"Taking candy from a baby," Luke said.

On the other side of the creek, Juice stared at the water then behind him, back and forth, back and forth, like he was ready to turn tail for the truck.

Orion nodded at George. "Let's go."

George was aghast. "You want to leave him?"

"He can ride all the way back to his sainted mother for all I care. We're doing what we came to do." Orion kicked his horse, who pinned its ears but moved forward. He wasn't winning any points with the animal, and George knew that if it got the chance to ditch Orion, it would.

Luke followed Orion. George hesitated, blocking the trail. Juice could try to ride back, but the truck was locked. George wasn't about to give him the keys, either. But lack of shelter and a ride weren't going to be Juice's problem, because there was no way his horse was going to stand for being separated from his buddies. Not by a novice and a stranger in an unfamiliar place.

One way or another, with or without Juice, that horse would be coming with the group.

"Where are you going?" Juice screamed after Orion and Luke.

Luke turned his bloody face back to his twin brother. He grinned, exposing red teeth. "Don't get eaten by a bear, you big cry baby." Then he faced the trail again, bouncing along behind Orion.

Juice's horse started huffing and pawing. "Hey, you, trail guy. What's wrong with this horse? He's going crazy."

George shouted, "Hang on tight."

The animal exploded across the creek as Juice screamed like the hounds of hell were on their heels. George wasn't even sure if more than one of the horse's hooves touched the water, which was a good thing, since the panicked animal was past being careful about footing and could have broken its fool leg. George lost sight of it for a split second, then it was up the bank and shaking water off like a dog. The horse trotted straight over to Junior, and George grabbed one side of the reins, which were still looped over its neck.

Juice was not with the animal.

George didn't care what Orion and Luke did. He couldn't leave a man behind, fifteen hundred dollars or not. Especially not a man who was on the ground, possibly injured. All he could hear from the creek was groaning. But groaning noises meant Juice was alive and probably conscious.

"Juice? You all right?" he shouted.

The clattering hooves of two horses told him that the other men hadn't stopped.

"You guys, wait up," George said.

No one answered. The hoofbeats continued up the trail.

George sighed. He walked Junior back to the creek, tugging three horses behind him. Just as he got to the edge of bank, Juice's head appeared above it. He crawled over it on all fours. He was covered in mud, including one whole side of his face. Otherwise, he appeared all right, without a drop of blood on him. Slowly, shakily, he stood, not meeting George's eyes. He delivered a few choice words to his horse, then snatched the reins from George.

"Need a hand?" George said.

Juice ignored him. He spent the better part of the next minute trying to climb on, first pulling the saddle sideways and having to right it and tighten the cinch with George's coaching, then slipping through the stirrup with his wet city boots. Finally, he led the horse to a fallen log and climbed on. Without a word to George, he took off after his buddies. His horse decided to set the pace and broke into a fast lope, with Juice's legs bouncing like they were on marionette strings.

"No, no, no," he shouted, in perfect cadence with the horse's stride.

"Nice, buddy," George muttered. *Maybe I should have just left him.*

He turned and rode after the men. He hadn't gone fifty yards before the trail split. To the left was a short cut up to Highland Park. It was poorly marked and too boggy for wet weather use. To the right was the trail they needed to take today.

Muddy hoof prints led to the left. They had taken the wrong fork.

George looped the reins over his saddle horn and cupped his hands around his mouth. "Hey. Hey, you guys. You went the wrong way. Come on back."

"George?" a man's voice said from his right.

George hadn't heard the man and horse approach. When he turned toward them, he saw a rider with a low-slung hat protecting his face astride a nice-looking young gelding, but George couldn't help noticing the frothy sweat on the horse's neck and sides. The man lifted his hat brim.

George smiled at the familiar face. "Henry Sibley. Hello, sir. Heck of a day for a ride, isn't it? What are you up to?" Henry owned the Piney Bottoms ranch, and he'd had George out to do some electrical work a few months before.

"Sorry to be brief, but I'm hustling down the mountain. Got someone injured in our party, and I'm going ahead to arrange for a ride."

That explained the animal's signs of exertion. "Anybody I know?"

Henry paused, then said, "Perry Flint got his mouth busted up. And we ran into some other trouble up there. I'd tell you more, but I'm in a huge hurry."

"Jiminy crickets!" George hit his forehead with his fingers. "That's right. You were coming up here with them. I was just at their house yesterday. How can I help?"

"The rest of the group is further up this trail. Tell them you saw me and that everything is on schedule."

"I will. Listen, my truck and trailer are down at Hazel Park. I can give you my keys. I'd take you myself, but I'm up here searching for some missing persons with a paid group that just ran off and got themselves a few hundred yards down the wrong trail."

"That would be much appreciated. But I don't want to leave you stranded with your clients. I'll only use your rig as a last resort. If I do, I can have it back in a few hours at the most."

"Don't worry about it. Just leave the keys on the back passenger side tire of the trailer, if you would." George retrieved the keys from a zippered pocket inside his jacket and handed them to Henry.

Henry nodded. "Listen, I really need to go, but I sure thank you for your help."

"No problem. Good luck."

Henry saluted him and took off, his horse loping easily toward the creek. George caught a last glimpse of the animal's rump and tail as it descended the bank, and then they were gone.

Seconds later, Orion and his crew rode up behind him from the left fork of the trail.

Orion said, "Whyn't you tell us which fork to take?"

George turned back to his clients and forced a smile. He was fast growing sick of this man. He muttered, "Because you probably wouldn't have listened to me anyway."

"What?"

"I said let's make up some time. Follow me. Yah." He slapped Junior on the rump. Junior hopped in surprise before settling into a lope, jerking Yeti and The Lunker along with him up the narrow trail. Trees limbs smacked George in the face, and from the sounds behind him, were hitting the others, too, but he didn't slow down.

He wanted all the distance he could manage to put between himself and the disagreeable men from Chicago.

CHAPTER NINETEEN: CONSIDER

UPPER LITTLE GOOSE TRAIL, CLOUD PEAK WILDERNESS,
BIGHORN MOUNTAINS, WYOMING
FRIDAY, AUGUST 12, 1977, 3:15 P.M.

Patrick

PATRICK LED Reno and Eddie past the cairn that marked the start
of Little Goose Trail. The group was single file behind them, heads
down. With nothing to slow it down, the wind barreled through the
saddle. He started across the ridgeline and trudged through it. Ahead
of him, he could see the trail winding its way into a boulder-strewn
meadow.

"I'm really starting to hurt, man," Eddie said.

Patrick wanted to tell him to suck it up, but his medical training
and ethics kicked in. There were many days when he cursed the
Hippocratic Oath. *First, do no harm. Yeah, right.* Its guidance had
caused him and the people he loved plenty of harm. Yet how could he
ignore a person in pain? Wasn't that in and of itself causing harm,
when he had the ability to help? It was this exact phenomenon that

drove him to risk his life for others, time and again. Even to rescue murderers who might not have been the most deserving of his mercy and assistance.

He sighed and halted Reno. "I thought you said you were okay?"

"The pain is getting worse. My shoulder and my elbow especially." Eddie clutched his arm.

Patrick turned to the others. "Hold up, kids."

"It's so c-c-c-cold." John's shaking had gotten worse, and Patrick didn't like how sallow his skin looked.

He looked around him, down the trail in front of them, behind them, and up the small summit along the ridge to their right. His eyes stopped there. He thought he saw a small cave up in the boulders, ten or fifteen yards off the trail. It would only take a minute to hobble the horses. The others could take shelter there with him while he took care of Eddie.

"Let's get out of this weather. Follow me," he said.

He walked Reno up toward the rocks. As he got closer, he saw that the cave was more of a west-facing overhang, really, but deep enough that it would provide shelter from the wind and the wet. He set Trish and Perry to work hobbling the horses while he retrieved his medical kit from Reno's bags. By the time he had it out, John and Eddie were already under cover. Patrick helped his kids finish the hobbling job, then the three of them scrambled under the overhang. Trish sat by John, and Perry perched on a rock a few feet away from them.

Patrick didn't even look at Eddie. "I need your shirt off so I can get a good look at you."

Eddie tried to lift it over his head, but he grimaced and stopped. Patrick shook his head. He'd messed up. He should have forced Eddie to submit to an examination up on Highland Park. Adrenaline can mask pain and some serious injuries. The incident with John and Perry, the storm, and the crash had distracted him. And maybe his dislike of the man had made him easier to distract.

Patrick peeled the shirt off of Eddie, who hollered something blue as it jostled and lifted his injured arm. "Sorry."

With his shirt off, Eddie's stomach was concave, and Patrick could see a lot of it. His too-large jeans rode low on his hips, exposing the waistband of his underpants. Patrick wondered why he didn't wear a belt. He hated that his daughter was in here and could see the man. He tossed Eddie's shirt to the ground. It felt heavy, and it hit the dirt floor of the cave like it was holding something heavy. Patrick glanced down and saw what looked like a bundle of money sticking out of the breast pocket. Eddie reached out with his foot and pulled the shirt over to himself, covering the bundle in the process. If it had been a bundle. *None of my business. Not illegal to be carrying cash.*

Patrick pulled a pen light out of his bag and shined it in Eddie's eyes. The pupils reacted normally. Next, he did a visual examination of Eddie's head, neck, extremities, and torso. The man had several gashes and would have some wicked bruises on his left side. He uncapped the hydrogen peroxide. Its slightly sharp odor was fleeting. He put some on a cotton ball and cleaned the cuts with it, then applied antibacterial ointment and some adhesive bandages.

He moved on to the joints, deciding to start from the bottom. He reached for an ankle.

Eddie jerked it away. "What? No, man. It's my side that hurts."

"I need to be thorough. I should have done this at Highland Park."

"And I need you to quit wasting my time. Get your hands off my legs. Nothing below my waist, understand?" Eddie's glare was malevolent.

What the heck is his problem? But Patrick had already known Eddie was not a nice person and prone to behavior that didn't seem rational. He thought back on Eddie's movements. He'd had plenty of time to observe him, walking, getting on and off Reno, and riding with his feet in the stirrups. He hadn't seen any signs of foot, ankle, hip, or leg injuries. He didn't want to be negligent, but it wasn't worth a violent confrontation.

"Fine." He began rotating Eddie's arm joints, one by one, saving the obviously injured left shoulder and elbow for last. When he got to them, he clucked.

"What?" Eddie flinched as Patrick touched his elbow.

"Hold still."

Patrick palpated up and down the arm first, looking for signs of obvious breaks and finding none. He turned his attention to the swollen elbow and sagging shoulder. It looked like Eddie had taken the brunt of an impact with the arm.

"Well, I can't do an x-ray to be sure, but I don't think you broke anything. Looks like a hyperextended elbow and a subluxation."

"A what?"

"Shoulder dislocation. Do you have a history of them?"

"A few."

"So, you're familiar with putting it back in place."

"Yeah, and it hurts like mad."

"Yes, it does. It will be even worse because your elbow is hyperextended, too. But we need to do it first. Then I can put you in a sling for the elbow. You ready?"

"Now?"

"Now. The sooner it goes back in, the easier." It was already more swollen than Patrick liked. This wouldn't be easy for either of them. "Lie down on your good side for me."

Eddie did, gritting his teeth. Patrick grasped the man's wrist and pulled the left arm down and out, slowly and steadily. The muscles resisted, spasming in protest. Patrick kept up the pressure, willing the ball of the shoulder joint back into the socket, but, still, it refused to cooperate. Sweat had beaded on Patrick's forehead. After what felt like an eternity but was probably only about thirty seconds, he finally felt a clunk as the shoulder re-located.

Eddie's shriek rattled Patrick's skull. For a tough guy, he wasn't very stoic. Patrick looked at him closely. His skin had grown pale, which wasn't surprising. Patrick guided him back up to a seated position and pushed his head between his knees. While Eddie was recovering, Patrick retrieved an ace bandage and some old rags out of his kit. Patrick helped him put his shirt back on. Now, Patrick could see the breast pocket sagged with a stack of bound bills. He was surprised at the amount of cash the man was carrying, but he supposed it was because he was traveling. Working fast, he bandaged the elbow then fashioned a crude sling and slipped it over Eddie's wrist and shoulder.

Again, Eddie let loose a string of unprintable words.

Patrick started re-packing his bag. "The good news is that I can't find anything seriously wrong with you, besides the elbow and shoulder. The bad news is that riding down is still going to be painful." Patrick rifled through his supplies. He'd given Eddie ibuprofen earlier. "Do you have any problem that you know of taking painkillers? I can give you some Tylenol with codeine."

"Just give them to me, man."

Eddie downed two pills with the canteen of water Patrick handed him. Patrick closed the bag. Only then did he think about his audience of teenagers. Eddie had probably added color to their vocabularies. Trish saw him watching her and looked out of the cave. He turned his attention to the boys. John's pupils were still dilated. His shaking was a little less noticeable, though. Perry's lip was twice it's normal size, but his bleeding had stopped.

It was like he was running a field hospital up here on the mountain. He shook his head. "All right. Henry's going to be waiting for us with our ride. We have to get moving. Anybody need anything else before we go?"

The kids shook their heads. None of the bright eyes and bushy tails of that morning when they'd left Park Reservoir. Or, at least, when Perry and John had left it. Trish had been flat all day.

He decided to unhobble the horses himself to give everyone else a little longer out of the elements. "Okay, then. Everyone wait here for a minute."

Patrick adjusted his slicker and marched out. The weather hadn't improved. Sleet and wind, which drove cold deep into the bones. He shivered. His thoughts turned to Susanne as he unhobbled Reno. He hoped she was having a better day than him. He missed her, at the same time as he was glad she wasn't here. He would have hated to put her through another bad mountain experience. She was probably having a great time with her friends. Holding babies and throwing a party—two things she loved. He would have loved to be back there with her. He wanted to wrap her warm body up in his arms, to soak in her heat. He stopped himself before he could take the thought further. Now was not the time to be thinking about his wife's warm body. Next, he wondered if Henry was making good time. But from Henry his mind quickly turned back to Eddie Blackhawk. And the more he thought about Eddie, the angrier he got.

He didn't trust the man.

He moved on to Goldie's hobbles. Eddie had given Patrick plenty of reason not to trust him before. Eddie frequented the Fort Washakie Health Center during Patrick's visits, not because of medical issues, but to hit up his sister Constance for money. Then there were the illegal poker games he ran at the T-ton Ranch. And the threats he'd made against Patrick.

Patrick leaned down and unfastened the hobbles around Duke's legs. Now here Eddie was, the only survivor of a plane crash in the Bighorns, supposedly onboard to visit family in Buffalo. But Patrick had racked his brain, and he couldn't think of any Blackhawks in Johnson County. As a doctor, he crossed paths with just about everyone sooner or later. It didn't mean there weren't any, but it seemed unlikely.

Still, what was there not to believe Eddie about now? So, he'd jumped off a horse without telling anyone to run into the woods to relieve himself. That was hardly a crime. And the man had survived a high-altitude plane crash. He needed their help. Patrick should be concentrating more on that and less on reasons to doubt him.

He just couldn't shake the distrust he felt.

Holding four sets of reins in his hand, Patrick unbuckled the last set of hobbles—from Plug—and returned them to the saddle bags.

"Let's go, everybody," he called.

The kids and Eddie made their way from the overhang to the horses, hunched in their slickers. The group was dragging more all the time. For once, he wasn't sorry they weren't going to be camping out that night. He couldn't wait to get home—after a trip to the emergency room—and sleep in his own bed with his beautiful wife. He wouldn't have admitted it aloud, because he didn't want to make John feel any worse, but he was freezing cold without his jacket under his slicker.

As he held out his hand to give Eddie a leg up onto Reno, a man's voice called his name.

"Patrick."

Patrick turned toward the voice as Eddie grunted and lurched back to the overhang. *What the heck was wrong with him now?* Patrick tented his eyes to see better through the sleet.

George Nichols was riding up the trail, ponying a big draft horse and an oversized nag.

CHAPTER TWENTY: SURPRISE

Flint Residence, Buffalo, Wyoming
Friday, August 12, 1977, 3:15 p.m.

Susanne

WHEN SUSANNE WENT BACK into the house to see who had driven up and come inside, the first thing she heard was a baby whimpering. "Ronnie?"

There was no answer.

Susanne hurried into the dark living room, restraining Ferdinand by the collar. A form shifted on the couch. A baby hiccupped and whimpered again. Then she heard the soft sound of crying. Not from an infant, but from a woman.

She lowered her voice and walked closer to the figure and the baby. "Ronnie?"

The voice that answered was choking on tears. "I feel like such a failure."

Susanne sat down by her friend on the couch. "Place," she said to the dog.

He whimpered.

"Place," she repeated.

He slunk to his pillow on the far side of the living room. She heard him collapse onto it with a sigh. Her eyes were adjusting, and she could just make out Ronnie's long blonde French braid and pale face.

"You're no failure. What would make you say that?"

Ronnie crumbled into a sob. In her arms, the baby continued to make unhappy noises.

Susanne pulled the two of them into an embrace, careful not to smush the child. Ronnie smelled like coffee and spoiled milk. It reminded Susanne of the days her own children were infants. "There, there. It's going to be all right." She rubbed circles on Ronnie's back. "You're going to be all right."

The sobs tapered off. Ronnie drew in a deep, shaky breath. "I'm a fraud. I couldn't have a baby of my own, and there was a reason. It's because God knew I would be a terrible mother. Like I am to Will."

"That's not true."

"This is the first time he's stopped crying in days. And I'm s-s-s-so tired."

"That's the first thing you've said that I can agree with. Newborns are exhausting. And if he's crying all the time, are you sleeping at all?"

"No. None. And I thought I would love this. I . . . I . . . I don't."

"Well, of course not. Not yet. When he's past this stage, it will get better. He'll smile and laugh and sleep and you will, too. You'll see."

"Is it wrong that I want to go back to work?" Ronnie was a well-respected deputy. Tough. Calm. Fair. The quintessential Wyoming rancher's daughter. So competent that Susanne had been intimidated by her and resisted her friendship for a long time. She was glad she'd gotten over it, and she marveled at the complete role reversal between them. That she was helping Ronnie for a change. "It's so much easier than being home with Will."

"You probably never thought you'd be saying that, did you?"

Ronnie laughed and sniffled. She disengaged from Susanne and wiped her eyes. "No. I was a parenthood snob."

"If it's any consolation, every mother goes through this."

"Really?"

"Doubts? Of course. Maybe when they're newborn, maybe when they have trouble at school or when they're surly teenagers. But at some point, we all find ourselves crying on our knees in a dark room, begging God for a do-over."

"Thanks for saying that."

"It's true. I promise."

Ronnie shook her head. "I can't believe he's not screaming. I'm a wreck for the party, and everyone will be telling me what an easy baby he is."

"Of course. Kids specialize in making their mothers look and feel stupid."

Ronnie's amazing blue eyes shone even in the low light, magnified by her lingering tears. "I worry that he . . . that he . . . that he acts like this because of his mother—his birth mother—and that maybe there's something wrong with him. What if he turns out like her?"

"Don't you believe that for a second. You and Jeff will give him the love and environment he needs. He'll be wonderful, like the two of you."

"But her genetics. She could have passed *something* on."

Susanne hurt for her friend. "Ronnie, I went to grammar school with a boy whose father kidnapped, tortured, raped, and murdered three women. The son grew up to be a model citizen."

"Is that supposed to make me feel better?"

"Maybe not completely. But I just want you to know Will is not his mother any more than that boy was his father. Will is a unique human being, and he has wonderful parents. All parents worry about how their children will turn out. Patrick and I do all the time."

"Your kids are perfect."

Not by a long shot. But that wasn't fair. They were great kids. Just not perfect, because no one was, no kids or adults, even if Patrick sometimes *acted* like he was. The thought made Susanne smile with affection. A pang of longing to have her husband home zinged through her. And her imperfect kids. She always thought she needed more time to herself, and it was lovely at first when she got it, but it grew old quickly. *See there? I'm not perfect either.* She hadn't been appreciating the blessing of Trish and Perry like she should. And when it came to her own childhood—she'd been far from perfect. She'd disobeyed her parents at times, disrespected them occasionally, and ultimately defied them to elope with Patrick when she wasn't even out of high school yet. Her kids were normal and—knock on wood—unlikely to turn to lives of crime.

"Trish and Perry are good kids. Sometimes they make me a little crazy, but you're right, Patrick and I are very lucky."

"I've always believed you make your own luck by working hard and making good choices. At least mostly."

"There you go."

Ronnie snorted. "I should listen to myself then."

"You said it." Susanne squeezed Ronnie's hand. "Ronnie, Will is going to disappoint you and break your heart. But he's also going to light up your life and bring you incredible joy. In a few months, anyway."

The doorbell rang. Guests already? Sometimes the women in Susanne's Sunday school class drove her nuts. She wondered which one of them couldn't tell time. It couldn't be later than three-twenty.

"People are here? Ugh. I look awful."

Susanne reached for Will. "You want to let me hold him while you freshen up in my bathroom? It's more private back there."

"Yes. Thank you. For that and for talking to me."

"Any time. Especially after all you've done for me." Talking her friend through a mothering crisis was small potatoes compared to the time Ronnie had dragged a terrified Susanne through the mountains to find Patrick and the kids, only to get cold cocked by multiple murderer Billy Kemecke and nearly lose her job over it, too. Susanne stood, cuddling Will to her chest. Her second baby to hold in an hour. It was shaping up to be a great day.

The doorbell rang again as Ronnie grabbed her handbag and hustled toward the master suite.

"Hold your horses out there. I'm coming after I put the dog up." Susanne led a dejected Ferdinand to the garage. He balked at the door, and she gave him a push. As soon as she closed the door behind him, he bawled a mournful howl.

"That dog. Right, Will?" She hurried toward the door.

The doorbell rang a third time. She wrenched the door open, mustering her biggest welcoming smile.

Her sister-in-law stood on the front stoop. Her face was white and pinched, her eyes huge. The Suburban was parked in the driveway facing the house behind her. So was a white Chevy pickup. Its engine was running and the door to the driver's side was open. Susanne didn't recognize the vehicle. A delivery perhaps?

She tried to dam up the exasperation that wanted to come flooding out at her sister-in-law. A little of it slipped over anyway. "Patricia. You could have just let yourself in."

Patricia opened her mouth, but no words came out.

"Hello, Susanne." A red-haired woman stepped into view from where she'd been standing just out of sight. She lifted a gun barrel from Patricia's back to the side of her head. "I've come for my son."

It was Barb Lamkin.

At first, Susanne's brain struggled to process the scene. This couldn't be happening. This couldn't be real. But there she was. Barb. It was real. Terribly, horribly real. And she wanted Will.

Susanne clutched Will to her chest. She was *not* handing this baby over to a killer.

Barb cocked the hammer on the revolver with her thumb, a big smile on her face. "Hand him over slowly."

Would Barb really blow Patricia's brains out? Surely not. But what would Susanne do to get her own kids back?

Anything. She'd do whatever she had to do, no matter the cost. Of course Barb would kill Patricia.

But she wouldn't kill her son.

Words flowed from Susanne's mouth, unconnected to her brain. Automatic, desperate words, stalling words. "Don't do this, Barb. You don't want to do this." She clung tighter to Will.

"Now," Barb screamed, the sudden change in her tone making Patricia and Susanne jump and Will squall.

"Please, no . . ." Patricia said.

Barb lunged at Susanne, reaching for Will as she smashed the barrel of the revolver across the side of Susanne's head. For a split second, Susanne wondered how she would grab the boy. Barb only had one hand. Patrick had hacked the other off when she'd been trapped in a burning truck. But reality was an ugly interruption to the thought. Barb's blow made a loud THWACK sound in Susanne's head. Her jaw dropped, her head whipped around, and she tumbled to the side. Her vision was a field of stars. She was dimly aware of the muffled sounds of a dog snarling and barking, of trying to hold on to the baby, and of the absence of his warmth in her arm as Barb wrenched him away.

"No." She tried to scream the word, but it came out like a whisper. Everything around her was moving like a jerky reel-to-reel film. She realized she was still upright, that she'd caught herself on the handle of the open door. Was propping herself up. As if in a dream, she forced herself to turn back toward Barb. She gasped in a breath.

Barb was backing away, the gun trained on Patricia. She put Will in the white Chevy pickup, jumped in after him, and gunned it out of the Flint's driveway.

Susanne gave her woozy head a shake. *Will. No.* She snatched the keys from Patricia's trembling hands, and, without a word, ran for the Suburban.

CHAPTER TWENTY-ONE: THREATEN

Perry

PERRY HEARD A MAN SAY, "PATRICK FLINT." The voice was
coming from down the trail.

Perry had just made his way across the rocks from the cave to
where the horses were ready and waiting to go. Duke smelled awful,
although it was mostly his wool blanket. It smelled like a sweaty gym
sock. Perry had been about to put his foot in the stirrup to mount
Duke, but he paused. He knew that voice. He grinned, getting a cold,
painful blast of wet wind to the gap in his gum, and turned toward
the ridge, waving.

Sure enough, George Nichols was riding toward their group,
pulling two big horses along behind him. One of them was monster
sized with fuzzy black and white hair. So much hair. Hanging off its
chin, its belly, its legs. Long, thick hair covering its hooves. A heavy

mane on either side of its neck and a thick black and white tail sweeping the ground. It was the coolest horse Perry had ever seen. It looked like the ones in the beer commercials, only a different color than they were.

"Hi, George," Perry shouted. "Is that a wooly mammoth behind you?" It didn't even embarrass him that wooly came out like "woowy."

"That's Yeti. Don't hurt his feelings." George grinned and waved back. "Mrs. Flint said to tell you all hello."

"Did you get the electricity back on?" Perry's dad asked.

"No, sir. I'm sorry to have to tell you that, but I had to bring some guys up the mountain to Highland Park. I told Mrs. Flint I'd get it fixed up on Monday."

Perry wondered where the guys were. It looked like George and the horses were all by themselves.

"But her party . . ."

"I think she had it under control, sir."

Perry believed that. His mom could handle anything. On the other hand, she didn't like to be disappointed, and he guessed she'd make George sorry on Monday. The thought made him smile.

A dark-haired man with a round belly rode into view. *One of the guys George had brought up?* He interrupted their conversation without being introduced. "Have any of youse guys seen a coupla men out here that weren't dressed for this weather?" He waved his hand at the sky and the sleety rain. Something about his weird accent and forceful tone made Perry's mouth go dry.

George looked at the pushy guy like he'd burped out loud during silent prayer time in church. Perry snuck a glance at John and Trish. John was staring at the ground. Trish's mouth was hanging open.

His dad spoke. "I'm Patrick Flint. These are my kids and their friend."

Two more men rode up and stopped by the dark-haired man. These two were bald men who looked just alike, except that one of them had a weird eye. They were big like Yeti and made the Quarter horses they were riding look undersized. The horses sighed, lowered their heads, and closed their eyes.

"Uh, Dr. Flint, this is Orion Cardinale and his . . . friends Luke and Juice." George frowned. "But, Orion, didn't you say your friend and his girlfriend—"

Orion held up a hand. "Like I was saying, we're looking for some guys. You either seen 'em or you haven't. End of story."

Perry's insides tightened up.

"We have not." His dad's voice was no nonsense, like he used when he'd say, "This is not a negotiation," to Perry and Trish when they argued with him. It surprised Perry, because he would have thought his dad would tell the truth, which is that they had seen one guy—and Eddie definitely hadn't been dressed for the weather—who told them two other men had died in a plane crash. His dad had a thing about telling the truth all the time. So, when he lied, Perry knew something big was up.

One of the men—Luke or Juice?—put his hand under his rain poncho. Perry heard a zipping sound. The man left his hand there, which was really strange. Was he trying to dry it off? Keep it warm? Or . . . did he have a gun holstered there? Lots of people in Wyoming kept their guns in chest holsters. Perry hoped that wasn't it.

"Uh, Dad." Perry kept his voice quiet, hoping only his dad would hear. His dad didn't seem to notice.

"You sure?" Orion smiled with his mouth, but it didn't reach his eyes. "There's a cash reward in it for some lucky person. We're very worried about them."

George's forehead folded up like the wings of a paper airplane.

Perry's dad said, "We're sure."

Orion shifted in his saddle. "They would have made quite an . . . entrance. Loud. If you know what I mean."

"I'm sorry. I don't."

"And you haven't seen or heard anything else unusual?"

"I'm sorry, did you say you're with law enforcement?"

This made the meatheads laugh. Orion held a hand out and

pushed it at the ground, like he was telling them to stop. Which they did. "I didn't say. But you can consider me the law of the land out here."

"Well, all right then." Perry's dad tipped his cowboy hat. A little waterfall ran off of it. "You fellows have a nice day. George, good seeing you."

"And you, too, sir," George said.

Perry's heart was pounding so loud now he could barely hear himself think. He'd been around plenty of creepy people in the last year, and this guy ranked right up with the creepiest. What he'd said to Perry's dad sounded an awfully lot like a threat.

Perry had thought George was a good guy. His friend. So what was he doing with creepy people?

Then again, Perry had thought John was tough.

He pressed his fingers against his torn, swollen lips. He guessed today was just a day full of surprises and disappointments.

CHAPTER TWENTY-TWO: SPILL

Patrick

PATRICK'S LIPS moved feverishly as he watched George lead
Orion and the other two riders away. He'd thought better of George
than to associate with men like them. The young man was a hard
worker. Conscientious and smart. He and Patrick had become
friendly when George had been working on a job at the hospital.
They'd had some great conversations about George's time as an outfitter. Then, one day George had arrived at the hospital at the same
time as another truck had entered the parking lot. Instead of pulling
into a space, the truck careened toward the building without braking.
George had pulled open the passenger door and leapt inside. He'd
managed to stop the vehicle before it crashed into the entrance.
George had put the truck in park and carried the man into the ER. It
turned out that the driver had been having a heart attack and lost

consciousness. The incident had cemented Patrick's good opinion of him.

So, now, to discover him mixed up with thuggish big city men? It was disappointing. And, while Patrick didn't like to speculate without all the facts, Orion's accent had sounded like Chicago. The men looked Italian, Orion with his dark hair, all of them with olive-toned skin. Their clothes had been distinctive, too. Black leather jackets peeking out from under their slickers. Shiny shoes, ruined by the rain. They couldn't have looked and acted more like gangsters if they'd been toting machine guns. Chicago, Italian, and gangsters. Patrick's conclusion? Mobsters, in Wyoming, with George.

As Patrick watched, George stopped the group at the rock cairn, then turned onto the Solitude Trail to the right. Patrick frowned. He thought George had said they were heading up to Highland Park, which was to the left. After Orion's comments, Patrick had expected them to be looking for the wrecked plane. But maybe they weren't. Or maybe they didn't know where it had gone down.

"They went the wrong way, Dad," Perry said. "Should we tell them?"

"George knows what he's doing, son." Or, if he didn't, that was okay, too. A bubble of hope rose in his chest. He wanted the men as far away as possible, and he prayed they would take the Solitude Trail all the way back to where it began, at Coffeen Park, miles past where his group had joined it earlier that day near Bighorn Reservoir.

"I guess." Perry sounded as disappointed in George as Patrick felt.

When they were out of sight over the saddle, Patrick handed Reno's lead line to Perry. "Hold him, please."

"Yes, sir." Then Perry blurted out, "Why'd you lie to those guys, Dad?"

Patrick lowered his voice. "I think you can figure out the answer to that one, buddy." Perry's eyes were wide, but he nodded. Patrick raised his voice so Trish and John would hear him. "Be ready to ride out. I'm just going to get Eddie."

John's voice trembled. "Were they bad men, Dr. Flint?"

"Well, I'm not sure, but I don't want to hang around until they come back to find out." He winked at the boy.

Trish moved closer to John, her stance protective. "It will be okay, John. We're heading in the opposite direction."

Patrick looked at his kids and his chest felt tight. Then he pushed his emotion aside and stalked toward the overhang to get Eddie. Immediately, his mind started racing again. The gangsters had looked so out of place that it would have been funny if he hadn't seen one of the musclemen reach for a piece in a shoulder holster. And Eddie. He'd been right not to trust him. These guys were after Eddie and the other men in the plane. Eddie had put his family at risk, smack in the middle of whatever it was he was involved in. Which was what, exactly? What in the world would have a trio of Chicago wise guys looking for Eddie and two other men in a downed plane in the middle of Cloud Peak Wilderness?

He peaked in the overhang. "Eddie?" His voice echoed back at him.

No answer. Eddie wasn't in there.

Patrick shook his head, his teeth grinding together. Had he made a run for it? But, while Eddie couldn't be too smart if he'd gotten on the wrong side of the mafia, Patrick didn't think the man was foolish enough to run off injured, alone, unprepared, and lost in the wilderness with mobsters on his tail.

Patrick turned away from the cave and raised his voice. "Your friends are gone. I lied to them, and you're safe for now. You've got until the count of five and then I'm leaving you up here."

Still, Eddie didn't appear.

"Fine." Patrick couldn't believe he was having to count backwards, like Eddie was a naughty child. "Five. Four. Three. Two."

There was a scrambling of rocks. Eddie stumbled into view from around the far side of the cave. "I'm here."

Patrick advanced on him, fists balled. "What have you gotten my family into?"

Eddie dropped his chin. "We've got to get out of here."

Patrick was dumbfounded. He'd expected Eddie to fight back, not yield. "Yes, we do. But do you care to clue me in so I can be prepared first?"

Eddie stared back at the mouth of the cave. "I . . . I . . . I saw something I shouldn't have. Those men want to kill me." He turned back to Patrick.

Patrick pinned him with his eyes. "Go on."

Eddie shrugged. "What else do you want to know?"

"What else should I know?"

Eddie rolled his lips in and rubbed them together. "Nothing."

Patrick leaned toward Eddie with barely controlled fury, their eyes locked on each other's. "If you want any help from me, you'll tell me the truth, the whole truth and nothing but, right now."

Eddie didn't back away. He smelled like blood, fear, and sweat. The silence seemed to stretch on forever, with neither man breaking eye contact. Finally, Eddie sighed.

He said, "The other guys in the plane . . ."

Patrick closed his eyes for a moment. "Go on."

"They weren't dead. They were in bad shape, but not dead. One of them is Elvin Cross. You remember Elvin?"

Patrick went on high alert. Yes, he did, from as recently as yesterday, when Constance had told him in Dubois that the dead Jimmy Beartusk was Elvin's cousin. "Yes. But you told me I didn't know the guys on the plane."

Eddie shrugged one shoulder, like his lies were no big deal. *They're a big deal to me.* "Elvin begged me to go on without him."

Blood rushed in Patrick's ears. Two men were behind them on the mountain, severely injured and alone. "And you think Orion and his thugs are looking for the plane?"

"Yes. And they'll kill them."

"You abandoned them there. I wouldn't think that would matter to you."

"They were trapped in the wreckage. I couldn't get them free or down the mountain. But I told them I'd get help and come back for them."

Patrick raised his hands, then dropped them. "Yet, when you found help, you didn't."

"Man, I was scared. I was lost and confused. The weather. The mountains. And I knew those guys would be coming."

"How did they know where to find you? Did the pilot radio the airport for help?"

"No. We were—he was—flying off radar. But they'd hired him. They were waiting at the airport in Buffalo. They'd set up a channel to communicate on. We were close enough that he could radio Mr. Cardinale we were going down. He told him we would be on Highland Park."

Patrick rubbed his chin. "Where exactly did the plane go down?"

"I don't know man. Way up on some rocks, past a pond and some trees. I had to run across this giant open area with the hail and lightning. It was hard to get my bearings."

Not much to go on. "Could you find it again?"

"I guess. If I had to."

"Where were you really headed?"

"Buffalo. To meet them. That part was true."

Patrick spoke slowly and firmly, his finger pointing at Eddie's chest in rhythm with his words. "What was on that plane?"

"Me and Elvin. They, uh, wanted us. But, man, if I tell you anymore, you'll be in as much trouble as me."

"I'm already in as much trouble as you, Eddie, and so are the kids." Patrick shook his head, huffing.

Suddenly, from behind him, he heard Trish say, "Dad, George is back."

He turned. She was standing five feet from them.

Eddie's eyes grew wild.

"Are the others with him?" Patrick asked.

"No, sir. George said to tell you he sent them in the wrong direction. But he looks really scared."

"Are you going to help me?" Eddie said. "I told you everything."

Patrick pointed at him. "You. You either come with us now, or not. But I'm not coming back for you again. You run away, you stay away."

Eddie nodded slowly. Patrick trotted out after Trish without looking back.

George was there with one of his giant horses. "You gotta get out of here, Dr. Flint. Something's not right. I'm so sorry. I thought they were looking for their friend and his girlfriend, but I don't think so anymore. I took them the wrong way and then pretended I was having an appendicitis attack. I made a deal with them to forfeit my fee. They made me leave Yeti. And I loved that horse. But I was scared of them, and—" He stopped, pointing at Eddie. "You. Are you one of the ones they're looking for?"

Eddie didn't speak.

"He is." Patrick took a deep breath. He hated what he was about to say. He hated what he was about to have to do. But he had no choice. "There was a plane crash on Highland Park. That's what those goons are looking for. And we have to go back for the survivors." He turned to face Eddie. "Eddie and me."

"We can't!" Eddie said. His eyes darted, like he was looking for a place to run. Again.

George nodded. "Now I understand what Henry meant. About you guys running into a mess of trouble."

"Henry? Where did you see him?"

"Back on the trail. But the Chicago guys didn't." He smacked his forehead with the palm of his hand. "I was supposed to tell you I gave him the keys to my truck and trailer down on Hazel Park."

"Good. He'll be waiting," Patrick said.

Eddie grabbed Patrick by the elbow. "Dr. Flint, if we go back up on that mountain, Orion will kill us."

"George sent them on a wild goose chase. They're flatlanders lost in Cloud Peak Wilderness."

"They're determined and they're smart."

Patrick patted his chest. "I have my knife, my revolver, and plenty of ammo."

"What about us?" John sounded close to hysteria again. "I can't go back up there. And Eddie said they'll kill us."

Trish whispered, "Calm down, John. My dad has a plan. He always has a plan."

Patrick didn't have a plan. He felt as sick as John.

"What do you need me to do, Dad?" Perry seemed to stand two inches taller before his eyes.

George's saddle creaked as he shifted. "I, uh, I could take the kids down to meet Henry, Dr. Flint."

Patrick felt a stabbing pain in his chest. He didn't want to separate from the kids. Hadn't he learned his lesson about sticking together earlier that summer in the Gros Ventre Wilderness? Splitting up had led to bad, bad things. But he couldn't take them back up to Highland Park. John was coming apart at the seams. Perry needed medical attention. Trish was strong and tough, but no match for the kind of trouble they were likely to encounter. And they all needed dry clothes, food, and sleep.

He stared at George. His earlier doubts had been allayed when George ditched his shady clients. While Patrick didn't trust anyone else completely with the well-being of his kids—except for his wife—George wasn't a bad choice for a stand-in. He was an outfitter. Paid to lead inexperienced people in and out of the mountains, often in extreme and mercurial weather. He'd risked his life to save a stranger at the hospital. He had heart and was courageous and resourceful.

So, instead of saying no, he said, "Are you armed, George?"

George dipped his chin. "I was born and raised in Sheridan, Wyoming. I'm always armed, sir."

"But, Dad." Trish looked at John. His face was pale and drawn. She buttoned her lip. Her eyes, though, continued to plead with him. *Don't go, Daddy.*

He forced a smile and a warm, calm tone. "I'm going to be fine,

Trish. All of us are. Use the buddy system. You've got John, George has Perry."

She shook her head, her mouth open. Then she sighed. "Yes, sir."

"She can't have me. She isn't a grownup." John's voice was shrill.

Patrick nodded. "But George is, and he'll be in charge. You'll be fine."

"I can come with you, Dad. I can help." Perry straightened his shoulders. His soft, boyish face was slimming up. His stern expression made him look older.

Patrick pressed his lips together. "Not this time, buddy, but thanks. All right. It's settled, then. Eddie, you're with me. Everybody else, get your horse and go."

"I can't." John was shaking his head rapidly and backing up.

Patrick deepened his voice. "You can, and you will, John. You have to."

Trish grabbed Plug's reins. "I'll lead him, John. You'll just ride him right behind Goldie and me."

John stopped. His face was uncertain.

Trish took his elbow. "I'll help you mount up before I get on Goldie."

Patrick swallowed hard. He turned away to gather himself. When he turned back around, all three kids were on horseback. Trish had looped Plug's lead rope around her saddle horn. She looked stricken. Perry looked forlorn. John had dropped his face toward the ground.

"Ready to ride out?" George clucked to his horses. They started moving back toward the ridge.

"Do what George says, you guys." He turned to Eddie. "You'll ride behind me." Reno was eighteen hundred pounds of muscle. He could handle a double ride. Because of his old injury, Patrick would take it easy on him, though. As easy as he could.

George pulled up. "Do you want The Lunker, Dr. Flint?"

"What's the lunker?"

He held up the pony line. "The big horse attached to the end of this. You need him more than I do right now. The only thing is whoever rides him will have to go bareback."

Eddie snorted. "I grew up riding green broke colts without a saddle. Bareback is better than double, man."

They'd make better time and have more horsepower to get the injured survivors off the mountain. "Fine with me," Patrick said. "Thanks, George."

"No bridle?" Eddie asked.

George shook his head. "Just a halter and lead. Sorry."

"Even better." Eddie grinned.

George led The Lunker over, and Eddie grasped the horse's lead rope in one hand. Then he led him to a boulder, climbed onto it, and vaulted onto the animal's back. The Lunker snorted and hopped.

Eddie patted his shoulder. "Settle, big boy."

Patrick climbed onto Reno's saddle and snatched the lead rope away from Eddie.

"Hey!" Eddie said, scowling.

Patrick tied the rope onto Reno's saddle horn, like Trish had done with John. "So we don't get . . . separated." He turned in the saddle to face the others. "Take them straight down the mountain, George. Tell Henry the kids need to go to the hospital, and then he needs to call Susanne. She'll know what to do from there. I'll be seeing you back in town."

He kicked Reno forward, and the horse pushed off. At first, The Lunker resisted, splay legged, head down, heavy footed, wanting to stay with George and the horse he knew. But Eddie goosed him on the sides, and the animal jumped forward, giving in, mostly. Reno trotted off with his ears up, back toward the basin leading to Highland Park, dragging Eddie and The Lunker behind him.

CHAPTER TWENTY-THREE: CLASH

Patricia

PATRICIA HUDDLED IN A ROCKING CHAIR, her arms around herself. Ferdie had his large, hairy body plastered against her leg. The frantic animal hadn't left her side since she'd let him out of the garage. She wasn't quite sure which of them was consoling the other, but she did wish that Patrick and Susanne placed a higher value on keeping him bathed, since he was an inside dog. The day before she'd seen him rolling on a baby bird that had fallen from a nest and rotted for a few days or weeks before he'd found it. *Pee-yew.* She couldn't really blame Susanne, though. Patrick had always been animal crazy. Her mother had to put up with baby alligators, raccoons, and snakes, in addition to normal pets, and all of them came with odor. At least Ferdie, stinky as he was, was helping keep Patricia from going out of her mind with worry.

Johnson County Attorney Max Alexandrov paced the Flint living room back and forth in front of her. Under normal circumstances, she would have considered him handsome. Light hair. Thinning, but not showing the top of his scalp like Patrick's did. A dark three-piece suit. Flat stomach, nice eyes, and long-fingered hands. *Stop it. These aren't normal circumstances,* she chided herself.

Max—was she supposed to think of him as Attorney Alexandrov or the County Attorney or Mr. Alexandrov?—dodged people with every step. The room was literally brimming over with humanity, not to mention the dozen or more party guests gossiping in the yard and reluctant to leave. Patricia surveyed the crowd. Police officers. Personnel from the sheriff's office, there to help but also in support of the Harcourts. And, of course, Jeff and Ronnie, who were dazed and stricken. Vangie, with Hank in her arms, was sitting beside Ronnie, trying to comfort her friend.

Patricia wished Susanne was there. Wished she hadn't taken the Suburban to go shopping. Wished she'd never gotten out of bed. But she wasn't getting any of her wishes. Susanne had torn out of the driveway in the Suburban, gravel flying, as soon as that woman—Patricia could barely bring herself to call her Barbara Lamkin—had snatched little Will and taken off. It was utterly terrifying to think about what could be happening to that baby and Susanne right now.

"Tell me what happened, Ms. Flint." Max's voice had a slight accent. Russian, maybe? Patricia was a sucker for a man with an accent. Usually. But not now, of course.

Ferdie's head cocked one way, following Max with his eyes. A gawky young officer still fighting teenage acne was trying to keep pace with Max, too. He gave up, sitting down on a chair across from Patricia. He pulled out a notepad and pencil.

"My last name's not Flint. It's Sand." Her response was quick and automatic. Patricia hadn't reclaimed her maiden name after her divorce the year before. In her life in Austin, people expected her to be a Sand, so she never had to explain. Never had to face the issue.

"Mrs. Sand. My apologies."

"Not Mrs." She blurted it out, then her cheeks flushed with heat. She wished she'd just let Max think her last name was Flint. Maybe he would think she was a very young widow. But why did it even matter what he thought? Being divorced was nothing to be ashamed of. Not everyone mated for life like Patrick and Susanne, who'd started dating when they were children of fourteen and fifteen. She lifted her chin.

His eyes locked on hers for a few seconds. "Gotcha. *Ms.* Sand, please tell me how you met Barbara Lamkin and talk me through everything that transpired from that moment forward until law enforcement arrived."

Patricia dropped her eyes. She knew she looked like a mess. Her eyes were probably still red from crying. But she wasn't made of stone like her older brother. Patricia felt things with great big, unstoppable feelings. It was just who she was. She reached for Ferdie and massaged his ears. He liked it, and it soothed her. "I drove Susanne's Suburban into Sheridan to go shopping, then I came back to Buffalo after lunch. I had a little time left before Ronnie's party, so—"

"By yourself?"

"Yes. I had just parked when—"

"Where did you park, Ms. Fli-Sand?"

"Behind the courthouse. I couldn't find a space on Main Street, so I went around the block and parked back there. Susanne had shown me that lot before and said it was her secret parking place."

He nodded, frowning. "Go on."

The man hadn't been the least bit encouraging or friendly since he'd arrived. Did he blame her for this fiasco? Sure, she felt terrible about it. Awful, awful, awful. But from what she'd heard so far, a dangerous murderer had escaped from custody right under his and everybody else's noses. So, whose fault did that make it? He might be cute, but she wasn't going to let him try to make her feel worse than she already did.

She took a deep breath. "I parked. I wasn't sure how to get to the street, and I got kind of lost in some trees on the side of the building. She was there." Her voice started shaking, which was embarrassing.

"Barbara Lamkin."

"Yes, but at the time I didn't know that's who she was."

"Of course. How was she dressed?" He started walking to and fro again. The man was wound tighter than Patrick.

"At the time, she was wearing some sweatpants with a matching sweatshirt—plain gray—with really long sleeves that covered her hands. Her hair was in a ponytail." Patricia leaned forward. "Honestly, she didn't look very good. People have been talking about how beautiful she is, but I just didn't see it."

One of Max's eyes twitched. "Keep going."

"She pointed at the Suburban and said something like 'you don't look like Susanne.' I told her that Susanne was my sister-in-law, and that I was just glad I didn't look like my brother. We laughed, and she said she was friends with Susanne and that her name was Heather. I told her my name was Patricia and that I was lost. She looped her arm through mine and said Buffalo was too small a town to get lost in if you had friends, and that any relative of Susanne's was a friend of hers. She invited me for coffee."

"Where?" He stopped pacing for a moment.

Ferdie sat up straighter and whined.

"She said her favorite spot wasn't downtown. She was so . . . friendly, I couldn't say no. She said, 'Let's take your car.' We got in the Suburban, and she gave me directions."

"Where to?"

"First, the grocery store. She asked if I'd mind if she ran in for something. Of course, I thought it was strange since I'd only just met her, but I didn't really *mind*. But when she got out of the car, she said she had forgotten her purse and asked to borrow money. I lent her ten dollars." Patricia shook her head in embarrassment. "I should have known something was off, but, well, I didn't have any reason to think an escaped killer was on the loose, did I?"

Max didn't answer, but she thought he looked a bit uncomfortable. *Good.* Ferdie settled back against her leg until Max started pacing again.

Patricia continued. "She was back in just a minute, and she gave me some change. About thirty cents. And then she directed me to a house."

Max stopped short, eyes bright. "Wait. What was in the bag?"

"Well, I don't *snoop*." Patricia examined her nails. The light pink polish she'd applied that morning was already chipped. "But it was lipstick and hair dye. L'Oreal. No wonder she didn't have much change."

"Color?"

"I only got a peek. But a white blonde, I think. The woman on the box had hair like Marilyn Monroe."

He nodded. "Okay."

"Where were we?"

"The house." He paced again. She was finding it very distracting. So was Ferdie.

"Right. I didn't realize until she unlocked the front door with a key from under a flowerpot that it wasn't a coffee shop."

He frowned and froze in his tracks. "Where was the house?"

"Kind of behind the grocery store. In that neighborhood. It was an old house. White siding, two-story. Very nice, actually."

He groaned. "Green shutters? A really big spruce tree in the yard?"

Ferdie sighed and flopped onto his belly, seemingly exhausted.

"Yes. The tree was enormous."

He rubbed his eyes. "Then what?"

"She put a pot of coffee on to percolate and said she'd be back in a flash. She went into a bedroom for about five minutes. When she came back out, she had changed clothes and had a duffel bag with her." Patricia's voice hitched. "If only I'd known she put a gun in that bag. But I had no idea." She paused, hoping for a little reassurance. None came. "She looked completely different."

"In what way?"

"Well, she had put on some baggy jeans, cinched with a belt to stay up, I'd guess, and another big sweatshirt. A brown one that said Cowboys on it in yellow. And she was wearing a baseball cap. Green and yellow. It was covering her hair. Which needed to be washed, by the way."

"And?"

"And, then we had coffee and some little cookies she got out of the pantry. It was all very pleasant."

"And you didn't think it was odd she used a key she found under a pot?"

Patricia's cheeks warmed. "Well, no. She'd forgotten her purse, after all."

He made a rolling motion with his hand. "Anything else?"

The county attorney was rubbing her the wrong way, handsome or not, accent or no accent. "I asked her if it was her place, and she laughed like that was a big joke. She winked and told me that she made the best coffee in town. 'Never spend more for someone else to do something you can do better yourself,' she said."

"What did you talk about?"

"My visit to Buffalo. Where I was from. That I taught school and so did she. That kind of thing. And that I had to get going to Ronnie's party for Will. Heather—Barbara—said she was going to it as well, and that she would just follow me." Patricia frowned. "There *was* one odd thing about her."

"What was that?"

"She kept one of her hands in her pocket all the time. Like it was hurt or she was hiding it or something."

"She doesn't have one of them."

"One of them what?"

"A hand. Your brother chopped it off. Field amputation when she was trapped in a truck. He saved her life."

Patricia's jaw dropped. How had she not heard about that before? "What did he use?"

Max paused, then said, "An ax."

She nodded. "Wow." Her brother had always been something of a hero. She supposed that was what made someone think they should be a doctor.

"Anything else at the house?"

"It was time for the party, so we left. She followed me in her truck."

"Where'd she get a truck?"

"From the garage."

Max's face turned splotchy red.

Patricia couldn't figure the man out. When he didn't speak, she said, "She also brought the duffel bag, which I thought was weird. I asked about it as we were leaving, and she said Will's present was in it. But when we got here, everything changed. She pulled a gun out of the duffel, pointed it at me, and took Will. Then Susanne went after her, and Vangie called 911."

Max stood with his back to her, then turned. He sighed. "It's not her place, you know. Or her truck."

"What?"

"The house you were in. It isn't hers."

He'd told her about the green shutters and the big spruce, though. She frowned. "Then how did you know what it looked like?"

Ferdie looked up at Patricia, then at Max.

"Because it belonged to me and my ex-wife."

"You're divorced?" Patricia suddenly felt better about life and herself. She'd worried what Max thought about her, when he was divorced himself.

"We used to live there together. Last year she moved back to Virginia. I got the house and truck when we split up." Max turned and stalked back across the room, one hand pressed against his forehead. He barked out a license plate number. "Put out an APB on it. STAT."

"Then it's . . . your house. Your truck."

Max didn't answer.

Holy smokes. Ferdie let out a booming bark. The officer looked up from his notes, mouth hanging open. His pencil fell from his hand to the floor.

Patricia knew just how they felt.

CHAPTER TWENTY-FOUR: BUMP

Hazel Park, Bighorn National Forest, Wyoming
Friday, August 12, 1977, 4:00 p.m.

Ben

BEN HELD onto the steering wheel with both hands. He couldn't believe the old truck and trailer had made it this far. The roads from Red Grade down to Little Goose Creek had been bad. Cruddy, even. It still smelled like something was burning after the workout he'd given the brakes. Then the truck had almost swamped in the stream but going up the rocky incline after the crossing was the worst part of all. Poor Jackalope, back in the trailer, surfing the bumps from the ruts and washouts. He felt almost sorry enough to stop and ride the horse instead. But the further he drove at a speed faster than the horse could walk, the shorter the time until he caught up with Trish. And that's what this was all about. Trish.

He rounded a curve, splashing through a mud puddle the size of a small pond. For a moment, the windshield wipers did double duty against mud and the rain or sleet or hail or whatever the thick wet stuff falling from the sky was.

He slowed down until his visibility improved. When the glass was clearer, he saw he'd come upon a meadow with a truck and stock trailer parked up against the tree line, right where it looked like outfitters occasionally camped, given the fire rings and poles in the trees for hanging elk and deer and anything else the hunters had shot.

This road wasn't going to get any better. He took his foot completely off the gas. He wasn't sure how much further he could drive. The parked rig was pretty clear evidence that someone else had thought they shouldn't drive any further. If he got Henry's truck and trailer stuck or broken down, he'd have big problems. It might slow him down so much that he missed Trish completely. No one even knew he'd come up here. Help would be slow coming. Maybe he should have left Vangie a note, but he hadn't, and it was too late to fix that now. For a moment, guilt ate at him. He wasn't used to having people concerned about him. Was out of practice being cared for. She'd be alone and worried when he didn't show up at home that night. He would have a lot of explaining and making up to do.

But if he caught up to Trish, it would all be worth it. And Henry would be there, so he could help make things right with Vangie.

Mind made up, he whipped the steering wheel to the right and pulled in to park ten yards away from the other vehicle. Moving fast, he put on his outerwear and hopped out, locking the truck, and turning to jog back to the trailer. The weather was horrible, but he wasn't going to let it stop him or dampen his mood.

He was doing the right thing. Trish would see how he felt, and he could explain himself. Everything between them would be great again.

"Where do you think you're going?" a voice asked, as he nearly ran smack into an unhappy horse and an even more unhappy Henry Sibley.

CHAPTER TWENTY-FIVE: PUSH

Highland Park, Cloud Peak Wilderness, Bighorn
Mountains, Wyoming
Friday, August 12, 1977, 4:00 p.m.

Patrick

PATRICK HAD to hold Reno back as he began the climb from the East Fork of Little Goose to Highland Park. The horse was a powerhouse. Solid muscle, even after a year of mostly lounging in a pasture five thousand feet lower in elevation than where he was now, and he loved to attack on the uphill and ride the brakes on the downhill. It had only been about three quarters of a mile since they'd departed from the kids and George, but it was tough going—six hundred feet of steep, narrow, rocky descent. They were now facing the same up the other side of the basin.

All day, Patrick had been hypervigilant to the slightest falter in his horse's stride. Any hesitation. Any unwillingness. But, as counterintuitive as it seemed, Reno appeared stronger with every mile, like he was enjoying using his body for something other than as a hay receptacle. His head was high, his ears alert. His step on the flat sections, a prance. Patrick suspected this was in part a show for The Lunker. Reno was always the dominant gelding in any herd, and he clearly enjoyed forcing the other horse to match his path and pace.

Around them, the sleet had left a rapidly melting blanket, and water cascaded down the mountain. Reno splashed up mud with every step. Behind them, Patrick could hear The Lunker's heavy breathing. He glanced back. Eddie was riding with no hands, using his good arm to brace the injured one. The lead line was icy but still snug around the saddle horn. The weather had started easing up, though. It was no warmer, but the precipitation intermittent, the sky lighter, the wind less gusty. Patrick was relieved. Their work at the crash would be hard enough without fighting the crazy storm.

Eddie hadn't spoken during the ride. The quiet gave Patrick time to think about what to say to him. He still didn't believe he had gotten the real story out of him. He felt like he needed it, for their safety and the safety of the other survivors, if they were still alive. Questions wouldn't necessarily yield truthful answers. Chewing Eddie out wouldn't do anything except make Patrick feel better, and only a little bit at that.

The grade of the trail increased, and Reno sped up. Patrick shifted his weight back. The horse didn't know when to say when. Patrick hated to pull on the horse's mouth when he was expending so much effort, but he needed to be smarter than the horse. To not let him hurt himself or spend all his energy. So, Patrick used the influence of his body mechanics to coax Reno into a slower pace. It worked, but only a little, and Patrick smiled as Reno resisted. He liked "try" in an animal. He liked it in a person, too. Try, truthfulness, and honor. Maybe that was why he'd never liked Eddie. Or Elvin for that matter. When he'd known Eddie, the man had never held an honest job. He'd acted like his sister was his personal piggy bank, and Elvin had treated her with appalling disrespect. When Patrick had seen her in Dubois, Constance claimed Eddie and Elvin had gone legit, but, based on what he'd seen so far today, he found it hard to believe.

He shook his head. And it was for Elvin and a pilot working for the goons that he'd handed his kids off to George Nichols and ridden back out to Highland Park with Eddie? He knew God had a plan for everyone, and that His plan was for Patrick to be a healer. Sometimes, though, he had trouble believing in the wisdom of that plan. He supposed that was what faith was all about. He just hoped that this was not a situation that would put his faith to the test.

Reno stopped to catch his breath and The Lunker bumped into him. Reno pinned his ears back and shot the other horse a malevolent glare.

"Easy," Patrick said in a firm voice.

There was no sound from Eddie or The Lunker except the horse's heavy breathing.

Reno sucked air like he'd sucked water at the stream a few minutes before. Patrick cocked his head and listened to him. The altitude was hitting him. Patrick had only taken him up over ten thousand feet once before this trip, on the night Reno had broken his leg. And, while horses acclimate to altitude faster than humans, it's still not automatic for them. But Reno's breathing sounded normal, if winded. Patrick nodded, satisfied. He would have enough problems transporting the injured men off the mountain on two horses. He'd never needed Reno's size and strength more.

Reno gave The Lunker another dose of the stink eye. Patrick patted his neck, looked up at the final ascent to the saddle onto Highland Park. It was the steepest section yet, and he knew Reno would try to lope it unless he kept him in hand.

"All right, boy. Let's finish this." He gave the horse a gentle tap in the flanks. As expected, the gelding lunged upward, but Patrick held him to a fast walk. "Easy, easy."

Reno snorted and pulled at the bit, but Patrick stayed firm. He tried to imagine running up this trail like his horse. *No way.* He was a darn good hiker—accused of being a mountain goat by his family, who always lagged behind him and begged him to slow down. He couldn't help it. Between his slow twitch endurance muscles and his goal smashing personality, pushing into the inclines was the only way he knew how to climb. *Like Reno. Except he's got me beat.*

Suddenly, yellow sunlight flooded the hillside in front of them. The heat of the sun on Patrick's wet cheeks was so intense, that it felt like they were venting steam. Everything seemed to smell clean and fresh again. How was that even possible so quickly? He snuck a glance over his shoulder. A dark gloom still clung to the mountains below, but it gave way to wispier clouds that rose to meet skies as clear and blue as his daughter's eyes. He hoped it would clear up for her and the rest of the group at lower elevations soon, too.

Then Reno was cresting the ridge in a final push. Patrick reined him in for another rest stop, then looked up. His jaw dropped. He let out a low whistle. Highland Park stretched out before him. He'd known it was a big park. He'd seen it from above. But it was hard to believe a meadow of this size, with such hearty grass, existed at the tree line.

"This is where we were?" Eddie said. The Lunker had pulled up beside Reno, and Reno, for once, wasn't telling the other horse to back away.

Patrick had forgotten the other man was with him for a sweet moment. "Hard to believe, isn't it?"

"It sure looks different."

The view of the massif that had been obscured before by the weather dominated the skyline. The peaks were shockingly close, and yet, at the same time, still a long distance away. Dark and imposing, it wasn't hard to pick out Black Tooth's rocky, jagged profile from the others. From the plane, Black Tooth had been beautiful, but different. Flattened out. Here at its foot, Patrick could appreciate every inch of its additional three thousand feet of elevation from where he sat astride his horse. He remembered the name Perry had given the mountain earlier—Snaggle Tooth—and Perry's missing tooth, which had given him a matching profile. It almost made him smile. Almost.

"Jeez. My butt hurts almost as much as my arm. Got any more of that codeine, man?"

Anger flared in Patrick.

This. This view and this ruined moment were what he had come for. To enjoy this place with his friend and his kids. Not to be carting around Eddie Blackhawk while mobsters hunted for him and his injured buddy. A sense of loss replaced Patrick's anger. The more of his birthdays that passed, the more he realized that time lost couldn't be recaptured. The opportunity for the time with his kids, *this* time, was gone forever. Taken by Eddie, because of whatever it was he and Elvin had done that had brought the mafia after them.

"Which direction to the plane?" Eddie asked.

Patrick tried to shake off his anger. It wouldn't help him find the survivors and get them safely off the mountain. His lips were tight when he answered, though. "I thought you knew. We were still climbing that last pitch when you went down. When we got up here, the park and the peaks were completely socked in with clouds. Then Henry went after John's horse—I'm not even sure in what direction—and half an hour later, he showed back up with you, over there." Patrick pointed to a stand of trees to their right.

The Lunker inched forward until Eddie was even with Patrick. Reno dropped his head to graze. Patrick loosened the pony line, and The Lunker did the same.

Eddie said, "I don't see the plane."

"Neither do I." Nor did Patrick see smoke or broken timber. Nothing to identify a crash site.

Eddie nodded. "I'm a decent enough tracker. I'll find it."

"After a storm like that one?"

He shrugged. "It makes it harder. I need to be on the ground to do it, though."

Patrick thought about the men looking for Eddie. George had sent them on the wrong path, but they were bound to figure that out sooner or later. They were delayed, not thwarted, and they would be coming for Eddie, he felt sure. "It will slow us down if you walk."

"Not as much as wandering in circles without getting anywhere will."

That was true. "Do you need help?"

"I know how to get off a horse." Eddie slid feet first down The Lunker's rump. The horse didn't stop chomping grass or even flinch. Eddie cradled his injured arm in his good hand. "This way." He struck out to the right of the trail, his knees bent and his eyes intent on the ground. Within seconds he was moving at a brisk pace toward the trees where the group had sheltered earlier.

Patrick eased Reno and The Lunker forward. "I know we went there."

"I know you know. But I want to get familiar with the prints so my eyes will know what to look for when we strike new ground."

It made sense. Patrick kept the horses well behind Eddie. Now that they were getting closer to the crash, it was time to learn more about what he would be facing. Maybe there was something he could do to prepare "How badly were Elvin and the pilot hurt?".

Eddie didn't look up. "Bad. I couldn't get Elvin's seat belt to release. He was unconscious and it looked like his ankle was broken. And his arm." After a moment he added, "The pilot was trapped, and his head was bleeding. He wasn't conscious either."

It sounded to Patrick like they'd be towing down travois, which meant they would also be carrying them like stretchers through the worst terrain. Evading mobsters wouldn't be easy. But Patrick couldn't think about that. One problem at a time. Right now, that problem was to find the plane. But then it registered on him that Eddie had just described Elvin as unconscious. It gnawed at him. Earlier, when he admitted his friend had survived the crash, Eddie had claimed Elvin had spoken to him.

Patrick spoke casually. "Did Elvin wake up before you left him?"

Eddie's steps didn't falter. "No."

"But I thought you said he begged you to leave him and get help?"

Eddie kept his eyes on the ground. "He would have, if he'd been awake. I know him."

Patrick's voice rose. "Do you ever tell the truth?"

"I guess."

Eddie sounded so blasé that Patrick itched to jump off his horse and give him a pummeling. These were men's lives they were talking about, even if one of them was a man Patrick didn't like. But Eddie was his friend. The man was trapped in a wrecked plane, deserted by his friend in a strange wilderness. With friends like Eddie, a man wouldn't need enemies.

Patrick clenched his jaw and closed his eyes for a moment. He prayed Elvin and the pilot were still alive when they finally reached them. Otherwise, leaving his kids with George wouldn't have been worth the risk.

CHAPTER TWENTY-SIX: SHADOW

Susanne

DRIVING EAST DOWN Main Street past interspersed little hotels and storefronts in jauntily painted old houses, Susanne's Suburban might as well have been a flashing neon light in Barb Lamkin's rearview mirror. Barb knew the vehicle. Susanne eased off the gas to let it fall as far back from Barb as she could get and still follow her. Nearly two blocks. A tractor without its trailer—how many wheels did that make it?—turned onto Main between them. It belched out a cloud of smelly black smoke as it accelerated. Susanne couldn't see around it, and she bit her lip. Barb could turn off on a side road and be gone in a flash.

Susanne never drove aggressively. But that didn't mean she wasn't capable. Her father had kept roadsters when she was a girl. She'd learned to drive in a race car, and he'd made her prove to him she could put it through all of its paces, on and off the dirt track.

Mashing her accelerator, Susanne whipped around the truck, earning her angry beeps from an oncoming sedan.

"Thanks, Daddy," she said aloud.

Adrenaline pulsed in her veins. She squinted, looking ahead for Barb. Her glasses. She didn't have her glasses. Her far-vision was terrible. The white blob in the distance had to be her. She gave the Suburban some gas so she could get close enough to be sure. She tried to recall ever seeing Barb drive a white Chevy truck before but came up empty. In fact, Barb had totaled her *brown* Chevy truck the night she'd tried to kill Susanne and the kids. From there, Barb had been transported to the hospital, then to jail after she was released from medical care. She probably didn't even own a working vehicle anymore. Had she stolen this truck? Maybe from a tourist. The plates were from out of state. White with Columbia blue lettering. Virginia, if Susanne's eyes didn't deceive her.

They were on the outskirts of town now, near the fairgrounds. Ahead was the junction of the interstates—90 north to Sheridan, east to Gillette, or 25 south to Casper. As the gap between their vehicles closed, Susanne's adrenaline slowed. It was definitely the white truck ahead of her. She hadn't lost her. Luckily, Barb was easy to follow. She was obeying the speed limit and traffic laws, obviously taking care not to attract the attention of cops. *Her being a wanted fugitive and all.* Anger boiled up in Susanne. She squeezed the steering wheel so hard it hurt her fingers. Barb had better drive carefully, because Will was in that truck.

Susanne didn't trust Barb with a baby, even one she'd given birth to. She pictured the infant thrown off the seat and tumbling to the floorboard. Or being catapulted into the dash. The thought made her shudder.

Up ahead, Barb put on a left blinker, then red lights flashed on her bumper. Susanne applied her brakes. Where could Barb be going? She clearly wasn't headed to her old house, a tiny rental near the hospital. It was now occupied by Mayor Martin Ochoa's aged parents, who had recently been convinced by their son to move into town from their remote ranch, nearer to community assistance and medical care. There would have been nothing for Barb at her old house.

Barb didn't appear to be driving toward a friend's house either, at least no one Susanne had known about. Barb's best buddy had been Tara Coker, another young teacher at the high school, who'd lived in a duplex further south. But Tara had left town after she was fired for having an affair with a student. And not just with any student. With Trish's ex-boyfriend, Brandon Lewis. He'd been seventeen at the time. In Susanne's opinion, that constituted abuse of a child, and the woman should have been prosecuted. She'd pled the case to Max Alexandrov, but he'd stood firm that the damage to Brandon and the school from bringing charges would be greater than the gain. As the parent of teens and an aspiring educator herself, it had made her sick.

Other than Tara, Barb had mostly associated with her former lover, Judge Renkin, up until their mutual incarcerations. Hers, pending the trial she'd run out on. His, after pleading guilty as an accessory after the fact in Barb's murder of his wife. Plus, the Renkins had lived next door to the Flints. Barb definitely wasn't headed there.

The white truck turned left onto Airport Road. Who did Barb know out in that area? Susanne had exhausted all of the contacts she could think of who might have helped Barb make her escape or who might harbor her now. This was the Flints' old neighborhood and the only route to the county airport. *Dear God, don't let her be meeting someone with a plane.*

Susanne eased her big vehicle slowly into the turn, hanging as far back from Barb as she dared get. The road would wind through a rugged gulch for the next mile, then open up onto a plateau with multi-acre properties and an unfortunate amount of visibility between the homes on them. No trees, unless you counted the occasional oversized chokecherry bush or buckbrush. Not much for the pronghorn antelope and white-tailed deer to hide behind except rocks. Wyoming wasn't renowned for its lush vegetation, except in the mountains. In fact, pretty much any land where trees grew naturally belonged to the state. Because of the terrain, Susanne would have to stay close enough that she'd see Barb in case she turned off the road, but, because of the lack of cover, far enough behind that she didn't attract her attention. It would be hard to balance and not something Susanne had any experience with. She was a homemaker, for Pete's sake. A soon-to-be college student. A wife and mother. Not a police officer.

So, what the heck was she doing following this woman? It had been a rash decision. Not even a decision, really. Pure instinct. She'd been dazed at the time, still reeling from the blow to her head. She touched the knot on the left side of her forehead gently with her fingertips. It was tender and as round and raised as a grape. The blow hadn't helped her headache, that was for sure. The hole in the light had returned, and she knew the migraine would come barreling in behind it like a freight train soon. And she was on the trail of a murderer, albeit one with a missing hand. Not that it seemed to have slowed Barb down much. Susanne had no weapon. She didn't have her purse—glasses—or medicine. She had no idea what she'd do if she caught up with Barb, or, worse, how she'd defend herself if Barb realized she was being tailed and turned on her.

All she knew for sure was that she couldn't let Barb out of her sight. At this point, Susanne was the only person who knew where Barb and Will were. She felt a strong sense of responsibility to herself and her family and the state of Wyoming to thwart Barb's escape. It might sound crazy, but she was the only one who could. But she felt an even stronger sense of duty to Ronnie not to let Will out of her sight. Because it was Susanne's fault. Barb had taken Will right out of her arms.

She still couldn't believe it. How could she have let it happen? Why hadn't she fought back harder? Would she have done something differently if it had been one of her babies? She hoped not, but she'd never know. A sobering thought struck her. What would she have done in *Barb's* shoes, if she had given birth to a child, then had a chance to escape from life in prison or a death sentence, to get the baby back? For a fleeting second, she felt something like sympathy for Barb. It had to have been and must still be incredibly difficult to be forced to give the boy up.

But the moment ended as fast as it had begun. *That's what happens when you murder your lover's wife and try to kill the witness and his family.* Barb had forfeited her right to freedom by her own choices, even the freedom to raise her son. Prison was no place for a baby. No place for a child. The State was working in Will's best interests, to give him a chance at a normal life. A good life. That sweet little boy didn't deserve to be kidnapped from the good people who were giving that to him. He didn't deserve to suffer because of who gave birth to him.

Ahead of her, Barb's truck disappeared from sight into the ravine. Susanne goosed the accelerator. Around the next curve, she caught sight of the truck's bumper again. She was not letting this woman get away.

A low, furry body waddled into the road. She slammed on the brakes, biting the inside of her lip so hard that she drew blood. A badger.

"Go, go, go," she screamed.

The badger didn't look at her, didn't hurry. When it had cleared her lane, she stomped on the gas pedal. The Suburban's tires laid rubber on the asphalt. She didn't let off the gas until she caught a glimpse of Barb's taillights going around a bend. Her speedometer had climbed to fifty, and she eased back on her speed as she entered the curve. It didn't matter that she didn't know what to do. She was doing the only thing she could, the thing she had to, which was *something*. Even if all she could do was not let Barb out of her sight. But that also meant she couldn't blow a tire or wreck the Suburban. Wherever Barb went, Susanne, if no one else, would know about it. Will would not be missing. He would be kidnapped, but he would not be missing.

The road climbed out of the ravine, spitting the Suburban out onto the vast, barren expanse of the plateau. Susanne scanned the road ahead.

No Barb.

She whipped her head back and forth, checking the long rural driveways from the road to the small acreages and homes along it.

No white truck. How could she have lost her so quickly?

She looked ahead further, to the limits of her terrible vision, to the last turn off from the road before it crested the hill toward the airport. Barb could have accelerated up the straightaway and be half a mile ahead by now. She could be almost to the entrance of the airport. Susanne smashed the gas pedal down again, heedless of the ninety degree turn ahead in the road. Her tires squealed around it, and her back end slid onto the gravelly shoulder of the road. The smell of burning rubber filled the interior. She hung on tight to the wheel, muscling the Suburban straight again, holding her breath, spraying gravel. Then, as she was gathering speed, she darted a glance to the left, down the dirt road she, Patrick, and the kids had lived on until they'd bought their house on Clear Creek. Where Ronnie and Jeff Harcourt had been their next-door neighbors and still lived.

She hit the brakes. Ronnie and Jeff lived out there. Will's home was down this road.

She peered into the distance. And there it was—the white blob, pulling into a sheltered parking area on the south side of the Harcourt house. Blood ran from her face, leaving it cold. Was Barb going to lie in wait for the Harcourts to come home and then do something horrible to them?

Susanne slammed the Suburban into reverse and smashed the accelerator. The vehicle lurched and weaved as she backed up. She stomped the brakes to the floor, shifted before she was fully stopped, and gunned the engine into a turn to the left, fishtailing onto the gravel. *If only Daddy could see me now. Or Patrick, who likes to think he's the better driver. Fat chance.*

But now that she was barreling down the dirt road, indecision and self-doubt hit her full force. She couldn't just drive up to the house. Barb had a gun. And there were plenty more in the Harcourts' house, since Ronnie was a deputy and both she and Jeff were hunters. What Susanne really needed to do was inform law enforcement of where Barb and Will were. But there were no pay phones out here. No stores where she could borrow one. There were phones, however. There was one right next door, in fact, at the Flints' former home.

Susanne had met the family who had moved into it. She could ask them to call the police. Barb would be next door. Susanne could keep one eye on her and leave the Suburban running. She nodded. It was her best option.

She drove past the entrance to the Harcourt place and on to her old driveway. The Suburban bumped and jolted up the familiar path as memories swirled in her head. Good ones, like walking the kids to the bus on their first day of school in Wyoming. Watching Patrick set up a triangular pattern of barrels for Trish and Goldie. Perry running down the hill, racing Ferdinand, who had been just a gangly puppy. And bad ones, like the night of terror she'd spent tied up in her bedroom, hostage to Billy Kemecke, until Ronnie had found her the next day, after Kemecke had gone after Patrick up on Walker Prairie in the mountains.

When they'd moved to their dream house, she'd been so excited that it hadn't registered with her then how many important moments had taken place here. Tears threatened, but she swallowed and willed them away. This was no time to give in to emotion. She whipped the Suburban around the circle drive in front of the house, leaving it poised to make a quick exit, but out of sight of the Harcourt house, engine running.

She ran to the front door. A mat with a picture of a fat black bear on it read WELCOME TO OUR DEN. She took a deep breath, then rang the bell. "Come on, come on, come on."

She looked to her right, toward the Harcourts' house, but it was set back further on its property than this one was. She couldn't see it while she was standing at the front door. Her breathing sped back up again.

There was no answer to the doorbell.

She rang it again. As she waited, her vision dimmed out. *No. No. Not again. Not now.* She threw her hands up and braced herself on the door. Images flashed through her head. At first, they were the same ones she'd seen earlier. Patrick and an American Indian man. Trish and Perry standing by a stack of felled timber. Henry and Ben riding full speed through a forest. And Barbara Lamkin, holding a baby in a dark parking lot. Then they changed. A church next to a motel. George Nichols with tears in his eyes. A crumpled figure on a mountain trail.

She cried out and slumped forward against the door. The images faded. Her vision returned to normal. Why was this happening to her? Was she losing her mind? After a few seconds, she forced herself to stand up. To get control of herself.

She started knocking. When that didn't yield immediate results, she pounded on the sidelight window with her palm. She shouted through the glass. "Hello in there. Is anyone home? Emergency. Help. Hello!"

Still, no answer.

She tried the doorknob. Everyone in Wyoming left doors unlocked. She could run in and use the phone, even if there was no one home. The owners wouldn't mind. Wyomingites looked out for each other, like with the little cabins up in the mountains stocked with firewood and water in the winter, in case people needed them.

The doorknob didn't give. Of all the bad luck, the new people locked their doors. What were the odds?

She backed away, looking for a rock or a brick. She'd have to bust out a window. Movement in her side vision caught her attention. The white truck. It was backing out. Barb was on the move again. Whatever she'd been doing in the house, she didn't plan to wait around to kill Ronnie and Jeff.

That was good, right? But Susanne hadn't been able to call the police.

And now she had to go. She couldn't let Barb and Will get away. She ran back to the Suburban, threw it in gear, and floored it. The big vehicle bumped down the driveway, on the teetering edge of control, like Susanne herself. In her rearview mirror, Susanne saw the front door to her old house open. A woman of about her age stepped outside, a toddler clutching her leg. She waved. *What had taken them so long?* Susanne screamed and pounded the steering wheel. She let off the gas, tempted to turn back and make the call.

Then Barb turned right back onto Airport Road. In seconds, Susanne knew, she would disappear into the gulch. It was possible that even if Susanne hurried, she would lose her. Would let Ronnie and Jeff down. Would never see Will again. Would only be able to tell the cops that Barb was gone.

She accelerated after Barb, praying she was doing the right thing.

CHAPTER TWENTY-SEVEN: HURT

Upper Little Goose Trail, Cloud Peak Wilderness,
Bighorn Mountains, Wyoming
Friday, August 12, 1977, 5:00 p.m.

Perry

AS HIS GROUP rode down the Little Goose Trail, Perry was bringing up the rear. If a starving mountain lion came after them, it would jump from the trees onto his and Duke's backs. Everybody knew it was always the last one in a line that got eaten. But he didn't care. He wanted to be there. He could hang back as far as he wanted, away from John. Because Perry wasn't speaking to his friend. Not anymore. He'd tried to talk to him over and over when they were still up at the cave. He'd told him that he wasn't mad about his tooth. He'd promised not to tell any of their friends about how things had gone. He'd even asked him about Kelsey, in a last ditch effort. John had acted like he hadn't heard him, which was impossible since Perry had been standing right beside him the whole time.

And it wasn't like John wasn't talking at all. A few times, Trish had asked John stuff, and John had answered her, like everything was normal. That really hurt Perry's feelings. Talking to Trish and not him? He hadn't done anything to John. John was the one who'd kicked Perry's tooth out and busted his lip, and Perry wasn't even mad about it. Not that he was happy about it, but he didn't blame John. Accidents happen, and John had been scared. Perry had done dumb stuff before when he was scared. Like once when he'd been really little and was riding on his dad's shoulders, a dog had charged at them and Perry had accidentally wet his pants. Except his pants were on his dad's neck, so it was like he had peed on his dad. It was an accident. His dad hadn't gotten mad.

Perry hadn't been mean to his dad about it like John was being to him. Why was John giving Perry the cold shoulder? That wasn't what best friends did to each other. So, not another word. Not until John spoke to him first, anyway. Then, Perry would consider it.

Perry pressed his fingers against his busted lip, very gently. No scab yet. Still oozy. But his gum wasn't bleeding anymore. The bloody wad of gauze had started to stink, and every time he caught a whiff, he'd gagged. The last thing he needed to do was barf. He'd thrown it away ten minutes before. His mouth was really starting to hurt, though. He wished his dad had given him some more Tylenol for the ride down.

Mind over matter, his dad would have told him if he were there. But he wasn't there. He'd left them. And he hadn't even bothered to act like he was considering Perry's offer to help rescue the plane crash survivors. He'd just sent Perry away like he was some little boy. *I'm no little boy*. He was thirteen and a half, nearly a man, and he'd proven himself, hadn't he? When his mom and his sister would have burned up in Coach Lamkin's wrecked truck, who had saved them, with no help from anyone?

He had.

He straightened his shoulders and ducked away from a tree

branch. This trail was a harder ride than Solitude had been from Park Reservoir. The branches were lower, and the path was lots more narrow. He glanced to his left, past the steep drop into a valley, out over a row of low rocky summits along a ridgeline. They looked like ant hills to him. Lots and lots of giant anthills, with no ants. Like some giant anteater had come along and slurped them all up. Bing, bang, boom, no more ants. It was a glum thought. And a glum ride with no talking or singing. He even would have liked to hear his dad singing his dumb songs right now. "Thank God I'm a Country Boy." Or maybe "Rhinestone Cowboy." Instead, it was just the thwap, thwap, thwap of wetness falling from the sky.

"Everyone okay back there?" George called.

Natch, John wasn't going to answer George, so Perry did. "Yeah. Good."

"Is the pace all right for you?"

Perry wanted to say it was slower than Christmas, but he knew George was holding back for John's sake. It didn't make sense to Perry, though. When they'd gone on rides in town, John had been fine. He'd trotted, loped, even flat out galloped some. But he'd pretty much turned into a big, fat chicken on the mountain.

"Yeah, it's fine," Perry said.

Although at this pace they would probably still be riding down this trail after dark. *Let's see how much John likes that.* Perry wondered if this trip would be the end of their friendship. It would be the last time Perry would invite him up into the mountains, that was for sure. But he hoped they'd still practice ball together. Go to movies. Order an extra-large double cheese, double pepperoni pizza together and eat the whole thing. His eyes started burning, so he forced himself to run through plays in his mind instead.

Half an hour later, John started whispering something to Trish. Perry had been feeling calmer and less mad. He knew all the wide receiver routes cold, plus the special team trick plays the coaches loved to use him on. But the whispering set him off again. His blood boiled. Was this how it was going to be? If so, John could just be best friends with Trish for all Perry cared.

She shouted up the line. "George?"

Like a chain reaction, all the horses stopped as George pulled his up. "Yes, ma'am?"

"We need a bathroom break."

We. Ha. More like John.

George's mount backed up and tossed his head. "Okay. Here's as good as any place, I guess. I'll hold the horses."

Perry stopped Duke beside a big pile of fallen trees that someone had pushed off the trail. The forest service probably. His dad said when he got old enough, he could volunteer to help them clear trails in the spring, because every year more trees fell, during the winter especially. He thought that sounded more like something his dad would like him to do than what Perry would like to do himself. When he was old enough to get a real job, he was going to apply at the A&W so he could have all the root beer floats he wanted.

He slid off his horse. His legs were like jelly, and it took a second for him to get right with the ground. He walked Duke to George, who had also dismounted, and handed him the reins. Trish brought Goldie and Plug over, too.

George juggled the four sets of reins. "Probably best if you hurry. Junior is looking at Plug kind of nippy. Anytime there's a mare around, geldings lose their fool minds." He smiled at the horse. "Typical fella."

Perry thought about John and Kelsey. And now John and Trish. "Yeah. Typical." He gave John a slant-eye glare.

But John had already disappeared into the trees back up the hill a ways. Trish went off in the other direction. She picked a spot across the trail from George, up an incline and behind some rocks. Perry followed the trail about ten yards further than her. He wanted to be as far away as possible from his fair-weather friend. Normally, they would have gone into the woods together, had a contest to see which of them could pee the farthest, maybe snuck up on Trish and pretended to be bears. But no. Not today. Today Perry might as well have come by himself.

Grumbling, he climbed up the slope in the same direction as Trish, through the stubby, skinny trees, and across pine needles slippery and wet under his cowboy boots, until he found a big enough rock to give him some cover. It was a cool one, covered on one side in green moss and lichen in a bunch of different colors.

When he'd unzipped his pants, he called out to his sister. "Trish, can you hear me?" He kept his voice low, so that John couldn't.

"What?" She sounded irritated, which was normal for her.

"What's the matter with you?"

"You wouldn't understand."

He rolled his eyes. Her love life. It had to be. It always was. It sure wouldn't be about something important, like what was wrong with John, whether their dad was okay, or whether the people in the plane were all right. Okay, he hadn't been thinking about his dad or the crash survivors either, but he had an excuse. He was injured. John had weirded out on him. And did Trish even think to ask Perry how he was doing? Nope. With her, it was all Trish, all the time. Well, Trish and her boyfriends. She was so dopey. And now John had gone dopey, too. Again, the image of John mooning over Kelsey popped into his mind. He shook it away and refocused his ire on his crabby sister. The funny thing about her was that she thought no one knew about her secret boyfriend, but Perry did. He'd heard her on the phone, all lovey-dovey with Ben Jones, of all people. The guy who'd helped his dad and uncle kidnap her. Their parents would go ballistic if they found out.

But had Perry ratted her out? Had he even given her a hard time? No and no.

Pardon me if I'm not in the mood for this nonsense. "What, you mean about Ben?"

Her voice was low but screechy. "What do you know about Ben?"

He admired the waterfall he was creating against the rock. It pooled in a depression, then overflowed and cascaded into the pine needles below. "Oh, come on, Trish, my bedroom is next to yours."

She was dead silent for a few seconds. Her voice was nicer when she spoke. *Go figure.* "You haven't told, have you?"

The waterfall slowed to a trickle, then drops, then only a wet patch against the lichen. "Nope. So, you owe me."

"Fine." He could picture her arms crossed over her chest.

He zipped his pants, grinning. "My choice when and what."

"I said fine."

Perry imagined all the ways he could call in his favor. Trish had a driver's license and a truck now. He could make her take him to drag Main Street next Saturday night. Or he could have her do his chores for him when they got home. He could even save it for some time when he needed her to cover for him or—better—take the blame for something he'd done. He sure could have used it when he'd gotten nailed for pulling the fire alarm at school last spring. He grinned. He should ask John. John was really good at coming up with crazy stuff.

But, no, he couldn't, because he wasn't speaking to John.

He said, "What's the matter with John, anyway?"

"How would I know?"

"He's acting like he's mad at me. He won't say a word to me."

Trish sighed. "He's embarrassed, numb nuts."

Perry mulled that over. It was possible, but not a very good excuse, since he was talking to Trish. "That's no—"

His words were interrupted by the sound of hoofbeats on the trail. Loud, fast, and a little out of control.

Then they stopped. Perry frowned.

"Well, well, if it isn't Mr. Nichols. How's that appendicitis?" The voice was male, accented, and mean. Really mean. Perry recognized that voice—the man George had left up in the mountains. The one looking for the three guys. And he had those two other muscle men with him. Not good. "You musta thought we were pretty stupid, Mr. Nichols."

Perry wanted to whisper to Trish to stay down, but he knew she would. Trish was smart. And she'd been around bad guys before. But John! John was all the way up the trail, far from Perry and Trish, and he was not himself. Perry might be mad at him, but John had been his friend a long time.

Perry squeezed his eyes shut tight. Maybe the men would just ride on.

CHAPTER TWENTY-EIGHT: DISCOVER

HIGHLAND PARK, CLOUD PEAK WILDERNESS, BIGHORN
MOUNTAINS, WYOMING
FRIDAY, AUGUST 12, 1977, 5:00 P.M.

Patrick

PATRICK LED Reno and The Lunker toward the ring of peaks
behind Highland Park, following Eddie. Patrick had never had any
training or experience in tracking, unless you counted one desperate
night the year before when he'd been searching for Trish between
Walker Prairie and Dome Mountain. He'd been successful, but
lucky. Now, Eddie was creeping low to the ground with his face to
the earth, occasionally stooping to sniff like a bloodhound. To
Patrick's surprise, Eddie moved swiftly, traversing bogs, skirting
ponds and rocks, and, ultimately, forty-five minutes later, bee-lining
off to the far side of the park and up into a fringe of stunted trees.

There, Eddie dropped cross-legged in the wet grass, hurt arm
cradled in the other. Patrick was ten yards behind him, having
stopped the horses to drink from a pond. He took a swig of water

from his canteen then handed it to Eddie. It was nearly empty, although he had one more in a saddle bag. They needed more water for the other men. One of them would have to find a fresh-running stream and purify some more, after they located the plane.

"I need a rest, man. We're close," Eddie said, screwing the top back on the canteen and handing it to Patrick.

"I thought you didn't remember where it was."

"I don't, precisely, man, but I have a general feel. I know I've followed my trail back. Where I couldn't find my prints, I could smell fuel. I got some on me in the crash."

Patrick sniffed and detected a faint kerosene scent. The man was right. He'd been splashed with aviation fuel. It had been pounded by precipitation and was dissipating quickly in the open air, so he hadn't noticed it before.

"The indentations from my feet were pretty good in a few places, despite the storm. And I know when I left the plane that I came across some rocks, through some trees, and ended up here with a pond in front of me. This is the place."

Patrick rubbed his chin. "How high up in the rocks is it, do you think?"

"I was pretty delirious. I'm not sure. But it felt like a long way."

"I can't believe you survived."

Eddie looked off across the park. "Me either, man. The climb down those rocks or the crash."

"What do you remember about it?"

"The pilot was trying to put the plane down in the park. So, we were gliding low. It was just too cloudy for him to see anything. Then this horn noise went off before we crashed."

The stall warning, letting pilots know to push the nose of the plane down before speed reduces anymore or risk falling from the sky like a rock. Patrick pictured flying past this area with Trish a few days before. He imagined what it would have been like to fly blind over the mountains with the warning horn going off, knowing he'd lost lift and was going down at the base of Black Tooth Mountain. He shuddered.

"What are you saying, man?"

"Huh?"

"Your lips were moving like you were talking, but I couldn't hear you."

"Oh. Talking to myself. I flew past here on my way to Dubois on Thursday with my daughter. I was just thinking about what a crash like that would have been like."

Eddie frowned. "Yesterday?"

This time Patrick felt his lips move as he pieced together the timeline. Had it only been the day before? So much had happened that the intervening twenty-four hours felt like a week. "I guess so."

"Dubois?"

"Yes. I met your sister there, actually."

This time Eddie paled. "Constance was at the airport in Dubois yesterday?"

"To pick up an x-ray machine the Buffalo hospital donated to the clinic in Fort Washakie." Patrick looked hard at Eddie. "What's wrong?"

"I, uh, I just haven't talked to her in a while. She's always with Dann. Getting ready for their wedding."

Part of Patrick wanted to wrap up the conversation, but the larger part of him was on high alert, his sensors nearly humming with the weird vibe Eddie was giving off. "She told me about that. Actually, we had some excitement there. There was a guy in the middle of the runway, dead as a doornail. I nearly hit him on my landing. A cousin of Elvin's, Constance thought."

Eddie crawled to his feet, eyes averted from Patrick's. "That's a bummer."

Patrick's ears started ringing. Eddie hadn't even asked who it was. A cousin of Elvin's might be a friend of Eddie's. And hadn't Constance thought it was possible that Jimmy Beartusk worked with Elvin and Eddie? Either Eddie wasn't curious, or he already knew the man was dead. That was possible, since Beartusk had reservation connections, and news traveled like wildfire there. But not to even remark on it? Very odd.

Before he could push the issue, Eddie said, "Let's get moving. The sooner we get there, the sooner I can get some real rest." *So, does he expect that I'll do all the work of rescuing his friends by myself?* Eddie turned and pointed through some trees. "Broken branches. I came this way. But it's going to be tough going from here for the horses."

While he hadn't summitted Black Tooth, Patrick had hiked to the base of Cloud Peak nearby. Eddie was right. The horses would reach a point of no return. Patrick filed the topic of Jimmy Beartusk away for later. There were more pressing matters to tackle now. Like two men needing medical attention and rescue. And where and how to secure Reno and The Lunker.

He wouldn't tie them to a tree if he could help it, since, technically, it was against forest service and wilderness rules, because of the damage it causes to the trees. But he could hobble or highline them. There were two potential problems with hobbling, though. The first was that horses were fast ranging grazers and social creatures who would seek the herd they'd left behind. Even in his hobbles, Reno could move faster than Patrick could run. The second was that the two horses were as big as moose and hard to miss. If the goons hunting Eddie and Elvin somehow found their way up to Highland Park, they'd know they'd hit paydirt as soon as they caught a glimpse of the horses. Then he thought of a third problem. He only had one set of hobbles. So, as much as he'd love to leave them hobbled in the good grass down on the park, he couldn't. That left him with only the option of highlining, which would keep them secure but wouldn't let them graze.

He'd just have to come back later and take the horses for food and water. "I'll highline them on the other side of the trees."

"Suit yourself."

The men and the horses pushed through the puny pines.

Patrick was actually impressed to find them growing at all at this elevation. The conditions were inhospitable at best nine months out of the year. And, given their experience earlier that day, Patrick thought that estimate was probably a little generous. These trees took the worst Mother Nature could dish out and survived, despite the odds. Like the wildflowers that bloomed in July in this park. Their season was short and filled with wind, hail, and the searing sun of high altitude. Yet every year, columbine, balsam root, lupine, and a myriad of other flowers forced their way up through the rocky soil and bloomed spectacularly, as if their brilliance was in compensation for their short life spans. These were no hothouse flowers. Or trees.

Meanwhile, humans at lower elevations—especially in the cities —were soft in comparison. A hundred years before, homesteaders had braved Wyoming winters in tents and sod houses. Trappers had lived and worked in these mountains year-round. The Plains Indians had been doing that and more for centuries. Yet people these days stayed inside with gas heaters if the temperatures were less than temperate and blasted air conditioners all summer long. His family wasn't much different. It was one of the reasons he liked to bring them on mountain adventures. To make them resourceful. To keep them tough and strong.

He smiled, proud of how they'd handled themselves today. No hothouse for his kids, either.

When he and Eddie broke from the trees, Patrick's jaw dropped. In front of them was a stretch of jumbled boulders that rose hundreds of yards before it curved away with no summit in sight. No trail either. The natural forces that had created this rockslide had to have been immense. And he knew they were always just a breath away from another event, with almost no ability to predict when it might occur.

"I'm going to take a leak, man." Eddie didn't wait for Patrick to respond, just headed back into the trees.

"Okay, then," Patrick said.

He tented his hand and looked up. *Amazing*. He had to come back and climb the peak someday.

A rhythmic sound caught his attention. He shifted his eyes toward it. A man was hopping from boulder to boulder, making his way down the field toward them with the speed and agility of a bighorn sheep. Patrick couldn't believe he'd been up in the massif in the storm. He saw Patrick and raised a hand in greeting without slowing down.

Patrick waved back

The man was close enough that Patrick could see his wide smile under a Denver Broncos cap. He was wearing sunglasses, rock climbing shoes, and a backpack with climbing ropes and a pickax swinging from it. A solo climber. Patrick was impressed and a little intrigued. This was the kind of person for him to befriend if he wanted information on climbing Black Tooth. Or maybe even a guide.

"Hello, sir," Patrick called. "Some weather, huh?"

"Nice enough now." The man was ten feet away.

"You didn't happen to see a plane on the ground up there, did you?"

Five feet. "This isn't Bomber Mountain." He pointed south. "That one's easiest to climb coming off 16 from Buffalo."

"No, I—"

The man passed him without stopping.

"I'm Patrick Flint." He turned, staring after the man.

"Be seeing you on the mountain, Patrick." The man again lifted a hand, this time in farewell, and disappeared into the stand of trees.

A minute later, Eddie re-emerged from roughly the same spot.

"Did you see the climber who just walked out?"

"No." Eddie didn't even appear interested in the topic.

"Well, I asked, and he hadn't seen the plane."

Eddie pointed up and to the right. "But there it is."

Patrick followed the line of Eddie's finger. "Well, what do you know."

The wreckage was in plain sight once you knew where to look, especially now that the clouds over the area had lifted. White and red metal were a sharp contrast to the black boulders around it. From this angle, he couldn't tell what type of plane it was. He wondered if it was visible from Highland Park at the right angle. If Cardinale and his men had binoculars, they might be able to pick it out from some distance away.

For a moment, the plane felt familiar to Patrick. "What were you guys flying in?"

"An airplane."

Patrick closed his eyes and breathed softly through his nose. "What kind of airplane?"

"Something that had two wings, a propeller, and was big enough for three of us and our stuff."

Patrick had an urge to punch Eddie. It wasn't the first time. He had a feeling it wasn't going to be the last. Clearly, he wasn't going to get any useful information from him. Not that it mattered. Patrick didn't know any reservation pilots, so he wouldn't know this plane.

Eddie tested his foot on the first boulder. "I don't remember how I climbed down this."

"Go ahead. I'll catch up. I have to get the horses set up."

Eddie nodded. "It will take me longer." He took a deep breath and stepped onto the first boulder. Patrick watched him for a moment. Eddie's balance seemed poor, but that was to be expected with one of his arms in a sling, tucked against his belly.

"Be careful." It was going to be hard enough to get two men down this rockslide. He needed Eddie's help, not for him to become another man down.

Eddie didn't answer.

Patrick retrieved a line from Reno's saddle bags and quickly fastened it between two trees about ten yards apart. Then he unsaddled Reno, took off his bridle, looped his lead through the line, and did the same for The Lunker. After he checked Reno's leg, which was good—great, really—he brushed the sweat out of the horses' coats.

Luckily, the two geldings were tired and ignoring each other. And with no mare around, he didn't expect much drama.

He gave Reno one last pat on the neck. "I'll be back soon."

He shouldered the bags with the food, water, bedding, and medical supplies and left the horse supplies bag. After a few steps, he had a wave of profound appreciation for Reno, and all ungulates. How could the hooved herbivores be so muscular and strong? Patrick considered himself in decent shape, certainly from a cardiovascular perspective. He'd just run his first half marathon that summer. But he wouldn't relish the thought of having to carry these packs—much less a saddle and full-grown man—up the mountain trails. Reno nickered. Patrick turned and waved, then felt a little silly.

Time to put his cardiovascular fitness to good use. He eyed the mountainside, tracing a line up it, then attacked the boulders. It was good to be stretching the kinks out of his legs after a day of riding, and it was an immediate and intense thigh workout. He'd been worried about footing, especially in his cowboy boots, but, fortunately, the sun had dried the rocks. He was careful to place his feet on the horizontal planes, ones with rough surfaces when he could find them. Unfortunately, the saddle bags wreaked havoc with his balance. One side of the bags hung heavier than the other, and he cursed his poor planning in not redistributing that weight while he was on flat ground. Injuring himself would be an even bigger catastrophe than if Eddie did. He slowed down to a near crawl.

Every ten yards, he stopped to catch his breath and recalibrate his route, so as not to climb himself into an untenable position. He stood tall and arched his back, drawing in deep lung-fulls of crisp, clean-smelling mountain air. Then he looked around. Black Tooth was hidden by the slide. Behind and all around him was clear, summer-blue sky. Below in the distance, the tops of the angry, black clouds were thinning and moving south. Above him, Eddie was a dot near the plane, but Patrick had closed much of the gap already.

He started climbing again. When he reached the outer fringes of the crash site, the smell of aviation fuel grew stronger. Eddie was sitting there with his legs splayed in front of him and his back against a boulder. Patrick leaned over, winded.

The other man's face was ashen. "I gotta sit here for a minute, man."

Patrick thought it was odd that he wasn't in a hurry to check on Elvin, no matter how bad he felt. "I'll go see about the others. Listen for me. I'll shout if I need your help."

Eddie nodded.

Patrick moved into the wreckage, paying close attention to where he put his feet. One misstep and he could rip a chunk in his hide on jagged metal, or, worse, fall against something lethally sharp. Twenty-dollar bills blew around his feet. *Strange*. As a pilot, walking through a crash site was beyond sobering for Patrick. He took a deep sniff. More aviation fuel, but there was no smell of anything burning. With all the precipitation, anything short of an explosion would have been extinguished quickly. Caution was always the best option, though, and he continued scanning for fire and smoke.

He eyed the remains of the plane as he headed for what was left of the cabin. It was a few sizes up from his Tri-Pacer. A Cessna 210 Centurion. Six seats, high fixed wings with struts—an old design, which told him it had been built before 1967—propeller driven, with a retractable tricycle undercarriage unlike his Tri-Pacer. It was a popular and reliable aircraft. Something had obviously gone wrong on this flight, though. Since eighty percent of plane crashes were pilot error, chances were slim that it had been this bad boy's fault.

Patrick patted the intact tail. The plane hadn't rolled. But it had crumpled. The undercarriage was flattened, the bottom of the fuselage ripped open, one wing broken off and the other crushed. Pieces of wing and fuselage littered the ground. He made his way toward the door. The entire propeller, nose, and cockpit were smashed between two rocks. It looked like the propeller had been thrown backwards into the pilot's seat on its impact with a boulder the size of a dump truck.

He stepped back, taking in the side view of what was left of the plane as a whole. Most of it was white, except its red belly. He turned and read the tail number, and the recognition he'd felt when he first saw the crashed plane from below suddenly made sense. N-BTF46. A heavy ball formed in the pit of his stomach.

He knew that call sign. The BTF stood for Bruce Timothy Folske, and 46 was for his year of birth. A vanity tail number, to match the confidence and ego of its Buffalo-based owner, Bruce Folske. Vietnam and civil aviation pilot. Wyoming aeronautical legend. Sometimes mechanic who maintained his own plane on a shoestring budget and had been battling a fuel leak in his Centurion.

Patrick's friend.

And a plane that had sputtered before crashing, suggesting that at least one of its wing tanks was empty. Then where had the aviation fuel around the site come from? The tanks required manual switching between them, and Patrick knew a plane could become fuel starved and still have fuel left in the other wing tank. He hated to think Bruce could have stalled and gone down with fuel left, but his mind went back to the sobering statistic about crashes caused by pilot error. Eighty percent. Eighty percent. Eighty percent. As a doctor, he was accustomed to his decisions meaning the difference between life and death for his patients. His feet were firmly planted on the ground when he made them. Not thousands of unforgiving feet in the air like when he was piloting.

Please, God, don't ever let me grow complacent.

A new thought struck Patrick, and it gave him pause. He'd thought the plane had come from the reservation. And Eddie had told him the two survivors were Indians—Dead Indians, originally, to be exact, until he changed his story. Another lie? Or was someone else piloting Bruce's plane? Patrick felt a flicker of hope.

"Bruce!" Patrick shouted.

There was no answer. Eddie had said the man was unconscious. Patrick leapt toward what was left of the front seats.

What he saw there stopped him in his tracks. He had seen plenty of gruesome dead bodies in his time, but nothing topped this one.

The man's shiny, bald head was lopped off partway and hanging to the side. His once-powerful torso was impaled on the yoke, and his intestines had spilled out over and around the column. The stench from the bowels made Patrick's eyes water. And an ungodly buzzing noise was coming from everywhere and nowhere all at once. Patrick's eyes adjusted to the dim light and he saw movement at Bruce's neck. *What the . . . ?* Then he saw the same type of movement on his belly.

Flies. His stomach lurched, but he was able to keep from retching. This wasn't his first rodeo. It just never got any easier, especially not when it was someone he knew. *A friend.* Because it was Bruce. There was no helping him. There wasn't even a way Patrick could envision recovering him and bringing down his body. It would take a team for that operation.

But now that he'd seen the man, his distrust of Eddie redlined. This man had died in the crash. He was nearly decapitated for God's sake. There was no way he had been alive, as Eddie had most recently claimed. But how had Bruce ended up here, crashing his beloved Centurion into the base of Black Tooth, with Eddie and Elvin onboard and three Chicago gangsters looking for them? Where had they been coming from, and where were they going?

And what was Eddie's game? Instinctively, Patrick patted his chest. His revolver was holstered and ready. He unbuttoned his jacket and overshirt for access, wondering if Eddie was carrying. He hadn't found a weapon on him when he examined him, but he would still have to assume the man had a weapon and be very, very careful.

His attention had zeroed in so quickly on the gory fate of his friend, that, for a moment, he'd forgotten about Elvin. Forgotten, that was, until a weak voice from the back seat said, "Help me. Please, help me."

CHAPTER TWENTY-NINE: FEAR

Middle Little Goose Trail, Cloud Peak Wilderness,
Bighorn Mountains, Wyoming
Friday, August 12, 1977, 5:15 p.m.

Trish

TRISH'S HEART was pounding so hot and hard in her ears that it hurt. The man with the Chicago accent was back, and he was really upset with George. From the sound of all the horse hooves, his two giant friends were with him, too. These were the men that her dad didn't like, and that George and Eddie were afraid of. Trish was scared of them, too.

She had to be silent as a mouse. She lowered herself to a crouch behind some rocks, trying to make her breathing quieter. She wobbled into the hard surface, brushing her face against it, getting a nose full of dirt and moss and . . . and . . . something that smelled like poop. She felt a sneeze coming and a gag. Grabbing her shirt, she wiped frantically until she'd dislodged whatever it was. She squeezed her nostrils shut with her fingers and swallowed the sneeze. Then she froze, listening to see if anyone had heard her. The noise wasn't too loud, was it? After a few seconds of no reaction from below, she relaxed. This was a good hiding spot. The rocks were big and thick. They'd muffle any sound she accidentally made, like the sneeze, and no one would see her. But the men would know how many people were with George just by counting the horses. They wouldn't know which people, though. Or where they were. If worse came to worst, she and Perry could make a run for it. Those guys were flatlanders. City slickers. They could outrun them in the woods. The men would never be able to find them. She felt good about that.

She listened for her brother and didn't hear him. That was good, too. She flashed back to the Gros Ventre Wilderness earlier that summer, when she'd been lost and responsible for her five-year-old cousin Bunny. The only thing that had kept her going when a strange man had found them and taken them was knowing she couldn't let anything happen to the little girl. And she'd kept her safe until her grandpa had helped them escape and find their parents.

Well, now she couldn't let anything happen to Perry. Her baby brother was completely annoying, but also, she had to admit, pretty awesome. When she'd been unconscious in the truck wreck after Barb Lamkin drove them off a cliff, it had been Perry who'd saved her. The little squirt had stepped up, big time. If he needed her today, she would do the same for him. She just hoped it didn't come to that. *Just go,* she willed the men. *Get out of here.*

Below her, George's voice was loud and high-pitched. "You guys must have gotten turned around. You're headed down the mountain, not up. Or did you find your friend?"

The accented man's laugh sounded malevolent. "We hired you to get us up to Highland Park."

"That's what I was—"

A second man said, "You took us in the wrong direction and left us out there. Pretended to be sick. Bad move."

"No, I had you on Solitude Trail. And I am sick. I'm just really tough."

A third man laughed. "Well, tough guy, we ran into some hikers who told us we should have gone left instead of right where Little Goose hit Solitude. Where you met up with your *friends*."

The first man cut in. "Speaking of which, where are Eddie, Elvin, and Bruce?" He raised his voice. "Yoo-hoo, guys. Come out, come out, wherever you are?"

"Who?"

"Don't play stupid with me. You're sneaking them down the mountain. Did they offer you more than I did?" He paused, then raised his voice. "If you come out now, everything will be okay. I'll pretend you weren't trying to steal my money."

Trish was so confused. Eddie was trying to steal this man's money? She knew her dad didn't like Eddie, but no one had said anything about him being a thief.

Up the trail, she heard a voice scream, "Don't hurt me. Please don't hurt me." John's voice. Branches snapped and feet pounded.

"No!" George shouted.

There was a deafening crack, quickly followed by another.

Gunshots.

CHAPTER THIRTY: CHARGE

Ben

THE UNMISTAKABLE THUNDER of gunfire erupted. Then an unworldly scream raised the hair on the back of Ben's neck. Ahead of him on the Little Goose Trail, Henry stopped Spot and held up his fist. His head whipped back and forth, searching for the source of the sounds.

Everything inside Ben wanted to gallop his horse at full speed up the trail. Trish was out there somewhere. What if it was her screaming? What if she'd been shot? But he followed Henry's instruction, waiting with him, while his guts turned inside out.

"I don't hear anything now," Henry whispered.

Ben cocked his head. He did. And it was getting louder. Tumbling, rumbling. Henry's eyes widened, and Ben knew he heard it now, too.

"Rockslide?" Ben suggested. "Mudslide?"

Henry leaned toward the noise, then he shook his head. "Hooves. Horses. Coming fast. Quick. Get off the trail and behind something. They'll trample us."

Ben reined his horse into the trees behind Henry. Less than a minute later, Trish's horse Goldie came tearing down the trail, fully out of control and leading several other equally panicked animals.

"Trish," Ben said, his voice caught in his throat. "That's her horse."

Henry turned on him. "You've got to keep it together, Ben. What did you see?"

"Goldie. No rider."

"And?" Henry prodded.

"Other horses."

Henry nodded. "Perry's horse, and two more. A sorrel the other boy was riding. And a buckskin. But what I didn't see is what has my attention. Patrick's Percheron."

"The other boy?" Ben asked.

"Perry's friend John."

"What does it mean?"

Henry drew in a deep breath. "I don't know. But the Flints and I weren't the only people out on the trail with horses today. I saw George Nichols near here when I was on my way down. That buckskin is his. He had some clients with him, and he was guiding them up to Highland Park. They had some pack horses, too."

"For what?"

"They were hunting for some missing people. I have a bad feeling Patrick might have found who or what they were looking for."

Ben didn't understand, but it didn't matter. All that mattered now was finding Trish and making sure she was all right. "So, what do we do?"

"Are you armed?"

"Yes, sir." Ben patted the rifle in the scabbard on his saddle, then the Smith & Wesson revolver in his holster. Henry had given him both of them for him to use on the ranch, despite the restrictions upon his release from juvie. "Can't turn you out without protection," he'd said. Riding out to check the Piney Bottoms herds could be dangerous. Mountain lions. Coyotes. Bears. Rattlesnakes. Rabid animals. Even cattle rustlers. The first thing he'd learned on the ranch was to always be prepared for the worst.

"We ride up the trail, then. Fast and quiet. Keep your safety on, but be ready, and watch your six. When we're close, we'll stash the horses some place safe and approach on foot."

Ben swallowed, and it felt like something big and dry was stuck in his throat. He struggled to get it down, finally winning the battle. He was all but coming out of his skin. He wanted to race up the trail screaming like a banshee, shooting first and asking questions later. If it was Trish who'd been shot, he'd kill whoever had done it, and he wouldn't be sorry.

He wasn't a killer like his dad or his uncle. He was nothing like them. Nothing. He would never kill without a good reason. But if someone hurt Trish, he expected that was reason enough.

He gritted his teeth and nodded at Henry. "Got it."

"And, Ben?"

"Yes, sir?"

"Think before you pull that trigger. It could change your life forever." Henry reined Spot back onto the trail and urged him forward with a slap of his reins on the horse's neck.

CHAPTER THIRTY-ONE: SHOT

Middle Little Goose Trail, Cloud Peak Wilderness,
Bighorn Mountains, Wyoming
Friday, August 12, 1977, 5:25 p.m.

Trish

A SCREAM RIPPED through the air. The horses echoed it and exploded down the trail, past Trish's hiding place. She looked down in time to see a flash of multi-colored Paint, golden Palomino, red sorrel, and buckskin race by in a blur of colors. Goldie. Goldie was all right. *Run, Goldie. Run.*

Trish clapped her hand over her mouth. She smelled gun powder, she'd heard three shots, and that had been a human scream. Was it George? Was it John? It couldn't be Perry, could it? He was still behind her, down the trail. *Oh, God. Oh, please God, let Perry still be hiding.*

"Stay down everyone." George's voice, deep and commanding. But he wasn't in the same place. He sounded closer to her. Up the trailside slope. There was a scrambling noise level with her. Then pebbles sliding and brush rustling higher than she was.

The boss guy spoke. "Don't be stupid, Mr. Nichols. That was only the semi-auto. Juice has himself a MAC-11. Don't ask me how he got it, because certain laws might have been ignored. It's not a civilian weapon. Trust me when I tell you that you don't want to see him firing it. How many rounds per minute, Juice?"

One of the other guys said, "One thousand one hundred forty-five." He sounded pleased about it, too.

Trish tried to comprehend a gun that shot that many bullets in a minute. And the fact that someone on the trail had a weapon like that and might fire it at them.

George said, "We don't mean you any harm, Mr. Cardinale. Just ride on by. Take my truck. I left the keys on the wheel. I'll forget I ever met you. That this whole thing ever happened."

"You say that, Mr. Nichols, but that boy on the ground isn't the one I was looking for, and that's a problem for both of us. I need you to send out the men I'm looking for or I'm going to have to let Juice have some target practice."

The boy on the ground? John or Perry? One of them was down. Shot? Trish heard a soft gasp behind her from Perry. *Thank you, God.* That meant it was John down, and that Perry knew it. Still, he had to keep quiet. She knew he was sad. She was sad. John was out there. Something had happened to him. But they'd all die if Perry lost it and those men started firing up the hill toward him. She wanted to go to her brother, to help him through this. To get him out of here. But if she did, she'd put them both in danger.

Her dad said that sometimes discretion is the better part of valor. She finally understood what he meant. She bit down on her bottom lip to keep from crying out.

CHAPTER THIRTY-TWO: EXAMINE

BASE OF BLACK TOOTH MOUNTAIN, CLOUD PEAK WILDERNESS,
BIGHORN MOUNTAINS, WYOMING
FRIDAY, AUGUST 12, 1977, 5:25 P.M.

Patrick

PATRICK CRAWLED through the hole where the passenger door used to be, batting his way through a curtain of flies. He'd been able to hear Elvin call for help, but he couldn't see him. The interior was dark and rank with the coppery smell of blood, human feces, and fuel. There were a myriad of sharp edges. Metal. Glass. God knew what. With each was the attendant risk of infection. So, Patrick moved slowly, letting his eyes adjust to the dim light inside.

Using what he thought of as his doctor's voice, he said, "Elvin, I'm Dr. Patrick Flint. I'm going to help you."

"Thank you." The man's voice was weak, but he'd survived a plane crash and being left to die. He had to be made of stern stuff. "Hey, I know you."

Patrick nodded, assuming Elvin could see him better than Patrick could see Elvin. "Yes, we've met."

Elvin's body and face started coming into focus. Patrick tried to keep a neutral look on his face while he did a visual assessment. Horror was definitely not the emotion he wanted to convey to his patient. Neither was panic. Or futility. None of the real feelings coursing through him. So, he focused on conveying nothing, while his mind raced.

Elvin's head and neck looked good. Some cuts and bloody spots, but his carriage was erect, and his head was moving and eyes tracking Patrick. His torso also looked fine, and he hadn't even sustained an injury from the handgun holstered to his chest and visible through his ripped shirt. He was trapped by a lap belt, but he was sitting up on his own. From there, things for Elvin went downhill. The lower right arm was definitely broken—no x-ray required— and his right ankle looked like it was on sideways. Broken, possibly crushed. The injury to this leg, to be followed by a long trip down a mountain, was devastating. Hypotensive shock, blood loss, and pain alone might kill the man. Goal number one would be to keep him alive. Make sure the bleeding had stopped, deal with the shock, and manage the pain. Then his mind went to stabilization. He hoped not just to keep him alive, but to avoid future amputation, which would probably be necessary, but which he wouldn't attempt on the mountain. He'd amputated Barbara Lamkin's hand in the field when she was trapped in a burning truck, and he'd sworn off field amputations for life. Elvin had to be hungry, exhausted, and dehydrated, in addition to everything else, but, overall, he looked like he was holding up, which gave Patrick hope that he hadn't suffered any severe internal damage.

He nodded at the man, trying to convey confidence and optimism. He would have preferred to work on Elvin outside the high-risk environment of the plane. But there was no way he could move him until he'd stabilized that arm and ankle, and then only after he'd dismantled the side panel. One small problem—he hadn't brought a blow torch on this little camping trip. *No Boy Scout merit badge for me.*

"Poker, right?" Elvin gave a weak grin. "You're a friend of Constance."

Not exactly on either count. He had met Elvin at a poker game on the T-ton Ranch, but only because he had been trying to help Constance shut it down. At the time, he'd been friends with the woman. But ever since she'd made her passes at him, he'd have to slot Constance firmly into the colleague category. But who was he to split hairs at a time like this? "Yes."

"You don't like me."

Patrick looked him in the eye. "I don't. But I'm going to save your life anyway."

Elvin nodded. "Good man. I gave you reason, but after this I'm a changed man. All you have to do is get me out of here so I can show you."

"One thing at a time. You'll have to stay strapped in while I work on you."

"I'm in no position to argue."

"Once we've got your arm and leg taken care of, Eddie and I will figure out how to get you out."

"Eddie?" He cursed, coughed, then spat on the floor. "He's still alive?"

"Yes. He ran into my party on the mountain when he was, um, going for help."

"Going for help. Leaving me to die is more like it."

"Well, he did bring me back here." It was a lie, but he needed Eddie and Elvin to cooperate with each other, not be out for each other's blood."

Elvin snorted. "He wants all the money for himself."

Patrick fought not to show any reaction. *He wants all the money for himself? Now we're getting closer to the truth.* He dragged his saddle bag through the door. As he did, he examined the ripped fuselage with his newly adjusted eyes. Again, he had to struggle to control the emotions that threatened to play across his face. Someone had installed a temporary skin inside the plane. Between it and the exterior, he saw bills. As in money. As in the plane was a flying piggy bank. *The source of the twenties I saw earlier.*

Patrick tore his eyes away. He handed Elvin the full canteen and a handful of pills—antibiotics and painkillers. Elvin drained the water, swallowed the pills, and handed back the empty canteen.

"If Eddie wants the money, he's got competition for it." Patrick kept his voice mild as he got out scissors, cleaning supplies, antibacterial ointment, and bandages. He didn't have an over-abundance of anything. If he ignored all the minor injuries, he should have enough for the major ones. "Now, after I give your vital parts a quick examination, I'm going to work on your arm." The arm would be easy compared to the ankle. "Tell me if any of this hurts."

Slowly and methodically, Patrick began palpating Elvin's abdomen, careful not to jar the right arm or ruined ankle. He wished he could examine his spine and back, but with pinpoint placement, he could check the kidneys from the front.

Elvin didn't register any complaints. "It's my arm and leg that hurt. Everything else is okay. Although I guess I got knocked out, so I must have hit my head."

Passed out from the pain, more likely. "Good. Let me take a closer look at your head and neck." He rotated Elvin's head gently, prodded and poked it, and ran his probing fingertips down the man's neck, then on down the collarbone and shoulders. Everything was intact.

Patrick settled back on his haunches. "All right. Let's get going on this arm. I'll clean it up, set it if I can, splint it, and sling it." The ulna fracture wasn't compound. If he couldn't get the bone completely into place, all he needed to do was immobilize it through the joints on either end, then sling it and secure it to his chest.

"Is it going to hurt?"

"Yep. But I'll warn you before I do anything crazy."

As Patrick cleaned the arm, Elvin changed the subject back to the money. "What do you mean about Eddie having competition for the money?"

"You know a guy named Cardinale?"

Again, Elvin swore. "What about him?"

"We ran into him on his way up here."

Elvin's reaction was lightning fast. He struggled against his seat belt. "I knew Bruce shouldn't have radioed in. He'll kill us."

Patrick put a hand on his chest and eased him back. "He has to find you first. A friend of ours sent him on a wild goose chase in the wrong direction. I'm hoping to have you out of here before that happens."

"Then hurry, doc. Please."

"I'll do my best." He pulled his hand away. "Now, this might smart a little."

"I'm ready."

"That's what they all say." Patrick straightened Elvin's arm, pulled his sleeve all the way to his wrist, and sandwiched his lower arm between two sticks, each extending past his wrist and his elbow. Then he secured the sticks with medical tape, to Elvin's shirt and each other, and taped two more in place. It would have to do as a splint. Leaning into the front passenger seat, he salvaged Bruce's windbreaker, silently apologizing to his friend. But Bruce had no use for it anymore, and Patrick knew he would have approved. He tied the garment by the arms around Elvin's neck, with the broken and splinted lower arm resting in the inside of the back. Not a bad sling, if he did say so himself. Lastly, he took off his own belt and strapped the injured arm snug to Elvin's belly.

When he'd finished, Elvin grunted. "Is that all you've got?"

Patrick chuckled. "The easy part is over. Now I've got to work on your leg. I hope those painkillers have kicked in."

"Do your worst."

Patrick was afraid that was exactly what it would be. Moving with care, he cut the denim away from Elvin's leg, from his ankle up to his knee, to free up plenty of space to work. Luckily, the man wore a loose-fitting pair of jeans, so Patrick was able to get his scissors underneath the fabric without pressure or contact to the worst of the injury.

When he'd cleared the area, he laid the fabric open like he was gutting a fish. The ankle was a bloody, gooey mess. Broken wasn't the right word for it, although he could see bits and pieces of bone in the open wound. Smashed, crushed, pulverized, twisted, and ruptured would be a more apt description. Like a tube of toothpaste that had been squeezed in the middle until it split, and the innards had leaked out under pressure. If he'd had a chain saw he might have gone back on his vow against field amputations, but he didn't have anything strong enough to do the job. What was most amazing to him wasn't the injury, though. It was that Elvin had survived it and was doing relatively well. Elvin was a tough son of a buzzard bait. It was going to serve him well in the next few minutes, and during the many hours it would take to get him down the mountain.

"Brace yourself, Elvin. I'm going to start cleaning this up now." Patrick poured a small amount of hydrogen peroxide into the last canteen of clean water, the half-full one he and Eddie had shared.

Elvin nodded.

Patrick tipped the canteen and let a stream of water flow into the open wound. It trickled around the bone, bubbling slightly. Using tweezers he sterilized with more of the peroxide and water solution, Patrick picked metal shavings, dirt, and what looked like insect wings out of the exposed tissue. Then he flushed the site again.

"How's it look?" Elvin's tone was nonchalant with an undercurrent of terror.

It was against Patrick's personal credo to lie to patients. Especially to one who was going to have to endure a hellish trip down the mountain. He paused from cleaning to make eye contact. "I'm sorry, Elvin, but it's not good. There's not much I can do for you except stabilize it and get you to a hospital. It's going to hurt more than I can imagine."

"I figured as much. Think I'll lose it?"

"I'm afraid that's likely."

"Can you take it here?"

"No. Or I would try. I'm sorry."

Elvin sucked in a deep breath. "So, what's next?"

Again, Patrick considered the possibility of fire. The risk was so low that he still thought it was better to stabilize the ankle before he moved Elvin. "I'll be gone for a while to go get the materials to build a box around your ankle. And a travois to transport you on. Then we'll get you out of here."

"We leaving tonight?"

"If we can."

"You have any more water?"

"Not with me. But I have food here. And a sleeping bag, too."

"I am a little cold and hungry."

Patrick got him a PB&J from the bags. While Elvin wolfed it down, Patrick draped the sleeping bag over him. "I'll be back as fast as I can."

Elvin's eyes fluttered closed. "I'm not going anywhere," he muttered.

CHAPTER THIRTY-THREE: BATTLE

Middle Little Goose Trail, Cloud Peak Wilderness,
Bighorn Mountains, Wyoming
Friday, August 12, 1977, 5:30 p.m.

Perry

PERRY TRIED his best to hold it in, but vomit spewed from his mouth anyway. It landed on the wet ground between his hands. Or mostly between them, and a little bit on them. He wiped the slime from his mouth with the back of his hand. The acid burned his nose and throat and made his eyes water. It didn't smell so hot either. But none of that mattered. What he cared about was that Mr. Cardinale and Juice and the other guy didn't find him and Trish. Had they heard him? He'd been as quiet as he could be. He listened carefully, but the men didn't seem to react.

A sigh eased out.

He felt like his brain was stuffed with cotton. Nothing was making sense. The horses had run away. And John . . . John had been shot, for no reason at all. His best friend was hurt and bleeding and

Perry couldn't help him because the bad guys were threatening them with a machine pistol. He wasn't even sure what a machine pistol was. Something for mobsters in the movies, or special operations guys in foreign countries, he figured. Not for people in the mountains of Wyoming.

Mr. Cardinale's voice rang out. It sent shivers up Perry's arms and neck. "We know where you are, Mr. Nichols. We heard your voice."

Perry saw someone moving to his left. Trish? No. It was too big to be his sister. One of the bad guys? He squinted. Caught a glimpse of hair blonder than his sister's but short. A man. George. Where was he going? He was hunched over moving uphill like Perry's dad whenever he did his dumb fox walk, trying to be as quiet as an Indian. But it seemed to be working for George, because the bad guys were still staring at where he had been, and he was fifty feet away from there now, heading up the steep trailside. They *didn't* know where he was.

Mr. Cardinale said, "Youse all got until the count of three to come out. Then Juice makes Swiss cheese out of everything within fifty yards."

George climbed faster, crawling on all fours with his butt up like a bear crawl now. To Perry, it was like he was watching this on a TV show where George was the hero, and he wanted to cheer. Taking the high ground to fire down on an enemy. It was sound military strategy according to all the shows he'd watched. That is, if George had a gun. He'd told Perry's dad that he did. But was it with him? George reached a rock ledge and scrambled onto it. It was the perfect perch for a mountain lion to pounce from. Or for a soldier to defend. George stretched out on his belly. He pulled a handgun from inside his jacket—*yes!*—and extended his arms. He sighted down toward the trail. He cocked the thumb hammer.

And then his trigger finger drew back.

The shot George fired wasn't nearly as loud as the ones earlier, but it must have been just as effective. A man grunted. Then there was a loud thud and the sound of a horse sprinting away.

"Big mistake." Mr. Cardinale's voice was really, really mad.

Bullets began firing from a gun, but so fast and loud that they were like popcorn on a hot stove, or a raft of firecrackers going up from one fuse. Perry flattened himself onto the ground and inched backwards. He barely noticed the puddle of sick as he dragged himself through it. He put his hands over his ears and glued his eyes on George. *Come on, George. Come on.* George had scooted off the rock and was crouched behind it. He was safe, and so far, so was Perry. But he hadn't heard a sound from Trish. His stomach started to churn. What if she'd been shot?

Finally, *finally*, the bullets stopped. The lingering gunpowder smell was so strong, even from a distance, that Perry could taste it. This was no TV show or dream. This was real, and it was happening to him.

Mr. Cardinale spoke again. "How do youse guys like the MAC-11?"

The silence after his words was complete, and that's when Perry realized the storm had stopped. Sunlight spilled through the tree branches and dappled the forest floor. There was no wind, no rain, no sleet, no hail. Just total stillness, without even the chirp of a bird. The shooting had probably scared every animal within a hundred miles, like it had scared off their horses.

Up the hill from him, he saw movement again. George was crawling back out onto his rock. Then Perry heard something. It was soft, but he was sure something was behind him, down on the trail. His heart lodged into his throat. If one of the men came from that direction, they would see him for sure. He had to see what it was. And he had to be ready.

If only his dad believed he was old enough to carry a gun—which he was—he could protect Trish and himself. Or if he hadn't lost his pocketknife last spring. He had a feeling his parents were giving him a new one for Christmas, but that didn't do him any good now. He dug his hands into the pine needles on the ground, digging under them until his fingers found a rock. It wasn't big. No more than half a palmful. But it was all he had. He clutched it and turned, ever so carefully, just enough that he had a view down the trail.

Two men were crawling up from the trail. He'd been right!

But it wasn't just any two men. It was Henry Sibley and Ben Jones. Perry's heart soared. For a second, he wondered why Ben was there and where he'd come from. But only for a second, because he was too glad to really care.

Henry and Ben were climbing on a diagonal now, aiming toward rocks at a higher elevation than George. Perry's eyes flitted from them to George and back again. A new worry had surfaced. What if George shot them, thinking they were the bad guys? Henry and Ben started spacing themselves out, so that one of them was above George on his right, and the other to his left. Perry cut his eyes back to George, afraid he'd see him taking aim at their friends.

Perry held his breath.

George nodded. First at Henry, then at Ben. He'd seen them.

A man's voice said, "Boss, I don't like this. It's too quiet."

Mr. Cardinale answered. "Nonsense, Juice. This is the sound of death. Isn't it beautiful?"

Suddenly, George, Henry, and Ben opened fire. Their cadence didn't rival the machine pistol, but it got the point across. Mr. Cardinale and Juice were up against multiple guns, from three separate locations.

The men on the trail screamed bad words.

Mr. Cardinale yelled, "Back. Get back up the trail."

Hooves clattered. George, Henry, and Ben stopped shooting. Hope rose in Perry. They were going to survive this. They were going to survive!

George shouted after them. "Your people aren't with me. And only cowards shoot children. If you come back, we're going to take you out."

There was no answer. The sound of the hoofbeats faded away.

Perry crawled to his knees. He whispered, "Trish? Are you all right?"

Her voice shook like she was crying. "I'm okay."

He jumped up and headed toward her, running, but not as fast as Ben, who came down the slope like a downhill skier, dodging trees and mowing down all the bush and brush in his way.

Trish's voice shook. "Ben? What are you doing . . ."

Ben disappeared behind the boulders Trish had been using as her hiding place. Perry didn't want to see them now anyway. They'd be making out, which was gross. Trish had Ben now. She didn't need him.

But John did.

He changed course. George and Henry were ahead of him, working their way down the slope.

Perry lunged toward them. "George. We have to help John."

George shook his head and put his face in his hands.

CHAPTER THIRTY-FOUR: CONSTRUCT

BASE OF BLACK TOOTH MOUNTAIN, CLOUD PEAK WILDERNESS,
BIGHORN MOUNTAINS, WYOMING
FRIDAY, AUGUST 12, 1977, 5:45 P.M.

Patrick

PATRICK FOUND Eddie sitting against a rock at the far edge of the wreckage, exactly as he'd left him. The blowing cash was nowhere in sight now. Gone, or picked up and stuffed in Eddie's clothes? Patrick glanced at his waterproof watch. Had it really only been twenty minutes since he'd arrived at the plane? He'd worked *lightning* fast on Elvin. But, the crush of urgency had spurred him on. He had to get them all off this mountain, ASAP.

Eddie didn't look up.

Patrick was tired. Tired of Eddie's deceit as well as physically, mentally, and emotionally wrung out. The man had done nothing but lie to him, and he hadn't lifted a finger to help Bruce or Elvin. Patrick could guess why now. Eddie hadn't wanted them to live, because he was planning on coming back for all the cash himself. Patrick remembered the modifications he'd seen Bruce making to his fuselage at the airport. A deep sadness settled over him. He'd been creating the storage space for the money. How much money was stuffed in the false skin in the plane? If it was all twenties, it could be hundreds of thousands of dollars. Bruce must have been every bit as broke as Ernie had told Patrick the day before to take a sketchy job like this.

Patrick remembered the bundle of twenties in Eddie's shirt pocket. And he pictured the man's sagging jeans—probably weighed down by more bundles in the pockets. He'd obviously tried to take some of it already. But not all of it. And he'd risked it being discovered by leaving the plane himself. Why?

He didn't have a way to get it all down the mountain, Patrick realized.

But now he did—the horses.

Patrick had walked into a trap of his own making by insisting he and Eddie come back to the plane with the two strong animals. Eddie now had the motive and opportunity to kill off everyone that stood between him and the money. But did he have the means? Patrick hadn't seen a weapon on him. But the man was clever and amoral. Patrick would have to keep his wits about him and his own gun in reach.

He slipped his hand inside his jacket and rested it on his holster, near the hand grip of his revolver. "I need your help, Eddie."

Eddie stood. His movements were stiff. "Is he all right?"

"He who—Bruce or Elvin?" Patrick's kept his face neutral.

"Bruce?"

"The pilot."

"You knew him?"

"You could say that." Emotions bubbled up, and Patrick pressed his lips together. When he had recovered, he said, "He was a friend of mine."

"Oh, uh, sorry, man."

"And he died on impact. Before you left."

Eddie held eye contact with Patrick. "Yeah, so?"

"I just want to be clear now what the truth was, and how far you were from telling it to me."

Eddie smiled at him. "I didn't owe you the truth."

"You were taking my help."

"I didn't ask for it, though, did I?"

The conversation was going nowhere good and wasting time they didn't have. Patrick ended the tangent. "Elvin will live, probably. But we're going to have to take that plane apart to get him out. And getting him down will be a nightmare for all of us, most of all him. What he needs first is fresh water." He handed Eddie the canteens. "I have a boiling pot in the bags down with Reno. What I need you to do is go find running water, boil it, and fill our canteens."

Eddie shrugged. He didn't say no.

Patrick pointed toward the boulder fall. "After you." He wasn't turning his back on Eddie Blackhawk.

"Where are you going?"

"I need materials to build a travois and a bracing box for Elvin's leg."

Eddie started climbing down. "Is he conscious?"

"Yes."

"Talking?"

Patrick started down the mountain. "Yes, and he had a *lot* to say."

"Did you tell him I went for help?"

"You can lie to him yourself." Patrick wasn't about to admit he already had, in the interest of maintaining order between the men.

"Man, I *was* going for help."

Help to get the money down. "That's why you didn't tell me about him?" Patrick snorted.

Eddie didn't reply.

"He would have died, you know. By the time you got back." He was gaining on Eddie, so he slowed down. "By the way, we have to hike out tonight. Now that I understand what your Chicago friends are really after, and just how motivated it will make them."

The silence was heavy for a few seconds.

Then Eddie turned to him and sneered. "You don't understand anything."

"Help me, then."

Eddie started back down the boulders. "For starters, it wasn't my idea."

Patrick drew in a soft breath. *It? What was "it?"* Eddie must think Elvin had spilled more than he did to Patrick. If Patrick wanted to learn more from Eddie, then his best course of action was silence.

He kept hopping down the rocks, but he stayed mum.

"Fine, don't believe me. But I was happy with the local poker games. I didn't need any more than that. Elvin was the one who wanted to expand. Bring in the high rollers. Satisfy more of their expensive tastes."

That explained the money. Some of it, anyway. But not the Chicago mafia involvement. Patrick held the uncomfortable silence as long as he could, hoping for more. "It's none of my business anyway."

Eddie's laugh was malignant. "A little late for that now, don't you think?"

Patrick did, and it wasn't a comforting thought.

CHAPTER THIRTY-FIVE: TUMULT

Trish

TRISH STOOD behind her little brother, her arms crossed over her chest. The two of them were off to the side of Little Goose Trail, turned away from the others. George, Henry, and Ben were a few feet up the trail, standing over John's body and talking softly. She leaned the front of her legs against Perry's back where he was sitting on the ground. She needed the human contact—a hug would have been even better—and she suspected he did, too, although he always complained when anyone hugged him.

She looked over her shoulder at John again. As much as she didn't want to, she couldn't help it. Had to keep trying to convince herself this wasn't just a bad dream. Her brother's best friend was dead.

She closed her eyes, but she could still see John. It wasn't like she'd never seen dead people before. She'd witnessed some awful things, including the death of Ben's father. She'd been through trauma, more than her fair share. But John dying was the worst thing she'd ever experienced. His body was curled up on the ground like he was sleeping on his side. He looked almost peaceful, except for a single hole in the side of his head with a little trickle of blood that had already dried. He had been spending the night at their house nearly every weekend for the last two years. He used to stare at her when he thought she wasn't looking, his eyes big and focusing on her chest. Younger boys were *so* goofy. But she hadn't really minded. She'd miss it now. She'd miss him.

Tears welled in her eyes, but she ignored them. She had to stay strong for Perry. If it was this bad for her, she knew it was ten times worse for Perry. There was so much more that he would miss. He and John had done everything together. All he'd done since he'd learned John was dead was stare at nothing, not speaking, not crying. She was worried about him. Without her parents here, he was her responsibility, and she didn't know what to do to help him.

She leaned more weight into her legs against his back

Hooves sounded on the trail, coming toward them. Trish's mouth dried in an instant. *They're back.* She grabbed Perry's arm. "Run, Perry. We have to get out of here."

He was limp. No reaction at all.

She jerked at him. How could such a short boy be so heavy? "Come on. Come *on*."

"Everyone off the trail," George yelled. "Into the trees."

"Perry, please. Please." She pulled with all her strength.

Perry fell over onto his hands and knees. She dragged him a step. A large body appeared beside her. Tall and strong. Her boyfriend. Ben.

Ben took Perry's other arm. "Move, Perry. Now." His height gave him a better angle, and his strength made Perry's resistance futile. Ben jerked Perry so far in the air that he landed on his feet.

Together, Trish and Ben dragged Perry behind them a few feet into the woods, without a moment to spare. A horse rounded the bend in the trail, barreling toward where they'd been. Trish dove behind a tree. Perry landed on top of her. Ben crouched behind them.

"Yeti!" George jumped back into the trail in front of John, waving both arms over his head.

The furry black and white draft horse sat back on his haunches, coming to a near sliding stop inches from the boy. His nostrils were flaring, his head tossing, and his ears flicked separately backwards, forwards, and side to side as he assessed threats. One foot of broken lead rope swung below his halter. His flanks were frothy white with sweat around his pack saddle and blanket. Trish could smell his strong horsey scent even from ten yards away.

A second horse trotted up behind him.

"Atta boy. Atta boy." George approached Yeti slowly, hand out and down.

Yeti danced from foot to foot like a hotblooded horse, setting the long hair around his fetlocks in violent motion. He whirled in a half circle, then turned back to his friend. George put a hand on the horse's muscled neck and rubbed in slow circles. Yeti lowered his head and huffed in George's scent.

"I'm so sorry. I'm so sorry." George's back heaved.

Was he crying?

The other horse stared at them all, wide-eyed, flanks heaving. A broken set of reins hung from its bit.

"Who is this one?" Trish said.

George seemed to notice the second horse for the first time. "The one Luke was riding."

"Do you think Luke is . . ."

George didn't answer. But Trish knew. He'd shot one of the bad guys. It was why they'd used the machine pistol. It was good news for her dad. One less of the horrible men for him to deal with. But where was Luke's body? Maybe the other men took him. He could just rot out here or get eaten by bears. She didn't care. He and his friends had killed John.

Ben helped Trish and Perry up. The three of them walked back onto the trail, Perry under his own power this time, where they met Henry.

George wiped at his eyes. "Anyone have an extra lead?"

"Our horses are just around the bend. I'll bring you one." Henry jogged down the trail.

"I should never have left you with them," George whispered to Yeti.

Trish pretended like she hadn't heard him, but his words choked her up. She looked at Ben. His face was pinched, like he was holding back tears, too. She put her arm around Perry. She was giving him that hug, whether he liked it or not. He didn't resist, just stared into the distance at nothing.

Henry reappeared, leading Spot and another horse Trish hadn't seen before. He unclipped the lead from Spot, then handed Trish Spot's reins and the other horse's lead.

He took Spot's lead to George and Yeti. "Here you go."

George unclasped the broken line and attached the new one. Henry walked to the second horse, palm down. The horse backed a few steps, then stopped. Henry untied its lead rope from the saddle horn and brought it to Trish as well.

Yeti shuddered and sighed. His agitated movements were slowing down.

George kept stroking his neck. "I think the big guy can help us with John now."

Henry nodded. "Seems like the best alternative." He raised his voice. "Ben, can you give us a hand with John and Yeti?"

They're going to carry John out on Yeti. With us. For a moment, Trish felt sick. Hiking out with a dead person. But she hadn't considered the logistics of John's death. They couldn't leave him up here. Someone had to carry him down. A wave of calmness washed over her. A big, gentle draft horse. It was the best alternative. It's just that no alternatives were good when someone you cared about was dead.

Suddenly, Trish thought of her own horse. Yeti had come back to George, but Goldie hadn't come back to her. She released her brother and turned to Henry. "What about our horses? Goldie's not a mountain horse. She lives in a pasture. With a stable. We feed her every day. She could die out here alone."

Henry's voice was soft, his expression kind. "Horses are self-preservationists. Two things I know because of that. First, those three are going to stick together. Second, they're going to follow the scent that George's horse laid down on the trail climbing up. That will lead them straight to his trailer. And I'll bet you dollars to doughnuts that's where we'll find them. Grazing near that trailer, which will smell nice and familiar to them."

"Really?" Her pitch rose. She wanted to believe him.

He gave her a thumbs up. "Wait and see."

Then he turned back to George and Ben and their grim task. He retrieved his sleeping bag from Spot's saddle bag and unrolled and unzipped it beside John. Henry took the slicker and jacket off John. Then the three of them lifted the boy onto the bag and wrapped it snugly around him. Trish knew the bag would protect John from protruding tree limbs or the hard, rocky ground if he slid off Yeti, but it was still hard to watch. Seeing his face and mouth covered made her feel like he was suffocating. Like she was. But he wasn't, of course. He would never breathe again. He didn't need air.

She did, and she gasped for it, relief mixing with the guilt of surviving when it entered her lungs.

Henry said, "If you could get on the other side of the horse, Ben. I'll put John on the pack saddle, and you can help me adjust him."

Trish swallowed a lump in her throat.

"Yes, sir." Ben's voice sounded thick. He moved to the other side of the horse. Yeti was so tall that Trish couldn't see him anymore.

George held Yeti's head. Henry grimaced, then he crouched down, slid his arms under the package that used to be a living, breathing John, and hoisted him high in the air. Henry's face turned red, and Trish realized how heavy John must be. Ben's hands appeared above Yeti's back and caught John. Then the two men maneuvered the boy into position with his stomach hinged over the saddle. Trish pressed a fist to her mouth, still holding the horses in her other hand. She couldn't watch John tied like a field-dressed deer. She turned and stared off into the forest at nothing with Perry.

Henry and George started talking fast and low. She ignored them. Then Henry took two of the horses from Trish. His and Ben's. She was left with only the scared horse Luke had been riding.

Her eyes had wandered off, but her brain couldn't escape the horror as easily. The gunshots repeated in her head. She winced at each one. Why had this happened? How had everything gone so wrong? And how were they ever going to tell John's parents their son had died? She wanted her dad back. She wanted her mom. She wanted none of this to have ever happened.

She wasn't going to get any of that.

A crashing sound jerked her back to harsh reality. She turned toward the noise. Henry and Ben had moved their two saddle horses up the trail. With George, they were now moving a big pile of downed timber onto the trail at a pinch point between two rock walls.

"You're going to block my dad in," Trish said to Henry.

He smiled at her. "Your dad will know what to do. He's handy. It will barely be a speed bump for him. But for those city folks, it will be quite an obstacle."

Ben cried out, "I found him. The guy."

Henry trotted over to Ben. The two of them gazed at something on the ground in the trees.

"Is he dead?" George said.

Henry turned, nodding.

"What do you want to do with him?"

Henry pressed his lips together. "We've got to leave him for law enforcement."

Trish's mouth dropped. Just leave him? But what if some hikers came upon him? They'd be scared out of their minds. She searched the area and saw the coat and slicker. "Can't you cover him up with those?"

George looked, and she pointed. He nodded. "Good idea."

Ben retrieved them and laid them over the body. Then the men got back to work on the timber like nothing had happened. Like they hadn't found a dead man who was lying on the ground a few feet away. She watched, numb, as they added log after dried log to their stack until they'd created a barrier four feet high that blocked off all access to the lower trail.

When they had finished, Ben walked over and claimed her free hand. "Hey."

She leaned into his side, not even caring that Henry could see them. "What are you doing here?" She tilted her face up to see his.

"Besides helping?" He crooked an eyebrow.

"No, I mean *why* are you here?"

"I came looking for you. I couldn't stand how we left things."

Guilt made her tear her eyes away from him. What if something had happened to him? He could have died, and she never would have had the chance to apologize. Which she needed to do before another second passed.

She took a deep breath. "I'm sorry."

"I am, too. What I said came out wrong."

Her forehead tightened. "Wrong in what way?"

"Well, I meant what I said about you not graduating early, but not for the reasons you think."

She jerked away from him, stung, but he kept his grip on her hand. "I thought you'd changed your mind, Ben. I thought because you came here . . ."

"Trish." He moved in front of her and the horse, his voice low, his eyes deep. "You are amazing. You have everything going for you. You could be valedictorian of your class. You're really good at cross country. You could go to state. I don't want you to give any of that up. I can't be responsible for ruining your life."

She jerked her hand away. The horse stepped back. "That's ridiculous! *You* are what I want."

"You say that now. But if it's meant to be, we'll be together anyway. . . Don't you see? You won't have to be any less of who you are to make it happen."

"I just have to give up time with you." *And risk you finding someone else in Laramie.*

"Not that much time."

"Too much. I can't do it."

"But I can't be part of making you less."

Perry's flat voice jolted Trish. "Will you two just shut up, please?"

She looked over at him. He hadn't moved and was still staring into the trees with glazed eyes. She clamped her mouth shut. Heat burned her cheeks.

"Time to ride out, Ben." It was Henry. He was right behind them.

How much had he heard of their conversation? Trish was horrified.

George called to Trish and Perry. "We're heading in the other direction. We need to get moving if we're going to make it to the truck by dark."

Trish looked from George to Henry. "Wait. Henry and Ben aren't coming with us?"

Henry put a hand on her shoulder. "We're going to stay between you and the bad guys, and head up to help your dad. George and I talked. He has everything covered."

"I'm going with you." Perry stood, fists balled.

Henry shook his head. "Your mom would never forgive me. I'm sorry, son. Not this time."

Perry glared at Henry, at George, at Ben, and finally at Trish. Then he wheeled and ran down the trail, reckless and out of control.

Trish wanted to go after him, but this was important, too. "But what if they come after us again? They think those guys they're looking for are with us." Trish was scared. She also couldn't stand the thought of Ben riding away. They weren't done. They were far from done. And if Henry thought they needed protection, he and Ben would have to stay.

George patted his chest. "I've got my revolver right here. But they won't be back, Trish. There's only one trail in and out of here. Henry's going to make sure they don't take it. And if they do, the logs will slow them down."

"They have a machine pistol." Her voice was shrill. "You guys don't."

"It's going to be okay, Trish. They're flatlanders. Greenhorns. I'll bring Ben and your dad back safe and sound, I promise." Henry walked to the log pile, signaling the end of the discussion.

She made one last desperate plea. "So that's it, Ben? You're just leaving?"

He pushed his hands in his pockets and looked down. Just when she thought he wasn't going to say anything, he took two quick steps back to her and kissed her on the lips in front of George and Henry. Then he and Henry scrambled over the logs.

Trish stood in the trail with the scared horse, mouth open, heart thudding to the sound of hoof beats as Ben rode away from her.

CHAPTER THIRTY-SIX: SEE

Susanne

THE DRIVE UP I-90 from Buffalo was torturous for Susanne. Her eyes were bleary from squinting into the distance to keep Barb's truck in sight, then refocusing on the road directly in front of her to watch for deer. If anyone ever wondered if there were deer in Wyoming, they just needed to drive seventy miles per hour down a road in the late afternoon or early evening. It was a failsafe test. And there were deer by the droves within a few miles north of Buffalo. Her fingers ached from her ten and two death grip on the steering wheel.

An eighteen-wheeler pulled around her to pass, slowing beside her. She could feel eyes on her, and she shot a quick glance over at the truck.

A man with thick glasses and greasy hair that needed a trim leered at her.

She jerked her eyes back to the road.

The giant bazooka sound made her jump in her seat. Pain shot through her left eye and her head. *The migraine. It's getting worse.* She pressed two fingers against her eyelid. What made a man think honking and scaring a woman would make him attractive? And what did he think she would do? Follow him to the next exit and climb into his rig?

If she was her daughter, she would have flipped him the bird.

Instead, she kept her eyes straight ahead and accelerated, leaving him behind her. A red light started blinking on the right side of Barb's bumper. Barb was exiting into Story! Susanne was gaining on her because of avoiding the guy in the big rig. She was close enough to see the license plate on the Chevy. Something about it looked different. It was just a normal Wyoming plate, but she was almost sure that hadn't been what was on the truck earlier. Hadn't it had Virginia plates? Virginia plates didn't make sense. Barb wasn't from Virginia.

Susanne had the sinking sensation that her brain wasn't clear. She wished her head wasn't hurting so bad. Everything was suddenly confusing. Maybe she'd just imagined the Virginia plates earlier.

In her rearview mirror, the eighteen-wheeler was catching up to her again. She couldn't wait to exit. Then the red blinker on the Chevy stopped, Barb sped up, and the exit came and went. The big rig bore down on her. Susanne pressed her accelerator, her eyes glued to her mirror.

Without signaling, the truck took the exit.

Susanne blew out a loud breath. *Thank, God.*

Her migraine was intensifying. She pressed the heel of her palm into the socket above her left eye. When she lowered her hand, she realized Barb had pulled far ahead of her. As Barb crested a rise, Susanne lost sight of her. Terror gripped her. Barb could pull off the interstate onto a dirt road. In seconds, she could disappear into the rugged hills and gulches. Susanne could lose her and Will and never find them.

She increased her speed, drumming her fingers on the wheel. *Where is she?* Then she spotted her, half a mile ahead. Tension released from her body. It seemed like a safe following distance, and she matched her speed to that of the Chevy's.

Miles and deer passed. Barb reached the outskirts of Sheridan. *Doesn't she need gas? And to feed the baby?*

Susanne eyed her own gas gauge. Less than an eighth of a tank. In an area where gas stations were few and far between, that was dangerously low. It wasn't even enough to get her back to Buffalo from Sheridan. Not enough to keep following Barb much further, and she had a feeling Barb was making a run for the northern border and the great expanse of Canada beyond. It was a long drive. Susanne would have given a kidney for her purse. Her wallet, her cash, not to mention her glasses and pills.

But she might have money in the Suburban. She stashed loose bills and change in the ashtray, since she and Patrick didn't smoke. She pulled it open, hope expanding in her chest. Keeping her eyes on the road, she dug her fingers in it, scooping out the contents. She turned her hand over and eyed the spoils.

A dollar bill and a handful of change. Not enough for gas and food. Her heart sank.

But it was enough, at least, to make some calls. That was a positive, and she had to hold on to anything positive she could dredge up.

She thought through the calls. A call to the police, to give them an update. Them first, before Barb could get too far away. Then a call home for help. She dreaded making it, although the time she'd have to was coming soon. An eighth of a tank soon. Patrick wouldn't be home yet. Maybe Patricia would pick up. If not, who could she call? Not Ronnie, whose child had been snatched while in Susanne's care. She'd probably be cloistered with law enforcement, anyway, monitoring the search for Barb. Susanne would call Vangie.

Barb's blinker started flashing. Susanne's pulse accelerated. She was going to stop! The Chevy exited the interstate and pulled up to a self-service pump in front of a gas station. Susanne followed, parking on the opposite side of the building and leaving her engine running and the nose of the Suburban pointed toward the exit. She lowered the sun visor to hide her face, then surveyed her surroundings. There was a pay phone in front of the station, but it was in clear view of the pumps. She didn't dare use it.

Barb got out of the truck and walked to the station carrying Will. Susanne's heart leapt at the sight of the boy, looking like he was fine. The two disappeared inside. *Should I make a run for the phone now?* Not enough time, she decided.

It turned out to be a good decision. Barb and Will were back in less than a minute. She put him back in the truck and started pumping gas, then kept glancing into the truck, smiling. It made Susanne's head hurt worse and her stomach burn. How dare Barb try to bond with Will? She'd forfeited the right to a relationship with him when she'd murdered Jeannie Renkin and come after Susanne and her family. And she was a horrible mother anyway. Will hadn't had his diaper changed in hours. He hadn't been fed in at least that long. Barb was so worried about snatching him and getting away that she wasn't even taking care of him.

Susanne scanned the street in both directions. Where was a police officer when she needed one? She started rocking in her seat. Why weren't the cops all over the roads looking for Barb? Or for Susanne? Surely they had APBs out on both vehicles? But Susanne hadn't seen a single one since she'd left her house. She heard a keening noise and looked around. It took her a moment to realize it was her own voice. *Get hold of yourself.* She put her hand over her mouth and stopped rocking.

Barb replaced the nozzle, got back in the car, and used the furthest exit to turn onto the street, heading away from the interstate. Susanne held still. *One one thousand, two one thousand, three one thousand, four one thousand, five one thousand,* she counted, then eased out and followed the truck. Barb didn't drive far before she turned right onto Coffeen, away from Sheridan College and toward downtown. Susanne was familiar with the area, since she'd recently registered for fall classes at Sheridan College.

She followed Barb down Coffeen and onto Main, pacing her

through downtown, where Barb turned on a left blinker, stopping for oncoming traffic in front of the Dairy Queen. Susanne eased past the restaurant and parked on the street front of a hotel. She watched Barb over her shoulder.

Barb made her left turn.

"Go in, go in, go in," she whispered.

The Chevy pulled into the drive-through.

"Spit in a well bucket."

Susanne had a few minutes to spare while Barb was in line. She looked around frantically for cops, a pay phone, or even a pedestrian. Someone. Anyone. But there was no one and no pay phones outside the buildings around her. A vehicle passed going the other direction. She considered getting out and flagging one down, but Barb might see her and drive off.

Her stomach growled. And there was that. Hunger. She wanted food and something to drink, too. *Fat chance.*

Barb slipped out of sight in the drive-through line. Traffic tapered off, and Susanne was alone on the street. She backed up, going the wrong direction on Main, until she could see the drive-through line from the other side. Barb was pulling up to the window. Out of nervous frustration, Susanne turned on the radio. Maybe one of the stations would provide updates on Barb's escape.

On the first station, Mac Davis was crooning "Baby Don't Get Hooked on Me." *No.* She spun the dial and found Abba and "Dancing Queen."

"Where is the news?" She turned the dial again and again until a staticky voice came through her speakers.

"—escaped from custody while on trial for first-degree murder in Buffalo. Shortly after her escape, Lamkin kidnapped an infant from his foster mother, Johnson County Deputy Veronica Harcourt. The boy is Lamkin's birth child but had been removed from her custody pending the outcome of this trial. Lamkin is five foot ten inches tall and has long red hair which she may be covering with a green and yellow baseball cap. She was last seen wearing baggy jeans and a brown Cowboys sweatshirt with yellow lettering. Lamkin is armed and considered dangerous. If you see her, call 911 and do not approach her. In other news . . ."

The Chevy rolled forward from the drive-through window to the street. Susanne ducked behind her sun visor and turned off the radio. They hadn't told her anything she didn't already know. Barb turned left. After a few seconds, Susanne eased behind Barb's vehicle. The truck turned east on Fifth, then got back on the interstate, headed north again. Susanne couldn't believe it. The woman still hadn't taken care of Will, unless she did it in the drive-through line at light speed. And could Susanne even afford to keep following her, or should she bail out now and make her calls? She stared at her gas gauge. It wasn't whether she could afford to follow her. It was whether she could afford not to, and the answer to that was easy.

She accelerated onto the interstate behind Barb. She had enough gas to make it to Ranchester, the next town. After that, well, she didn't know what she'd do.

She'd just have to think of something.

CHAPTER THIRTY-SEVEN: LEAD

Lower Little Goose Trail, Cloud Peak Wilderness,
Bighorn Mountains, Wyoming
Friday, August 12, 1977, 7:00 p.m.

Perry

PERRY STUMBLED OVER AN EXPOSED ROCK. He lost his balance, flailed his arms, then staggered a few steps, passing Yeti without looking up at what was on his back. The horse didn't react to Perry's herky-jerky dance.

"I'll take him." Perry held out his hand to George for Yeti's lead line.

George passed it over without a word.

Yeti shoved his nose against Perry's hand, drawing in a full breath of his scent. The horse nodded, as if deciding it would be all right to cede control to a boy. Perry's head swam. Maybe the horse was wrong to trust him. He had thought this was the right thing to do. John was his friend. He was up here because of him. He should be the one to lead him out. But now that he was standing under Yeti's head with the sleeping bag visible on either side of Yeti's round torso, it felt wrong.

"Let me take him," George said to Trish.

Perry glanced back at them. Trish gave George the line to the other horse. Then Trish marched up beside Perry. She'd stuck close to his heels on the way down, but she'd left him alone, not forcing him to talk about his feelings or trying to make things better. Or going on and on about Ben, which would have been just as bad.

"I'll walk with you, Snaggle Tooth," she said.

His throat felt tight and itchy.

They set out, George and the other horse in the rear. Perry hadn't cried yet, but tears were so close to leaking out that they stung his eyes. He wouldn't think about John behind on that horse. He just couldn't. Like he couldn't think about their friends finding out John was gone. Or John's parents. He couldn't think about all the plans he and John had made for the football season, or the way John had looked at that cheerleader Kelsey. He especially couldn't think about the fact that they had never gotten the football out of the saddle bag up on Highland Park. All he had to think about was putting one foot in front of the other and holding on to Yeti's rope.

At least for now.

The forest was growing dark. His dad had told him that the closer you got to the east side of the mountains, the earlier the sun set. Perry knew that was what was happening now, even though it wasn't time for sunset down in Buffalo. The sun had been warm since the storm broke, and then the temperature fell again. He was numb to it. The sounds around him seemed louder, and the clean forest smells stronger. This is when animals came out. He wondered if any predators were monitoring their presence. Bears, mountain lions, coyotes. Normally, he didn't think about them much. But he had John to protect. His eyes darted from left to right, scanning for any evidence they were being stalked and not seeing any.

He tripped again. Trish grabbed his arm. Yeti bumped him with his nose, exhaling a warm windstorm down his neck. It was getting hard to see where to put his feet. The moon was rising, but the trees blocked most of its light.

The tears burned but didn't fall.

He led Yeti past the wooden sign on a tree. CLOUD PEAK WILDERNESS, it read, going in the opposite direction. Did that mean this was the end of the line? He'd never been on this trail before.

George would tell them when to stop, though, so he kept going. The bottom of his feet ached, and the back of his heel stung from a new blister. Wet cowboy boots weren't made for long distance downhill hikes. *Don't be such a baby.* Aching feet were nothing. John wouldn't ever get blisters from the wrong boots again. Perry knew his friend would rather have had them than be killed by a bullet.

He tried to breathe and something went wrong. His lungs wouldn't work. He panicked for a second, then he bent over his knees. Trish put a hand on his shoulder. And then his breath came back like it had never gone. He gasped and started walking again. Trish did, too.

They passed another sign, again going the opposite direction. He turned to look. It announced the start of the trail and end of vehicle traffic.

A voice pulled him up short. "Whatcha got on that horse, son? It's not hunting season yet."

Perry whirled to his right. The voice belonged to a man. He was short and built like a bulldog. His thighs bulged so much Perry wondered how he kept from splitting his khaki pants. A shiny badge was pinned to his shirt pocket. *A deputy?* Behind him, a truck was parked by a cold campfire ring. There was a Wyoming Game & Fish decal on the truck door. *No, a game warden.* Perry looked at Trish. Her eyes were wide.

George hurried to the game warden, dragging the other horse, his arm out like he was putting up a wall between him and the Flints. "I'm George Nichols. These two kids are Trish and Perry Flint. Their father, Patrick Flint, is still up on the mountain. We've had a tragedy, sir. We were attacked by some men up on the trail. They shot one of our party."

The game warden's jaw dropped. "Come again?"

George dropped his arm and wiped his hand on his jeans. It was shaking. "I'm sorry. I know this is a lot of story to explain and even more to take in. But that's Perry's friend John on the horse. And I'm sad to say he's dead. We're packing him down."

The game warden turned to Perry. "I'm Game & Fish Warden Alan Turner. I know your father. I'm sorry about your friend." He stuck his hand out to Perry.

Perry shook the man's hand, trying to keep his own from being limp as a fish. When he pulled his back, he saw that it was stained with oily dirt from the horses. "Perry Flint."

The warden shook Trish's hand. "Ms. Flint."

Trish just nodded.

The warden said, "I apologize, but it's my job to make sure no one is poaching. I've heard wilder stories, so let me just take a look at what you're packing back here, and . . ." His voice trailed off as he ran his hand along John's body, from his waist down his legs and feet.

Perry was pretty sure a dead teenage boy felt nothing like an elk carcass.

The warden's face seemed to go pale, although it was hard to be sure in the low light. "Okay, then. Somebody needs to start over at the beginning and take me through this, real slow."

Perry wanted to be the one who did. He wanted to man up and prove himself like he had when Barb Lamkin had nearly killed his mom and sister. But when he opened his mouth to speak, no words came out, and the tears he'd been holding at bay finally broke through.

CHAPTER THIRTY-EIGHT: EXIT

Patrick

"PULL." Patrick put his weight into his pry bar. He'd fashioned two of them from strong, young trees he'd chopped and stripped.

Eddie grunted and strained against the other pry bar, with his one good arm. Sweat beaded on Patrick's forehead. That blow torch he hadn't brought would have finished this job in minutes, but all they had to peel back the plane's skin was ingenuity and sweat equity. The Centurion's torn metal siding squeaked and groaned. They were starting to make modest progress.

Patrick gritted his teeth and pulled harder. He'd hoped to get Elvin and his newly caged leg out through the opening where the door had been, but there just wasn't room to do it without injuring him further. *If* they could remove the side of the plane, though, Patrick would be able to ease him out and onto the ground without ramming him into anything. It would still be painful. It would still be difficult. But it would be far more humane.

If, being the operative word. *The good news is these planes are strong. The bad news is . . .*

With a screech, the tear in the panel gave way. Eddie fell on his rear, cursing. Patrick stayed upright, just barely.

"Out of sight." Elvin's sallow face was visible through the new hole in the side of the plane.

Patrick was worried about infection and sepsis. All of their efforts would be for naught if the man died. They had to hurry. For Elvin's sake, and because they would need some visibility to get down the boulder field, and the sun had all but disappeared.

"Almost ready for you," Patrick said.

"A hand?" Eddie glared up at Patrick from the ground.

Patrick clasped him by the wrist and hauled him up. *You're slowing us down,* he wanted to say. But better to be civil than to antagonize him and slow them down further.

"Eddie," Elvin said. It was the first time the men had laid eyes on each other or spoken since the crash.

"Elvin. Or should I say Deep Throat?" Eddie's voice was a hiss.

Patrick frowned. Deep Throat? It took him a moment to process the reference, but he'd heard it used frequently in relation to the informant in the Watergate scandal. Did Eddie mean Elvin was an informant? But an informant to whom and about what? The money? Clearly it wouldn't be hidden in the false skin of an airplane unless it was tainted. Stolen or obtained through illegal means.

Trouble seemed to be getting deeper by the second.

Elvin's voice was raspy and defensive. "Not me. We got rid of him."

The two of them had *gotten rid of* an informant? He glanced through the window at what was left of the pilot. Were they talking about Bruce? But his death had been caused by the crash. If not him, who, then? And when and where had they gotten rid of him?

Eddie glared at Elvin. "I was talking about everything *you* told Dr. *Flint*."

Patrick needed Elvin out of the plane so they could start their long descent. That meant he needed them not to kill each other right now. Answers to questions about informants would have to wait. He wished he could just leave these two up on the mountain. *Blast my Hippocratic oath. Blast it to hell and back.* "Come on. We've got to get him out of there, Eddie. Just a little bit more on the edges of this panel."

Eddie continued his staring contest with Elvin, showing no sign he'd heard Patrick.

Patrick sighed. Using his bare hands, he bent the metal back as far as he could. The panel ruptured, and twenty-dollar bills fluttered in the wind.

Eddie ran after the money, stuffing bills into his jacket.

Patrick worked on a sharp edge.

Elvin shouted, "Leave it, Eddie. Help get me out of here."

Eddie kept grabbing money. "A year of work. Nothing to show for it."

Patrick snorted, his disgust breaking through. "You'll *think* nothing if your buddies catch up with us."

Eddie disappeared behind the plane, still chasing the money.

Behind Patrick, a cheerful voice said, "Looks like you're in a heap of trouble."

Patrick wheeled toward the voice, hand instinctively going for his chest holster. But the accent didn't sound like the men from Chicago. When he saw the speaker, he dropped his arm from the draw position. It was the climber he'd seen earlier, still wearing the pack with gear swinging and clanking as he walked, his eyes hidden behind sunglasses.

The man adjusted his Broncos ball cap. He had a trickle of dried blood on his neck that Patrick hadn't noticed earlier. "Didn't mean to startle you. Can I help?"

Patrick frowned. The man hadn't said a word about the wrecked plane. Did he not see it and the injured man inside it? *How odd.* Disconcerting bordering on suspicious. "Hello, again. And thanks. I'm just trying to smooth this metal out enough that we can get the man inside out without hacking him up on the way. I need to curve it back. Like this." Patrick curled the metal outward until the lethal edge was neutralized.

The man nodded. "Doesn't look too hard." Without taking off his glasses, he set to work alongside Patrick in silence. Patrick couldn't tell where the blood was coming from, but the guy wasn't acting like he was in pain. There was an unpleasant smell to him. Not like body odor. Like garbage. Or death. Patrick switched to breathing through his mouth, which helped. He quickly realized the climber was very strong, although several inches shorter than his own six feet, without an ounce of fat on him. If he wanted to overpower Patrick, he might be able to do it, especially with the pickax in easy reach. Patrick kept an eye on him, just in case. A few minutes later, the men had an opening that looked safe enough to bring Elvin through.

Patrick shook the climber's hand, still wary. "Thank you. I'm trying to get him down the mountain tonight. Every minute gained helps."

"I wish I could stay and do more, but I have to get back to my family. I promised them I wouldn't be late. You got it from here?"

It wasn't as if the man *owed* Patrick assistance, but warning bells clanged inside Patrick anyway. Most people wouldn't just walk away from someone attempting to make a solo rescue of a plane crash survivor off a peak. He hadn't even offered to make a call or take a message down. It wasn't the Wyoming way. People here always offered their help and relied on each other.

Something about the man just seemed *off*. Could he be spying on them for Orion and company? It seemed unlikely. He was genuine, if . . . distant. Patrick tried to shrug off his suspicions. The man had helped him, after all. "Well, the other survivor is in good enough shape to walk out, so—"

"Great. Be seeing you on the mountain." The man turned to go.

An idea struck Patrick. The man seemed knowledgeable about the area. "I don't mean to slow you down, but do you know the easiest way to get down from here? I'm going to be carrying this guy out on a travois." Who knows—maybe he would offer help after hearing that.

The climber smiled. "Sure. It's a little longer, but there's a dirt path. Less steep and no bouldering until, oh, maybe eighty percent of the way down this pitch."

"Could you point me to it?"

He oriented his finger north. "Head straight across the boulder field. You won't be able to miss it. It'll switchback down and dead end back into the rocks above where you parked your rides."

"Thank you. That will be much easier."

The climber saluted and resumed his departure. *Nope. Not going to offer.* Patrick shook his head. Then he called out after him. "I didn't catch your name."

The man disappeared into the dark without answering.

Patrick shivered. The man hadn't been threatening, but something about him still set off Patrick's sensors. He glanced back at the plane, noticing a bag shoved behind Elvin's seat. *At least the moon has come up. We may be able to see where we're going after all.* He pulled the bag out and dug through its contents. Maps. Canteens of water. He could have used those earlier, although Eddie had refilled both of theirs. MREs. And a flare gun—a "Very" pistol model with a short, one-inch bore. He nodded. *Useful.* He tucked it into his belt loop. The MREs he stuffed in his shirt. Who knew how much longer they'd be up on the mountain? They might need the sustenance. He'd add them to the saddle bags later. The canteens he left, deciding they were too much to carry.

"You think you could stop talking to yourself long enough to get me out of here?" Elvin said.

"I wasn't—"

"Are we ready?" Eddie sauntered up, pockets heavier, hands full of bills that he was cramming down the front of his pants.

From one odd interaction straight to another. The climber and now Eddie, who was more concerned about the money than his friend. Who expected Patrick to take up the slack—not just the emergency medicine, but all of it. Patrick didn't normally assault people, but he was willing to make an exception to clock Eddie. Maybe when this was all over, he'd get the chance.

"Yes, *we* are. Time for *us* to get Elvin out. Wait here." Patrick walked around to the other side of the plane and climbed in. "Okay, Elvin. This isn't going to be much fun."

Elvin said, "Like the rest of this has been a party."

True enough. "I'm going to lower you to the floor, with your behind toward the opening. Then I'll go around and pull you out slowly. Your leg is going to take some abuse."

Elvin closed his eyes. "I'm ready."

"Eddie, can you help me with his leg?"

Eddie didn't look enthusiastic, but he leaned into the plane. "What do I have to do?"

"I need you to come in here and guide the box." Patrick gestured at the cage of timber he'd built around Elvin's leg and lashed to him with loose wiring he'd salvaged from the plane.

Eddie nodded. He disappeared for a moment, then reappeared beside Patrick inside the plane.

"Bite down on this." Patrick held up a stick.

Elvin opened his mouth. Patrick slid the stick in, and Elvin bit down. He'd used it earlier when Patrick had slid the cage up his leg, and it had worked well.

"Ready?"

Elvin nodded jerkily.

Patrick had tried the buckle on Elvin's seatbelt earlier, and it was jammed. He slid his six-inch pocketknife from its holster at his hip. The knife had been a gift from his friend and co-worker Wes Braten, who had engraved SAWBONES in the handle, his nickname for Patrick. Patrick had discounted the need for the heavy-duty pocketknife at first, but it had come in handy more than a few times. Now he'd no sooner get dressed without strapping it on than he'd dance into town naked. He opened it and carefully sliced Elvin's seatbelt in two.

Elvin grimaced and his face paled, but he nodded as if to say *keep going, keep going.*

Patrick stepped over him onto the outside edge of the plane. He put one arm under the man's shoulders and the other under his thighs. To Eddie, he said, "Get his leg."

Elvin nodded vigorously. He said something through the stick that sounded like *do it.*

"Ready, Eddie?"

"Yeah, man. Let's get this over with."

"I'm going on three. One, two, three." Patrick lifted Elvin as smoothly and carefully as he could. As soon as he had him off the seat, he turned him. "Now, Eddie."

The stick muffled Elvin's scream, but not completely. It tore into Patrick. He hated causing pain. He stepped backward out of the plane, being extra careful with his footing and balance, which were made difficult by his unwieldy load. Then he set Elvin in the place his own feet had been on the floor of the plane. It was a good thing the Shoshone man was lean, because there wasn't much of a gap between the front and back seats in the plane.

Elvin's head lolled forward.

"He's out cold, man," Eddie said.

"Let's work fast then. I'm going to lift him out. You guide the cage onto the seat, then come around and catch it on this side."

"Okay."

"Ready?" Patrick said.

"Go."

Patrick lifted Elvin's torso and Eddie balanced the injured leg across the seat. Then Eddie backed out of the plane and came around to stand beside Patrick. The two men nodded at each other. Patrick lifted again, dragging Elvin's uninjured leg out, while Eddie supported the caged leg down to the earth. Together they turned Elvin and propped him against the remaining intact siding of the tail.

Eddie stood with his hand on his hip. "Thank God he passed out."

"He might come to at any moment. Let's get him on the travois before that happens." Patrick positioned the contraption on the ground. It was his first travois, other than ones he'd made for fun as a kid, and he was satisfied with his work. He'd used a section of his tent as the bed and tied it by its straps to some good young trees like he'd used for the pry bars. He'd lashed the timber in place with the rope he always carried in his saddle bags. The travois was fairly long—as long as he could make it with his available materials—with the goal being to keep Elvin's caged leg off the ground, resting on the cross piece at the foot of the travois.

Eddie stared at it. Doubt was etched across his face. "How are we getting him over the boulders?"

"We'll use it like a stretcher. Boulder to boulder. Slow and easy. When we get him down to the trail, we'll drag him behind Reno. But we won't have to do much bouldering. That climber who was here a minute ago showed me an easier route."

"What climber?"

"Never mind."

Eddie grunted. "I'll bet Elvin's going to be passed out most of the way down."

Patrick hoped Eddie was right. "I'll get his shoulders, you take his legs."

They lifted and positioned Elvin over the travois, then lowered him onto it. The length seemed ample, to Patrick's relief. He tied Elvin in place with a long section of cable he'd liberated from the plane. As he did, he realized that visibility was getting better and better. After a day of horrible weather, God was finally showing signs of being on their side. A full moon was rising, nice and bright.

He nodded. "All right. Let's grab our things and get out of here." He opened the saddle bag, which tumbled over. *Horseman, Pass By* fell out, and he remembered Henry telling him how grim the book was. *Perfect for this trip, after all.* He stuffed the book and the MREs into the bag and closed it.

"Aren't we going to rest?" Eddie said.

"Nope."

"I'm hungry."

"We'll eat on the trail."

Eddie made an unhappy noise, close to a snarl. He took a last hard look at the money sticking out of the edges of the plane's false skin. He stalked over and pulled out a few more handfuls, then shoved them under Elvin's back.

Patrick wondered at what point Eddie would decide he didn't need Patrick's help anymore. He had to stay ready, because he knew they'd get there, sooner rather than later.

CHAPTER THIRTY-NINE: MISS

Dayton, Wyoming
Friday August 12, 1977, 10:00 p.m.

Trish

TRISH PICKED AT HER CUTICLES, pulling and tearing at them until blood seeped from the edges. Today had been horrible, and it seemed like it would never end. The sun had set nearly two hours before. Now, after a long, curvy, carsick ride, the little town of Dayton was only a mile or two away. Finally.

They would have made better time, but the game warden had slowed them down, a lot.

At first, she'd thought that because of Warden Turner, things might move faster and get better. He was a state law enforcement officer. John had been murdered. Her dad was somewhere up the mountain trying to rescue people from a plane crash—and so were Ben and Henry. Perry was hurt. If ever there was a time for help, this had seemed like the one.

She'd been hopeful when George had told their story. But the warden had interrupted him with so many questions that George's face had turned the color of the persimmons from Grandma Lana's tree back in Texas. Then Warden Turner had asked Trish to tell the story from her perspective. The peppering had started as soon as she opened her mouth. She was sure her cheeks had turned red, too. She'd put her hands to them, just to cool her face. All in all, it took them almost thirty minutes to get the story out. Perry was weaving back and forth, almost asleep on his feet.

The warden went to his truck to radio for help, only to discover the unit wasn't working. Another half hour passed as he attempted to fix it. After he finally gave up, he drove Trish and Perry to George's trailer, but so slowly that they'd only beaten George and the horses by a few minutes. There, Perry had laid down on the seat of George's truck while the men loaded John into the warden's truck bed. Trish took care of Yeti and the other horse, picking debris from their hooves with a stick, checking them for any ill effects of the day, and grazing them.

Yeti. She was pretty much in love with the Shire. He was the only horse that had come back to them. He'd been the perfect horse to carry John—kind, gentle, and strong. The other horse was a nice one, but Yeti was special.

She patted both horses, then said to Yeti, "Good job with John, big boy. Now, where's my horse? Where's Goldie?"

The horses ignored her, busy eating.

"I'm worried about Ben."

Yeti looked over his shoulder at her. His wise eyes and solemn expression made her feel squirmy inside.

"I know I should be worried about Dad. I am scared for him. But he's a grown man. Goldie is a silly mare and Ben, well, I just can't help it."

She closed her eyes. The thought of Ben riding toward that awful machine pistol . . . it was too much. She re-lived its awful noise again and again. Smelled the gun powder. Saw the bloody hole in John's head.

"Time to load them up." George opened the trailer gate.

Trish kept Yeti and handed the lead for the other horse to George. She walked the draft around the trailer. His strides were long and his turnover slow—so different from her little mare. Walking beside him made her feel small. He was even taller than Reno, and thicker, too.

George loaded his horse then turned to her. He patted Yeti on the rump. "He self-loads if you just take him up close and get out of his way."

But as Trish lined Yeti up, he stopped and threw his head in the air. His long, heavy mane whipped against Trish's face.

"What is it?" she asked.

He released a whinny from deep in his belly that shook his entire body. The horse in the trailer joined in. And they were answered. By more than one horse.

Trish wheeled around. A golden Palomino was prancing across Hazel Park, white tail fanned behind her. Goldie, beautiful and perfect. Squatty little Duke was fast trotting to keep up with her, Plug on his heels. Junior was bucking and running beside them.

"They're here!" Trish stroked Yeti's neck. The Shire was dancing in place and tossing his head. "Henry was right."

"Thank goodness," George said. "Junior's not mine. He belongs to the ranch I live on." He shook his head. "As do the horses Orion and Juice have. And your Dad. Man, I'm going to be in so much trouble." His eyes cut to the bed of the game warden's pickup. "Sorry. I know there are worse troubles than a few horses."

There was no loading the excited Yeti so quickly after the arrival of the other horses. Trish tied him off to the side of the trailer and went to catch the others. The horses were flighty, but Goldie was a sucker for a cookie. Trish soon had her tied up on the other side of the trailer from Yeti. With Goldie in hand, Duke, Plug, and Junior were easy to round up.

After they loaded the horses, George found a flat on his truck. Trish paced, rubbed her arms to stay warm, and watched the trail while the men changed the tire. It was eight-thirty when George finally rolled out behind the warden's truck. She'd expected they'd head down Red Grade. It was a major short cut. But they turned left.

"Why are we going this way?" Trish's stomach had been growling, and she was melting with tiredness.

"The trailer is too heavy, and the road is too steep. It wouldn't be safe."

"Where are we going?"

"Back up to the highway through the mountains. We'll pass through Burgess Junction, Dayton, Ranchester, and Sheridan."

"And then we'll go home?"

George shook his head. "Warden Turner needs us to all stay together until we meet with Sheridan County law enforcement."

"How long will that take?"

"Dunno. Maybe an hour?"

"And how far is it to Sheridan?"

"About two and a half hours."

She had groaned. A two and a half hour drive to Sheridan. An hour in Sheridan. Another hour back to Buffalo. So, it would be one in the morning, maybe, when they got home. Much later when they'd get to go to bed. And she and Perry had been up since four. She stared ahead through the windshield, dazed but unable to sleep, watching the taillights on the warden's truck for a long, long time.

An hour and a half later—had she slept or just zoned out?—the road leveled. She rubbed her face where it had been pressed against the door frame and came away with damp fingers. Drool. She'd been asleep. The lights of a town blinked in the distance. She shifted in her seat, worked her jaw to stretch her face, and started picking at her fingers. A sign announced the Dayton city limits. Warden Turner put on his blinker. George took his foot off the gas and set his right blinker, too. They pulled to a stop at a filling station.

Trish was dying to go to the bathroom. "George, I—"

The warden rapped on George's window. George rolled it down.

"I'm going to call in the incident from here," the warden said.

"Shouldn't we contact the boy's parents?" George asked.

Trish felt a sting as she pulled away cuticle. She looked down at her finger and saw blood. She stuck it in her mouth. It helped, a little.

"Let's wait and let someone with the county do that when we get to Sheridan."

George rubbed his forehead. It was a gesture her dad made all the time. George looked older all of a sudden—like her dad's age, even though he wasn't—with big dark circles around his eyes. She'd barely noticed him before, since he was a grown-up. But he was probably only a few years older than Ben. He was handsome, Trish realized. And nice. Like someone you'd want for a big brother.

She put her hand down and leaned forward so the warden could see her. "I need to call my mom." *And go to the bathroom.*

As soon as the words left her mouth, Trish felt her throat tighten and eyes prickle. Her mom would pick them up in Sheridan, take them home, and make everything better. Maybe not completely better, but at least a lot less bad. She'd be worried that Trish's dad was still in the mountains, especially after she heard what he was up to, but she'd know what to do. And they could call Vangie together and tell her where Henry and Ben were. Trish's heart ached at the thought of Ben.

"You can have her meet us in Sheridan at the Sheriff's Department."

Trish nodded. It's what she'd expected.

"Why don't you go first?" He pointed. "There's a pay phone over there. My call may take a little while."

Trish got out of the truck. The August air was warm, even with the sun down, especially after the cold of the mountain storm. Crickets were sawing and chirping, but otherwise it was quiet in the little town. Dayton was on the Tongue River, and it smelled a little like fish.

"I have to go to the ladies room." It was embarrassing to have to say it to the warden.

He nodded. "Sure. Meet me back at the phone." He pointed at it up against the building.

She hurried inside to get the key, then back out to the rest rooms. The ladies room was dark and smelled sour. When she sat, the toilet seat was so cold that she shot back up off of it. Hovering was smarter in a dirty place like this anyway. After she was done, she tried to wash her hands, but all she got when she turned on the taps was groaning pipes. She sighed and returned to the pay phone.

The warden was still on his call. She sat down on the curb to the building's sidewalk and hugged her arms around herself. Warden Turner's voice droned on and on. Sleepiness finally seeped over her.

"Your turn." The warden's voice startled her.

She jerked. "Okay." She stood and took the receiver from him, then touched each pocket in her jacket and jeans. They were all empty. She chewed her lip. "I don't have a quarter."

He dug in his pocket and came out with a handful of change. He selected a quarter and handed it to her pinched between his thumb and forefinger. "Here you go."

"Thank you." Trish dropped the coin into the phone and dialed.

The warden leaned against the wall to the filling station. He tipped his head back and closed his eyes. The phone started to ring.

After four rings, Trish decided she must have dialed the wrong number and hung up. "You don't have to wait for me."

The warden opened his eyes. "I'm not leaving you here in the dark by yourself. Is no one home?"

"I'm trying again." The pay phone spit her quarter out. She fished it from the change return and slid it into the coin slot once again, then dialed. It rang. This time she let it continue ringing. *Where is she?* Her mom never went anywhere on the weekends unless it was with her dad, and then it was usually to one of Trish or Perry's games.

On the eleventh ring, just as true panic was setting in, someone picked up on the other end. An eighteen-wheeler rolled by the filling station, downshifting loudly. "Hello?" a woman said.

Trish heaved a sigh of relief. "Mom?"

"No. This is your Aunt Patricia. I'm sorry, Trish, but she's not here."

"Where is she?"

"Honey, I think I should just tell you all about it when you get home."

Trish's mouth went dry. The warden seemed to pick up on her distress. He straightened and cocked his head at her.

"I can't come home. We've had . . . a problem. Perry and I need someone to pick us up in Sheridan."

"Sheridan? What? And why can't your dad drive you home?"

"He's still in the mountains. Can you come get us?"

"I would, but I don't have a car. Your mom took it."

Trish squeezed the receiver tight in her hand. "Where's my mom?"

Her Aunt Patricia sighed. "I don't want to worry you."

"Then tell me where my mom is!"

The warden's eyes widened. Trish knew she sounded snappish and disrespectful, but she needed to know where her mother was, and she needed to know right now.

"Oh, honey. Earlier today, Barbara Lamkin escaped from the courthouse. She came here and took her baby. Your mom went after them."

The receiver slipped from Trish's grasp and clanked against the phone booth. She scrambled to pick it back up.

"Are you okay?" the warden asked.

Trish put her mouth up to the phone. Her voice was hoarse. "Is my mom okay?"

"I'm sure she is. It's just that, well, no one knows where she went. She'll probably call any minute with good news, but, right now, that's all I know, Trish. I'm sorry."

Trish hung up on her aunt.

"What is it?" the warden asked.

Around her, the sky seemed impossibly large, the moon heavy with gloom. She felt lost in the vastness of the Wyoming night. As lost as her mother appeared to be.

She pressed her hands against her temples. "My mom is missing. Both of them—both my parents—are *missing*."

CHAPTER FORTY: TAIL

Susanne

WITHOUT A TURN SIGNAL, Barb's truck exited the interstate on Highway 14, west toward Ranchester, Dayton, and the Bighorn Mountains.

Susanne pounded the steering wheel. "Yes!"

Her gas gauge was hovering a hair above empty. She estimated she had thirty miles left before she'd be stranded. She'd have to fuel up in Ranchester. That was all there was to it. If Barb didn't stop, Susanne would try to catch up with her later—and pray she didn't pull off somewhere before then. Because there was no way Susanne was letting the Suburban run out of gas on a mountain road in the middle of the night. That wouldn't do anyone any good.

But before Susanne reached a filling station, Barb made another turn. A left, into a parking lot in front of an L-shaped building.

Susanne squinted at the sign, heart pounding in her throat. THE WESTERN MOTEL.

Thank you, God!

If Barb was getting a room, Susanne could go for gas, call the cops, get food. First, though, she had to park where she could watch Barb. To make sure she knew what the woman was doing. She sussed out her choices on either side of the road. They were sparse. It came down to a church or a bar. The last place Susanne wanted to be seen was the parking lot outside a skuzzy bar.

What better place to pray for the safe return of Will than a church?

The church it would be, then. She spun the steering wheel to the left. Her wheels squealed, which worried her—she didn't want to draw attention to herself. She pumped the brakes on the Suburban, pulling it to a stop. Her ears rang in the sudden stillness. She rolled down the window to let cool air in on her face. The migraine had made her dizzy, but she was determined to ignore it out of existence. She looked at the building. It had a large cross on the roof. A sign above the entrance read RANCHESTER CHURCH OF CHRIST. Not her denomination, but she felt sure God didn't discriminate.

As much as the pain in her head made her want to close her eyes, she kept them open and on the exit from the hotel parking lot. She prayed aloud. "Dear God, please let that heinous woman check in and take care of Will. And while you're at it, please help me figure out how to get him back."

She strained to see. Her eyes were bad, and it was so dark out. How she wished she had her glasses. She saw someone walking into the motel office, but not carrying a baby. Her mouth dropped open. Barb hadn't just left Will alone out in the truck, had she? Then she remembered Patrick kept binoculars in the Suburban, for wildlife spotting. She fumbled for the latch on the glovebox without taking her eyes off Barb. The hatch fell open—the compartment was over-stuffed—and binoculars tumbled to the floorboard along with the owner's manual, a wool cap and gloves, a flashlight, and miscellaneous papers.

"Spit in a well bucket!" Susanne ducked down, grabbed the binocs, and jerked herself upright. She adjusted the focus on the lenses.

A woman was clearly visible through the office window, talking to a stoop shouldered man with wispy gray hair sitting behind a counter. The woman was Barb, but if Susanne hadn't expected it to be her, she wouldn't have recognized her. She was wearing one of Ronnie's Johnson County Deputy uniforms, including a ball cap with her hair tucked into it.

"Gotcha!" Susanne whispered.

But that meant Will was outside in the truck. Susanne was torn between who to watch—Barb or Will—but opted for the baby. Barb had escaped to get him. She wasn't going to leave without him.

Susanne switched the binoculars to the truck. No one was near it. A few minutes passed, then Barb entered her field of view. The disguise was still jarring a second time. Barb opened the passenger door and grabbed a duffel bag, which she slung over her shoulder, then a brown paper bag. She set that on the ground. Lastly, she scooped something out of the floorboard. It was small and swaddled in blankets.

"Will!"

With Will tucked into the crook of the arm that was acting as a hook for the duffel, Barb picked up the grocery bag in the other hand and strode across the parking lot, disappearing from sight behind the building.

"No, no, no!"

Susanne needed to know which room was theirs. The blinding pain from her migraine made thinking difficult, so she acted on instinct instead. She wrenched the door open and ran across the dark parking lot in front of the church, past the office to the motel, then slowed to a walk. She peeked around the side of the building, the binoculars still in her hand, breathing hard. She was sure she was too late. They would already be inside their room.

But Barb was walking back to the truck.

Susanne gasped and retreated, running with her hand along the siding back to the other side of the building. From a safe distance, she watched through the office windows. Barb started the truck and backed it out.

Susanne whispered, "Where are you going without that baby?"

Her outrage gave way to a hopeful thought. If Barb left, maybe Susanne would have a chance to snatch Will back herself. She didn't know their room, but she could knock on doors until she got to one no one answered. Then she could smash out the window. *With what, dummy? Your bare hands?* She looked down at them and smiled. *With my husband's binoculars.* Now she willed Barb to leave. All Susanne needed was a few short minutes.

Barb turned the truck around and drove toward the back of the motel. Could she get out that way? Susanne crept to the corner of the building and peeked around it. If Barb circled the building to come around front, Susanne was exposed. There was nowhere to go, nowhere to hide. As she stood frozen in indecision, Barb appeared, walking from the rear of the building.

Susanne exhaled, the sound too loud in the quiet night. Barb had hidden the truck in back of the motel. She stopped at the last room, farthest from the road, and let herself in.

Susanne was lightheaded. She hadn't had a chance to take Will, but Barb was staying at the motel. That bought Susanne some time. But what should she do first? Get gas, to be ready in case Barb took off again? Call the police in Buffalo? Whatever it was, she needed her Suburban and she needed to move quickly, so she jogged back to the church parking lot and got in the vehicle. Her panting was loud in the closed space. She had a moment to gather herself, if only just one. She closed her eyes.

"God, thank you for bringing me this far. Help me not mess

things up. And please help Ronnie forgive me for letting Barb take Will."

Tears burned her eyes. Could she have stopped Barb? It had happened so fast. In the choice between Patricia's life and Will's, Susanne had hesitated. Yes, she'd fought, but too little, too late. Her moment of indecision had lost Will but bought time with no one getting harmed.

Except for Ronnie and Jeff. Pain stabbed Susanne through the left eye. How must they be feeling right now? *No.* She couldn't think about that. She had to remain at her best. She had to focus on getting Will back.

CRACK. A sharp sound on the window by her head seemed loud enough to shatter the glass. Susanne screamed. *Barb. Had she seen her? Followed her?*

Fearing the worst, she turned and was blinded by the high beam of a powerful flashlight.

CHAPTER FORTY-ONE: DEFEND

Base of Black Tooth Mountain, Cloud Peak Wilderness,
Bighorn Mountains, Wyoming
Friday August 12, 1977, 10:00 p.m.

Patrick

"CAREFUL!" Elvin's shout cracked with strain.

"Sorry." Patrick was doing his best, but he couldn't figure out a way to transport Elvin down the mountain pain-free. For either of them.

He set one end of the travois on the horizontal surface of a boulder, balancing the opposite end on another, then examined the ruptured blister in his palm in the bright moonlight. It smarted, no lie.

No one has ever died from a blister. And no real man ever got one so quickly. *Unless those real men work fifty hours a week as doctors.* Real men had hides like rhinos. Patrick envied the layers of calluses on Henry's hands. The hands of a rancher. But Patrick's mostly smooth hands couldn't be helped. And, unfortunately, a little thing like a blister could eventually render Patrick unable to carry the travois.

He'd have to do something about it. The saddle bags were balanced around his shoulders. He lifted a flap and pulled out his gloves. He hadn't wanted to wear them. The weather had warmed up, and the weight of the travois made it hard to keep them on. Now he didn't have a choice. He slipped them on, then rotated the upper end of the travois to the next boulder and repeated the process, holding on tighter than before to keep the gloves in place. Eddie had carried one end when they were on the dirt path—which had started and ended right where the odd climber had said it would. With only one arm, he'd been too unstable to continue after they'd reached the boulders, though. They'd nearly dumped Elvin twice before Patrick had come up with the rotation idea. His new method had turned out to be more effective and faster than carrying the travois together.

Only about twenty yards left to go until they were out of the rocks.

"Ouch," Elvin shouted again.

Eddie stumbled and kicked a few rocks in the direction of Patrick's head. Patrick whipped around. He'd been fighting off a recurring image—Eddie with a rock clutched in his hand above his shoulder, leaping from a ledge above him, legs splayed, lips drawn back in a scream—since they'd started their descent. It couldn't be lost on Eddie that Patrick was on edge about him. Frankly, Patrick didn't care.

"What's that at the bottom of the hill?" Eddie whispered.

Patrick stared down the hill. He'd been hyperaware of the threat Eddie posed behind him, but they were vulnerable from the front as well. The brilliant moon illuminating their path and bathing the park in a soft glow spotlighted them against the black rocks.

He whispered back. "Where?"

"Almost to the trees."

When Patrick couldn't find anything out of place by scanning, he slowed his eyes down. It was a trick he sometimes used. By keeping his gaze steady, movement would draw his eyes to it. This time, it worked immediately. Two large shapes were making their way along the line where the rocks and trees met, from north to south.

At first, Patrick was hopeful it was a few elk heading for the grassy park under the cover of the relative darkness, as they often did. There were plenty of them around. He'd seen fresh scat when he was highlining the horses.

But these shapes were too big to be elk.

Moose, then?

But moose were unlikely at this elevation.

Plus—and this was the clincher for Patrick—neither elk nor moose had camel-like humps on their backs. These animals were carrying riders.

No one needed to send him an engraved invitation. Patrick sank to the ground, minimizing his profile. "Men."

Eddie crouched near Patrick. His breath came out in a hiss. "I see them. Headed this way."

Patrick nodded. His palms started sweating inside his gloves. "This changes things."

Elvin said, "Hello, guys, what about me? I'm kind of exposed. Man, we should have just driven the money to Chicago."

Eddie sneered. "But we couldn't, could we? The Feds expected us. They would have been all over us."

"It wasn't my fault."

"You brought him in on the deal."

As much as Patrick wanted to know what the heck was going on, now wasn't the time for them to argue about the past. But Elvin didn't respond. Then Patrick heard the unmistakable noise of someone working the action on a gun. And it was close. His skin felt like it was on fire. *Eddie has a gun.*

He kept his voice calm. "Have you had that thing this whole time?" He stood and rotated Elvin down to a lower rock, did the same with the other end, then crouched beside the travois.

Elvin spoke for the silent Eddie. "He has. And I have one, too."

"I saw yours," Patrick said. "Chest holster. But Eddie didn't have one."

"He carries on his ankle. Help me get mine out."

Eddie had refused to let Patrick examine his lower extremities earlier. He'd been trying to keep his firearm a secret. Patrick felt foolish.

He seethed but tried to keep his voice light. "Don't forget, guys, I'm on your side."

Reaching inside Elvin's button-front shirt, he retrieved the gun, an old but well-maintained .44 Magnum. He handed Elvin the heavy revolver, then rebuttoned the shirt.

"Is it them?" Eddie said.

Patrick retrained his eyes on the moving figures. "I can't tell. Weren't there three of them when we saw them on the Little Goose trail?"

"I didn't stick around to take notes."

"There were three. Cardinale, the boss man, and two muscle heads."

Elvin groaned. "That would be Juice and Luke. His guard dogs."

What kind of man needed guards up in the wilderness? And why would Chicago mobsters be mixed up with two ne'er do well Shoshone from the res? Patrick intended to find out. But first he had to survive the night. He wondered if their group had been spotted from below. The plane, he felt sure, was shining like a beacon in the moonlight. He didn't care about the plane, though, other than his friend Bruce. He really didn't want the goons to desecrate the man any further than the crash had already done.

He focused on the riders. "It could be anybody. Two people from my group. Two strangers."

"Two from Orion's posse, with the third hiding and pointing a rifle at us right now," Elvin suggested.

Patrick didn't like Elvin's grim line of thinking.

Eddie, ever the cheerful team player, said, "Yeah, well, we're like dumb mule deer. Nothing but targets. I'm outta here."

He crawled past them, heading downslope, but to the right, in the opposite direction from the two men down below.

"Friends like him, I don't need no enemies," Elvin said, low enough that only Patrick could hear.

Patrick couldn't agree more. Except he was harboring no illusions that Eddie had ever been his friend.

CHAPTER FORTY-TWO: SCORE

Ranchester, Wyoming
Friday, August 12, 1977, 10:15 p.m.

Susanne

"ROLL your window down and put your hands on the steering wheel where I can see them," a woman's voice commanded. The kind of order a cop would give.

Susanne hesitated. Barb. It had to be Barb, even though it didn't really sound like her. Dressed as a deputy and impersonating one, maybe disguising her voice, too.

Susanne had a score to settle. Not just because of Barb taking Will, but what she'd done to Susanne and her kids. If only Patrick hadn't been so infuriatingly principled that he had saved Barb, Susanne wouldn't be in this situation right now. But then there would be no Will. The unborn child would have died, too. *Everything happens for a reason.*

Susanne rolled the window down as slowly as she could. Her

hands were shaking but she put them on the wheel. It was time for her to fight. Or was it? If she got herself killed, Barb would get away with Will. Maybe forever. Buying time had worked earlier. It was the smart thing to do now, even if it wasn't what she wanted to do.

The flashlight inched closer to her face. Susanne blinked and squinted. The light was making her head hurt even worse.

The woman's voice was harsh. "Who are you, and what are you doing watching people from the church parking lot?"

At first Susanne was confused. Barb wouldn't be asking who she was—she knew Susanne. Then she realized it wasn't Barb standing beside the Suburban. But if it wasn't Barb, who could it be? Someone with the appearance of authority. And the upper hand.

Susanne inhaled deep and long. "My name is Susanne Flint. I'm following a woman named Barb Lamkin. She kidnapped my friend's baby. She's a dangerous fugitive, and she's just checked into a room at the motel next door."

Silence met her words. Just as Susanne was about to blurt out more explanation, the woman said, "Driver's license, please."

"Are you a police officer?"

"Who else do you think would ask for your license?"

"I wouldn't know. You've been shining that light in my eyes, and I haven't seen you."

The woman—the officer—repeated, "Driver's license, please."

"I—I don't have it. When Barb took Will—the baby—I went after them. I didn't take the time to go back for my purse. I don't have my wallet and license. Or my glasses. I'm sorry. But if you call the police in Buffalo, they'll know who I am and what I'm talking about."

Silence again, like the officer was pondering her words. Then, "I'm going to need you to come with me, ma'am."

Susanne put her hands on the steering wheel and squeezed. "Please, if Barb leaves that motel and takes Will, she could disappear forever. Please help me. At least have someone watch to make sure she stays inside."

"Out of the car, ma'am."

Susanne swallowed back a wave of nausea. She grabbed her keys and opened her door, uncertain what to do with her hands. Was the woman going to handcuff her and arrest her?

"Do you have a weapon, ma'am?"

"What? No."

"Then have a seat in the back of my cruiser while I check your story, please." The officer lowered her flashlight. "After you."

Susanne's vision was a blinding array of spots. She hesitated. "I can't see."

"Take your time."

"I don't have time. Will doesn't have time." When there was no answer, Susanne stuck her hands out in front of her as feelers and took a few tentative steps.

The officer put a hand on her arm and guided her with pressure. "This way."

When they reached the vehicle, the officer said, "Stand with your legs apart and your hands on the roof while I pat you down, please."

"But why? I told you I'm not armed."

The officer didn't answer. Susanne put her hands on the car and widened her stance. The woman patted her down from head to toe, gently but firmly, and in places Susanne was very uncomfortable with. Her cheeks felt hot. When the humiliation finally ended, the officer opened the back door.

Susanne took a seat. The officer got in the front and radioed her station. Within a minute, Susanne's story had been confirmed. She should have felt vindicated, but badgered, sick, and frantic won out.

Over the radio, she heard, "Units en route from Sheridan and Buffalo. Please surveil the fugitive until assistance arrives."

After the officer ended the transmission, she turned to face Susanne, who was able to see her for the first time. She had a strong jaw with a dimple in her chin. Her dark hair was cut as short as a man's. "Thank you for your help, ma'am. I need to return you to your vehicle so I can get back to my job. And then you need to go home."

"Return me to . . . go home . . . can't I come with you?"

"No, ma'am. We'll take it from here."

Susanne was speechless for a moment. The officer opened up the back door. Susanne stayed put. "But I tracked her here. I kept her from getting away."

"And that's much appreciated, but you took a big risk. She could have killed you, you know."

"But she didn't. I need to know—I don't even—what is the plan?"

"Other officers are coming to join me. We'll stake out her room until she leaves. Then we'll arrest her and take the baby."

"She'll be wary. She's smart. And she's parked behind the motel. Are there windows from the rooms facing the back? If she's seen you, she could be leaving already."

"Yet we're still here talking. I need to do my job now. Good night, Mrs. Flint."

Susanne stood up and smoothed her skirt. With all the dignity she could muster, she marched to the Suburban. She'd been dismissed. After all the help she'd given them, she'd just been sent home like a naughty child from school.

The officer exited the parking lot and drove down the street. Susanne's eyes followed her, a hungry cat tracking a mouse. The squad car pulled in the bar parking lot, where Susanne lost sight of it. She retreated into the Suburban and drummed her hands on the wheel. The cops had the wrong strategy. Barb wouldn't leave through the front if she sensed anyone out there, and she wouldn't fail to notice them in a quiet town of this size. If she couldn't get out the back, it would be a standoff. It could take forever. Did Barb have the supplies to take care of Will if that happened? Susanne doubted it.

But she'd pled her case to the officer. Law enforcement had taken over, and, as a civilian, there was nothing more she could do.

She found a gas station across the street. One dollar wasn't going to take her very far, but it was better than nothing. Her migraine was nearly blinding her, and she longed to be asleep in her own bed. Maybe Patricia or Vangie could help her. She was about to use her quarter to call her sister-in-law, when Sheridan law enforcement vehicles began pulling into the bar parking lot with all the stealth of a Macy's parade. Her blood boiled. Unless Barb was asleep or in the bathroom, how could she not see them go by? And she was a fugitive, for goodness sakes. She'd be glued to the window, watching for exactly this.

Susanne's vision flashed white with migraine aura, and she saw a hand pulling a fire alarm in her mind. It was slender. Feminine. The skin of an adult woman. Perry had pulled the fire alarm at his school so he could get out of class early to go skiing one Friday the previous March. At the time, she'd been so angry with him. But, in retrospect, it had been clever, if devious and without forethought for the consequences. She smiled. The grown-up version of Perry's stunt might work. If Barb was faced with a real emergency, she'd be less careful. Less watchful. She'd feel like she had to run outside to save herself and Will. The cops could catch her unaware then. But it would have to happen soon, while there was still a prayer that Barb hadn't figured out they were on to her.

Was it her own hand Susanne saw in her vision?

She wished Patrick was with her so they could talk it through. They partnered on big decisions. Would he approve? Probably not. But after all the crazy stunts he'd pulled, after all the times he'd risked his life to save other people, how could he do anything now except wish her God speed when Will's life and Ronnie's happiness were on the line?

Of course, after it was over, Susanne might face consequences, like her son had. But it was a pittance to pay. This would work. It had to, and it would. Her own child had done it, after all, so she knew she could, too.

Energy built inside her—energy and *determination*. She put her quarter back in the ashtray. No phone calls. She was doing this. She'd check first that there really were law enforcement vehicles behind the motel, surrounding Barb's truck. Then, once she knew everyone was in place, she'd go back to the motel, pull the fire alarm, and get out of the way. She poked at her plan again, looking for holes. But she was satisfied with it.

She drove around the block, just under the speed limit, repeating instructions to herself like she was memorizing Bible verses for Sunday school. *Be observant, be careful, don't draw attention to yourself.*

In less than a minute, the Suburban was bouncing over potholes in the dirt alley behind the motel. The headlight beams jerked up and down on the back walls of the buildings. The alley seemed to dead end at the motel, where a lone white truck was parked. There were no officers in the alley. None she could see anyway. She bit her lip. What were they waiting for? She slowed the Suburban to let it waddle through a large hole. She didn't want Barb to get a glimpse of the Suburban, so she started eyeing the best spot to make a U-turn.

Suddenly, a woman climbed out a window in the back of the motel. Platinum hair shone in the moonlight. It gave Susanne pause. That couldn't be Barb. Barb had red hair. She'd seen it earlier tucked in her cap, and it definitely hadn't been platinum. But then the woman was running through the dark, outside of the span of the lights. A woman dressed as a deputy, with a duffel bag banging off one hip and a baby cradled in her arm.

"No!" Susanne screamed.

She stomped on her brakes, jolting the Suburban to a stop. She'd been right. Barb was way ahead of law enforcement.

Blonde Barb glanced down the alley, threw the duffel into the truck, and tucked a bundled-up Will in the passenger floorboard again. She hurried into the driver's seat and was backing the truck out before Susanne could formulate a new plan. Barb paused, idling, with the nose of the truck pointed at the Suburban.

Susanne looked up and down the alley for help, hoping for a last second miracle. There were no cops around. No humans around. No one except her and Barb.

Susanne had a little bit of gas and could follow Barb again, but not far. The woman would get away if that was all she did. Susanne had to do something *more*. Anything else was too big a risk to take with Will's life. Barb accelerated into the parking area on the side of the motel. She wasn't far from turning onto Highway 14 out of Ranchester. And God knew where after that.

It was time for action. Susanne mashed the accelerator all the way to the floor.

CHAPTER FORTY-THREE: FEEL

Trish

TRISH SHIELDED her eyes with her hand. The sudden glare from flashing lights was painful. Still, she couldn't help but look. George either, apparently, because he slowed his truck to a crawl. The light was coming from a motel parking lot. Trish rolled her window down and stuck her head out, catching a strong whiff of cooped up horse and the sound of hooves clanging against the metal sides of the trailer. She gawked at the drama—three police cars. So many for such a little town. Ranchester was half the size of Buffalo, and she'd thought *it* was small compared to Irving, the part of the Dallas metroplex where they'd lived before moving to Wyoming.

Two of the cop cars were parked inches away from the front of a white truck, one of its flat front wheels up on a curb. The third was beside it, doors open. Pressed up against the side of the rear bumper of the truck was a Suburban. A dark Suburban. Gray?

Trish frowned. It looked like . . . it couldn't be . . . it *was*.

"That's my mom's car!" she shouted.

"Where?" George asked.

A woman with long, wavy brown hair was holding an infant in her arms, her body turned away from a police officer, who appeared to be trying to take the baby from her.

"By the cop cars. And that's my mom. Stop!"

George stomped the brakes. His truck jerked to a stop. For a second, Trish felt sorry for the horses.

Beside her, Perry woke and rubbed his eyes. Then he sat forward, pointing. "What's Coach Lamkin doing here?"

An officer was on either side of a woman with long hair the color of Marily Monroe's, holding her arms. Coach Lamkin had red hair. And this woman was in an officer's uniform. She turned, and Trish saw her face. Trish's mouth fell open. Perry was right. It was her former coach.

"No. No." Trish jumped from the truck. The wind was intense, and grit pelted her face. She ignored it and ran toward her mom.

Perry scrambled after her. "Wait for me."

The officer talking to their mother intercepted them. At first Trish thought it was a man, but then she realized it was a woman with very short hair. "Stay back, kids. This is crime scene. It's not safe."

"Let them through. Those are my children," Trish's mom said.

Trish was so confused. What was going on? Why was her mom in Ranchester? How had Coach Lamkin escaped from custody? And why was her mom holding a baby? She didn't know why, but that seemed like the most important question. She leaned toward her mom. "Whose baby is that, Mom?"

The officer put her arms out wide. "I said stay back."

The baby started wailing. Its cry was surreal in the middle of all the strobing lights.

Trish's mom swayed and twisted, rocking the baby. "He's Ronnie and Jeff's baby. Will."

Trish stared at the baby, struggling to make sense of things. *Oh, my gosh. Coach Lamkin's baby.*

Her mom tried to pass by the officer to get to Trish and Perry.

The officer shook her head. "Mrs. Flint, stop right there. You need to leave the baby with us."

Her mom glared at the cop. It filled Trish's chest with something good. "This is no place for a baby."

"Ma'am, this is all going to end just fine for everyone, as long as you don't make me arrest you."

The two women locked eyes. There was something ferocious and unexpected in Trish's mom's face. Trish watched her in awe. *She isn't giving in.*

Tires screeched at the edge of the parking lot. Trish turned. Ronnie Harcourt, in her full Johnson County Sheriff's deputy uniform, jumped out of a car. She sprinted across the parking lot. Her face was tear-streaked, her braided hair loose and wild in the front. The tall figure of her husband Jeff was closing in fast behind her.

For a moment, all heads turned toward the Harcourts, even Coach Lamkin's, just as the two officers were lowering her into the back of one of their cars.

Trish's mom held the baby out toward Ronnie. "A baby's place is with its mother."

Ronnie snatched Will and pressed him to her chest. "Is he all right? Is my baby okay?"

Jeff put his arm around them both. His face was bright red, and his eyes were wet and shiny. He started murmuring something Trish couldn't hear.

The female police officer said, "Deputy Harcourt. Mr. Harcourt. Good to see you both. Will seems fine to me."

Ronnie nodded. She looked over Will's head at Trish's mom. "Susanne, I'll never be able to thank you enough."

The women embraced, with Will and Jeff sandwiched between them. When Will squalled, they laughed and backed away from each other.

Jeff wiped at his eyes. "You saved him, Susanne. You saved our little boy."

Ronnie frowned. "That isn't the outfit I had him dressed in for the party. But it's his. It was in his dresser at our house. How in the world . . . ?"

Trish's mom said, "The first place Barb headed when she left my house was to yours. I nearly made it to a phone to call the police from there, but she took off again too quickly. I'll bet she stocked up on Will's things from your place."

Ronnie shook her head. "I may have to rethink leaving the house unlocked after this." Trish had never understood why so many Wyomingites left their homes unsecured in the first place. Her parents sure didn't.

"And that explains why the plates off your county vehicle were on her truck, too, and why she was wearing your uniform," the female officer said.

"Wait—what?"

The cop nodded. "Apparently, she stole the truck she was driving from Max Alexandrov. The APB was out for a white Chevy truck with his plates. But when we apprehended her here, she had on a Johnson County Deputy uniform and had a different plate. Buffalo PD looked it up for us, and it's yours, Deputy Harcourt. Which you would see better if Mrs. Flint hadn't shoved her truck up on the sidewalk."

Her mom gave the cop a raised eyebrow look. "You're welcome."

"That . . .that . . .that horrible woman! She would have gotten away if it wasn't for Susanne." Ronnie turned back to Trish's mom. "But your kids." She pointed at Trish and Perry with her head. "I thought they were up in the mountains."

Trish and Perry were still rooted in place. The terrible things that had happened earlier had flown from Trish's mind once she saw her mom. They came crashing back all at once. She glanced at Perry. His face was as pale as the moon overhead.

"Me, too." Her mom crossed the invisible barrier the officer had established, but the woman didn't try to stop her this time. She hugged Trish and Perry to her, both at the same time. When she released them, she said, "What are you two doing here? Is that George Nichols with you?" She gasped. "Perry, what happened to your mouth? And where are John and your father?"

CHAPTER FORTY-FOUR: SLIDE

Base of Black Tooth Mountain, Cloud Peak Wilderness,
Bighorn Mountains, Wyoming
Friday, August 12, 1977, 10:35 p.m.

Patrick

SWEAT CASCADED down Patrick's back. He adjusted the travois, trying to keep Elvin's profile low. They were spotlighted and exposed against the slide of boulders, but he'd lost sight of the horses and riders below, about the same time Eddie had disappeared. He hoped they couldn't see Elvin and him either. He had to push on, down to Reno and The Lunker, and on down the mountain. But navigating the maze of boulders was arduous work. For every yard he gained down the slide, he had to climb back up half as much.

And it wore on him that he couldn't find the riders. Just because he couldn't see them didn't mean they didn't have him in their sights. Honestly, though, he was just as worried about an armed and combative Eddie. The man had declared his independence from Patrick and Elvin. Or maybe he'd been doing more than that. Maybe he'd been declaring his opposition to them. If he took them out, he would have both horses to himself. He could pack out a lot of cash on two animals of that size, without having to share the spoils, worry about Patrick turning it over to the authorities, or Elvin slowing him down. And eliminating Patrick and Elvin could make him an ally to the mobsters. Patrick was just surprised Eddie hadn't killed them before he left, or even up at the crash site and made a run for it then. Maybe hidden deep in Eddie's cold, dark heart there was a flicker of humanity, a concern for his friend's welfare.

More likely, he was waiting to see who came out on top before he picked sides.

From somewhere above, back in the direction of the trail they'd taken down from the crash site, Patrick heard a loud crack. Gunshot. He dropped into a crouch. A bullet ricocheted off a nearby rock, sending a chunk of it flying. His elbow stung. He hugged it to him. The chip had hit him. After a few seconds, he realized the injury was only a flesh wound. He released his arm and hunkered, waiting and listening.

"That was close," he whispered.

Elvin sounded rattled. "I'm a sitting duck up here."

Patrick eased an end of the travois lower. The man was right. There was no flat ground around to set Elvin on. Nothing completely covered by sheltering rock.

"Come on, come on," Elvin hissed.

"I'd have to unstrap you and take you off the travois. It would hurt, and you'd be stranded."

Crack.

Another shot. Another hunk of rock burst free and into the air. It clattered to the ground.

"They're going to get me. Do it."

"You'll pass out."

"Shoot at them already."

Patrick drew his .357 Magnum and checked the cylinder. It was fully loaded. "I can't take you off the travois and shoot at the same time. Can you fire, too, from that position?"

Elvin grunted. "I dropped my gun."

Patrick groaned. "Where?"

"A few yards back. I'm not sure."

Patrick felt his lips moving and pressed them together. He remembered the flare gun in his waist band. He hated leaving Elvin completely unarmed. While not a conventional weapon, it would be better than nothing.

He handed it over. "Keep this. It's only got one shot, so save it for when it really counts."

Elvin nodded.

Patrick took that for a thank you. "You're welcome," he muttered.

He peeked over a boulder toward the crash site, looking for a shape, for movement, for anything. Shooting back blindly was a waste of ammunition. Doing it while surrounded announced their position to anyone who hadn't already seen them. Eddie had headed in the opposite direction from where the shots had been fired. So, the shots had to come from the riders. And, based on where they were heading and the fact that they were firing, it had to be the mobsters. Patrick was sure of it. But just the two they'd seen? Or was the third man flanking them, even now?

Crack.

The bullet whistled over their heads, coming from their other side. *Eddie.* Was he shooting at them or the goons?

Crack.

Patrick drew in a sharp breath. That shot sounded like it had been fired from yet another direction. From down below them. The third mobster? Patrick realized there'd been no answering ping from bullet striking rock. Not near Elvin and him, and not anywhere else close enough to hear. Which didn't make sense, unless the person firing didn't know where they were or was a terrible shot.

Rat-a-tat-tat-tat-tat-tat-tat.

As unbelievable as it seemed, he knew it was a burst of machine gun fire, definitely coming from above them. His blood chilled. His Magnum six-shooter was no match for that kind of weapon. But he had to try, as soon as it was safe to raise it.

Elvin's voice was low and scared. "Ay, ay, ay, ay."

Rat-a-tat-tat-tat-tat-tat-tat.

The burst seemed to go on forever, giving Patrick time to fix on the goons' position. He was almost positive now they were climbing the dirt path up to the crash site, and that they had all but reached it.

The noise stopped. Patrick rose up and fired three quick rounds. *Three down, three to go. Then reload.* But a sick feeling washed over him. He hadn't packed any extra ammunition in his saddle bags, because on a normal ride into the mountains, he wouldn't have needed any. The possibility he'd be involved in a firefight had never occurred to him.

CRACK. CRACK. CRACK. CRACK.

More shots rang out, so close together that Patrick couldn't tell where they were coming from, only that they weren't from a machine gun. But, in the quiet after the firing ceased, the next sound was clear. Hooved animals, galloping. Horses, based on an intermittent metallic ring. Shoes on rocks. He cocked his head, judging location and direction. To his left and moving away from him, like the horses were hugging the tree line in an arc around the expanse of the park. Whether their riders were with them, he had no way of knowing. Then he winced. *Please don't let that be Reno and the Lunker.*

Footsteps approached, hopping from boulder to boulder. Patrick turned his head and his gun toward the sound. Eddie, ten feet away from them. He was visible to the shooters above, as was Patrick to him.

He grinned and aimed his gun at Patrick's head. "Got 'em, boss man," he shouted.

Crack.

Patrick ducked. *I love you, Susanne.* The hair on the top of his head fluttered. He couldn't believe it. He was alive. The bullet had missed. *Thank you, God.* But he didn't have any more time to marvel. He rolled over and lifted his revolver.

Before he could draw a bead on Eddie—or him another on Patrick—a new voice spoke. "Drop it, Eddie. I have a gun pointed at the back of your skull. Turn around and look if you don't believe me. I'd rather shoot you between the eyes anyway."

A broad grin stretched across Patrick's face. Henry. The shot from below earlier. It had to have been his friend's. And despite the dangerous crossfire, he'd scaled these boulders for Patrick.

There was a metallic clatter.

"Now put your hands on your head. Hand, I mean." A pause. "Good." Then, "Patrick, you okay?"

"A heckuva lot better now! But be careful. Those thugs are shooting at us from above."

"A machine pistol. I think I know where they are."

Henry had heard the rat-a-tat-tat, too, so of course he'd known it was a machine gun. But what made him think it was a pistol?

Before he could ask, Elvin said, "Not that anyone cares, but I'm fine, too."

Henry crawled into sight, staying low, and keeping his weapon on Eddie.

"Henry, you old devil, where'd you . . ." Patrick's voice trailed off. Henry wasn't alone. A boy crawled up beside him. A big, strong boy, also pointing a gun at Eddie. It took Patrick a moment, but then he recognized him. Ben Jones, the young man the Sibleys had taken in. "Oh, hey, Ben. Man alive, is it ever good to see you guys. This is Elvin."

Elvin waggled fingers on his uninjured side.

"Elvin, meet Henry and Ben." Patrick spider-crawled over to Eddie. "You won't be needing this anymore." He took Eddie's gun, which had fallen between some rocks, but was still reachable. He patted the man's waist, looking for a belt. He needed something to secure Eddie's wrists with. "Anybody got any rope? We need to tie this one up."

"I do. But keep your head lower. It won't take long to reload if they've got another magazine." Henry tossed a small coil to Patrick. It had been fastened to a belt loop on his jeans.

Patrick trussed Eddie's hands behind his back, keeping Eddie between himself and the shooter above.

Eddie cried out in pain. "My elbow and shoulder are busted up. You can't do this."

"You should have thought about that."

"Big mistake, man." Eddie shook his head.

"One I'm willing to make." Patrick jerked at Eddie's wrists, forcing the other man down beside him. Eddie hissed. *Yeah, that has to hurt like a son of a gun. Serves him right.* "What brought you back, Henry?"

There was a long silence. "The bad guys came down the mountain. We got one of theirs earlier. Luke, I think. Then we followed them up here. By the time we'd snuck up behind them, they'd already climbed up a ways. When they started firing, we returned the favor, then scrambled up here just as Eddie turned on you." He paused, listening. There were no sounds from above. "There's more to tell, but it can wait."

"But my kids are okay?"

"They're fine." Henry cleared his throat. "So, you think we scared them off? I can't believe they haven't shot again."

Patrick shook his head. "They won't leave. There's too much at stake."

"What do you mean?"

"A plane load of cash." Patrick gestured up the mountain.

Henry drew in a long breath. "That explains a lot."

"I'm willing to bet they're loading it into bags right now, which would explain why they're not firing. This could be our opportunity to get the heck out of here."

"It's an expensive bet if you're wrong."

"But it may be our only chance."

"All right then. How about I take our prisoner?" Henry grinned.

"Good. Ben, can you take one end of the travois? We need to move fast."

Ben nodded. "Yes, sir." He met Patrick at the travois, and the two men lifted Elvin.

"Let's stay as low as we can."

Patrick bent at the waist and flexed his knees, then started down the rocks. Ben kept pace with him. It was four times easier and faster with two men who could use both of their arms.

"Like riding in a Cadillac," Elvin said.

"Eddie and I are right behind you." Henry's voice was a low murmur.

"How did you end up here?" Patrick whispered to Ben.

"Uh, I was already on my way."

"By yourself?"

"Yes, sir."

"What for?" It wasn't hunting season yet. Late August fishing wasn't great. And from what Patrick had gleaned from Henry, Ben stayed really busy with work and summer classes.

"Uh, I was coming to see Trish, sir."

Patrick froze mid-step. His jaw tightened. Had he heard right? Ben and his daughter?

Before he could formulate a cogent reply, the horrible rat-a-tat-tat of the machine pistol started up again. Ben and Patrick crouched between boulders. Dust and rock chips flew up around them. Again, Elvin was left partially uncovered, and his tortured, terrified breathing was almost as disturbing as the sound of the weapon firing. Rock chips were flying from ten, twenty, even thirty feet away. Like the shooter was spraying the area. Patrick got out his revolver, ready to take a shot whenever the machine pistol paused.

"Argh!" It was Henry's voice.

"You all right?" Patrick called over the noise of the gun.

"A shot clipped me. I'm okay."

Why couldn't it have hit Eddie instead?

After what felt like an eternity, the firing stopped. Patrick peered

over a rock, searching for a target, revolver up. He had three bullets
left, but if the goons were at the crash site, he was too far away to hit
them.

"I'm firing," Henry said.

"Me, too." Ben pulled back the slide on his gun.

Even if Patrick couldn't hit them, he could help scare them back.
"Let's do it."

CRACK. CRACK.

Henry and Ben started alternating shots. Moonlight glinted off
the metal of the plane. Aiming there was Patrick's best bet. Maybe
he'd get lucky. He took two more shots, spacing them between the
other men's rounds. *One left.*

Patrick saw a flash from the downed plane. "Duck!"

Henry and Ben stopped firing just as Patrick heard the rat-a-tat-
tat-tat-tat-tat. He kept low to the ground, breathing hard. Elvin
screamed.

Patrick said, "Did they get you?"

Elvin kept screaming. The mobsters kept firing. How could they
stop the spray of bullets? Then Elvin stopped screaming.

CRACK.

A bright light streaked through the air toward the crash area, a
tail of smoke behind it.

"What in Hades?" Henry whispered.

The rat-a-tat-tat stopped. It took a moment, but then Patrick realized Elvin had fired the flare gun. Patrick groaned. A fireball. Aviation fuel. He wanted to shake Elvin, to slap some sense into him.
What had the man been thinking? But it was too late. The deed was
done. Luckily, the likelihood of the shot hitting the gas tanks in the
plane's wings was very slim.

Patrick held in a breath, watching. The flare seemed to move in
extreme slow motion toward its target. Elvin must have a dead eye,
because the fireball was tracking straight for the gleaming metal. *Not
good, not good.* Then it made contact. For a few seconds, nothing

happened. Patrick let himself feel hopeful. Maybe it had missed the tanks. Maybe it had even taken out one of the mobsters.

Then there was a blinding flash, a shock wave of air and debris against his face, and a bone rattling BOOM. Patrick hit the dirt face first. Elvin started screaming again.

"Who shot a flare gun?" Henry asked.

Patrick spoke through gritted teeth. "Elvin."

"My money." Eddie sounded like he was going to cry. "You blew up my money."

"Whoa, man," Ben said.

Whoa is right. Patrick pictured the nose of the plane wedged into the rocks. The wings attached to that nose held upwards of eighty gallons between them. There'd been a leak in one tank, but he knew from examining the site, from smelling it, that one of the tanks had still been carrying significant fuel. The force in the tight space . . . He lifted his head. The plane was burning like the Aggie bonfires he'd attended as a young boy, when his family had lived next to the Texas A&M campus. As he watched, another explosion rocked the sky. This time Patrick didn't duck. Pieces of plane shot upwards like oversized Roman candles. He tried to imagine the mobsters surviving the blast. If they were anywhere close to the plane, it seemed impossible. He couldn't muster up any pity for them.

A piece of flaming plane dropped to the ground thirty feet uphill from them.

"Take that, Cardinale." Elvin's voice tapered off as a deep rumbling started.

The rumbling turned to crashing and booming.

Patrick jumped to his feet. "Rockslide. Go!"

Patrick grabbed one side of the travois, and Ben snatched up the other.

"Hold on tight. I'm going to move fast," he told Ben.

Elvin moaned. "Hurry."

The crashing and booming grew louder, like an ominous drum roll working toward a crescendo that Patrick hoped was a long way off. Henry was shoving Eddie along. Both men were moving awkwardly. Patrick hopped to the next boulder across the slide. Ben jumped, and the travois jolted Patrick backwards, nearly dragging him over. Patrick righted himself and leapt again. This time, Ben was more in sync, making his way forward at the same time as Patrick's jump. They worked their way across the rock field in rhythm, away from the sound of rocks gathering steam.

"Too slow," Elvin said. "Too slow."

He was right. There was no way they were going to outrun the tons of rock hurtling down the mountain at their speed.

Patrick panted. "Faster, Ben. Faster."

One minute, Patrick's eyes were moving between the ground and Henry's back. The next, Henry and Eddie disappeared. Patrick hadn't realized he could be more terrified than he was until that second. A shout caught in his throat. Had they fallen off a precipice? He would have expected them to scream on the way down. He hadn't heard anything. But he couldn't dwell on it now. More and more dust and debris were pelting his face. The rocks were almost upon them.

Then Patrick saw his friend. Henry was huddled under a rock ledge, and Eddie was with him. In front of them was a sheer drop. If they hadn't had the light from the moon, then surely that drop would have been where they met their ends. But with the moon, they'd found cover and avoided the death plunge. Henry started motioning for them. Hope surged in Patrick. But if he didn't pull Ben along faster, the rocks would swallow them up.

"Shelter! Come on!" Patrick screamed. He gave one last desperate yank on the travois and leapt under the overhang.

The noise of the rocks catching up with them was deafening. Henry pushed backwards on Eddie, making space. Patrick dragged Elvin further into the shelter. It was only then that he realized Ben was no longer holding the other end of the travois.

The boy had vanished.

Henry shouted, "Ben!"

Around them and now over them, enormous rocks were careening. Cartwheeling. Leapfrogging. Crashing, splintering, pounding. Patrick closed his eyes and covered his head and ears by wrapping his arms around his head.

Ben. The boy had been coming to see Trish. The thought of the two of them together had nearly shorted out Patrick's brain. Now the thought of having to tell Trish that Ben was dead seemed far worse. *Dear God, please let Ben be all right,* he prayed, over and over.

The slide seemed to go on forever. Patrick wondered what fresh horrors it might wreak. An earthquake? Would it block their exits and make their sanctuary a tomb? They were powerless to do anything but wait and see.

He forced his mind back to his prayers.

And then, Patrick realized the vibrations and pounding had stopped.

His ears were ringing. He tried to swallow but couldn't. His mouth felt like he'd eaten a bucket of sawdust.

No one spoke. No one moved.

After close to a minute, Patrick raised his head, eyes open, arms down. He couldn't see to the end of his own fingers. "Is everyone all right?" He didn't dare call out to Ben by name. He could only hope the boy would answer.

"Yeah," Eddie said.

"No worse than I was," Elvin said.

"Where's Ben?" Henry's voice sounded on the edge of panic. "Where is Ben?"

Patrick winced. Henry and Vangie had grown to love the boy. For Henry to come all this way to help Patrick, only to lose the young man who had become like a son? It was unthinkable.

A rock fell off the ledge behind him. He heard coughing. *Not Elvin.* Then a groan and the sound of something shifting.

"I'm here," a voice said.

"Ben!" Henry's voice cracked.

Patrick crawled back around Elvin. Ben was wedged in a crevice, just at the mouth of the overhang. Patrick's eyes were adjusting to the conditions. The dust was settling. He could see well enough to check him for injuries. He sized the boy up and immediately reached for an arm. He started his prodding, palpating, rotating routine. "You're all right, Ben?"

Ben nodded, brushing dirt off himself with his other hand. "I'm okay." He jerked a thumb back toward the crash site. "But I'm pretty sure they're not."

A female voice rang out. "Hey! Hey up there! Are you all right?"

Ben and Patrick looked at each other. Patrick couldn't have been more surprised to hear a woman in the middle of the night at the base of Black Tooth than if the Pope had showed up at his home to play poker. Her voice sounded distant but clear.

"Trish . . ." Ben said.

But it wasn't her voice. Patrick called, "Hello—who's out there?"

"My name is Alicia." The voice was sounding closer. "I was camping on Highland Park when I heard shots. I saw an explosion and the rockslide. Then a climber came running through my camp shouting that people were caught in the slide. He said he was going for help and sent me to check the situation out."

Alicia. The name was familiar. Patrick remembered the black woman he'd seen hiking. It felt like a lifetime ago, but it had only been earlier that day. Something about her words jogged his memory. A climber. He'd seen one, twice. Could it be the same person?

"What climber?" he said.

"Some guy in a Denver Broncos cap with a lot of gear hanging off his backpack." Her voice was closer still.

The hair rose on the back of Patrick's neck. *The same one he'd seen earlier.* "It's bound to be unstable out there, Alicia. We're all fine. Get to where it's safe."

The friendly but embarrassed face he'd seen earlier poked into the opening of the overhang. "If it's unstable for me, it's unstable for all of us. I'll be careful." She smiled. "Hey, didn't I see you on horseback during the storm?"

"You did. Where's your trail buddy?"

She rolled her eyes. "He went on to try a morning ascent without me."

"Hopefully he was well above the slide, then."

She nodded. "He left hours ago. I'm sure he was."

Henry and Eddie had pushed up close behind Elvin. Eddie's hands were still bound behind him. Patrick made introductions.

Then Patrick eyed Alicia, thinking about their descent. With him and Ben carrying Elvin down the slide on the travois and Henry holding on to Eddie, an extra to their party would be a positive. "Do you shoot?"

She smiled at him. "I'm on leave from the Army. I work in munitions."

"That's music to my ears. Take this—" he handed her Eddie's revolver, "and keep it aimed at that guy." Patrick pointed at Eddie. "If he tries to make a run for it or goes after any of us, shoot him."

Her eyes widened. "What did he do?"

Patrick thought about Bruce. About Beartusk, the informant who he suspected Eddie had killed, or helped kill. About Eddie leaving Elvin for dead. About how he had turned on them and would have killed Patrick if Henry hadn't shown up. About the money and the mobsters, and how clear it was that Eddie's involvement was far from innocent. "It's a very long list. I'll tell you all about it on the way down."

CHAPTER FORTY-FIVE: FREE

Patrick

THE JUDGE CLEARED HIS THROAT. His voice was thready. His gray hair was unkempt, a far cry from the first time Patrick had seen him in the courtroom a few weeks before. He'd seemed younger then. This trial and Lamkin's escape had aged him. Patrick had felt younger then, too. So much had happened in such a short period of time. John's tragic death. The rescue at the plane crash. The rock-slide. And arriving home to find that his wife had chased a murderer across the state to take her friends' baby back. He was sure the judge had been having a rough time, but he'd put the Flints' week up against anyone's.

"Has the jury reached a verdict on sentencing?" the judge said.

The jury foreman—a thick-bodied woman in a worn sweater buttoned up to her chin—stood. "We have, Your Honor."

The long-legged bailiff took the verdict from the foreman and delivered it to the judge.

The judge read it and sent it back. "Go ahead and read it aloud, please, foreman."

The paper fluttered in the foreman's hand, but her voice was strong. "In the charge of murder in the first degree, we the jury sentence the defendant Barbara Lamkin to life in prison *without* possibility of parole."

Patrick squeezed Susanne's hand. A smattering of applause rang out from the gallery. The judge, who'd been a stickler for order throughout the trial, let it go. Patrick couldn't help checking Lamkin for her reaction. All he saw was the back of her platinum blonde head, but she seemed to be holding it high. She'd escaped the death penalty. After the jury's guilty verdict on Monday, death or life in prison had been the only options on the table.

"So say you all?" the judge said.

The jury answered as one. "Yes, Your Honor."

He nodded. "The defendant will serve her sentence in the Wyoming Women's Center in Evanston as soon as transport from county jail can be arranged. Bailiff, please escort the defendant from the courtroom." The bailiff ate up the space between him and Lamkin in three strides. He took her by the arm. The judge continued. "Jury, thank you for your service. Court is adjourned." He banged the gavel, stood, and exited the courtroom in a shuffle of black robes.

The bailiff hurried Lamkin through the defendant's door. She never looked back. To Patrick, the sentencing and her departure were so quick that they felt anticlimactic. But he'd take it.

Susanne exhaled, her shoulders rising and dropping. "It's finally over."

"I wish she'd gotten the death penalty." Perry hadn't gotten used to his missing tooth, and his speech was still strange and whistly. He'd have a long time to adjust. Their dentist had recommended waiting for Perry's mouth to mature before implanting a false tooth. Until then, the boy would make do with a retainer that had a false tooth attached, which wasn't ready yet.

Patrick closed his eyes for a second. Perry's injury resurrected the mountain in his mind. All that had led up to the rockslide. All that came after it. Getting off the mountain from Highland Park had been easier than getting up it, until they'd run into a literal logjam—a small mountain of downed timber erected by Henry, Ben, and George to slow the mobsters down in case they doubled back again. It had been there, as they removed the trees from the trail, that they'd encountered Search & Rescue en route. Henry had finally told Patrick everything that had happened. If Patrick could have grown wings and flown home to comfort his son and be with John's parents then, he would have. The many hours it had taken to finally get to them—even with George, Wes Braten, law enforcement, and ambulances waiting at Hazel Park to drive the group out—had nearly ripped his heart out. It was there they'd thanked Alicia for her kindness and generosity and bid her farewell. *Henry, George, Wes, Alicia.* Their very existence reminded Patrick that for every Herod, Lot, Jezebel, or Judas he met, the Good Samaritans outnumbered them a thousand or more to one.

Back at home, Patrick and Susanne worried night and day about their son. Perry's mood hadn't been exactly *black,* but it was definitely a dark gray. Loss was a hard, hard thing to come to grips with. John's parents were so shaken by their son's death that they'd declared their intention to move back east, away from the place that had robbed them of their boy. Patrick had wanted to try to convince them that mobsters from Chicago had been responsible, but, after years of delivering bad news to families, he understood grief couldn't be reasoned with. It just had to be endured. Perry wasn't immune to it. He had started threatening to drop out of football. Patrick and Susanne had persuaded him to hold off on a decision. The best way Patrick knew to honor the dead was to keep living, and they were determined to make sure Perry did that, with their help.

The living and the dead. Patrick's mind went briefly to the mysterious climber on the mountain. Two days after their return, he'd been drinking coffee on the deck and reading an article about their ordeal. It had laid out Black Tooth's deadly past and included a picture of Rocky Perritt, the Sheridan County deputy who'd fallen to his death less than two weeks before. Patrick had dropped his mug, scalding his leg. The man in the picture was the climber who'd helped Patrick find the easier trail, down to his Denver Broncos ball cap. There was no doubt in Patrick's mind. Patrick wouldn't have believed his eyes if it weren't for his past experiences, like the Shoshone man—seen separately by every member of the Flint family—who'd come to their aid in the Gros Ventre Wilderness.

Patrick had stared at the picture. *Thank you, God, for sending me a guardian angel.* If it hadn't been for Rocky, there wouldn't have been any way he could have gotten Elvin and the travois down the slope under fire from the mobsters. He smiled and looked up at the sky. Cerulean blue, without even a wisp of a cloud. For someone who didn't darken the doors of His church as often as He probably would have liked, Patrick got more than his fair share of help from the big guy up there.

His mind returned to the present. To Lamkin's sentence. To Perry's disappointment in it. To his rebellious daughter who hadn't said a word. He looked over at her. She hadn't really said much since the showdown she'd had with Susanne and him about her secret relationship with Ben. Wasn't it akin to the Stockholm Syndrome? He'd thought Brandon Lewis was bad, but Ben was even worse. How could a girl as smart as his daughter make such terrible choices about boys? True, Ben had shown incredible merit on the mountain. The boy had "try". Try, truthfulness, and honor. He deserved at least some of the credit for the multiple rescues. Could he be wrong about Ben? It wasn't something he was ready to think about just now. But their initial confrontation with Trish was nothing compared to the blowup they'd had after the school counselor called to get Patrick and Susanne's blessing to put Trish on an accelerated graduation program. *For no better reason than to follow Ben.* They'd said no, of course. And she hadn't spoken directly to them since.

It was a painful time for their whole family.

Patrick put a hand on his son's shoulder. He could empathize with Perry's desire to see Barb punished, although he had mixed feelings about the death penalty—the black and white he'd seen when he was younger was looking more and more like a million shades of gray. "Barb Lamkin is not our problem anymore. It'll be fine, Perry."

Patricia walked up to the family. She was leaving the next morning, and Patrick would miss her. With all the distractions, he felt like he'd hardly had a chance to reconnect with his baby sister. "Well, congratulations. I guess that's the right word for a situation like this? I don't know how you guys do it."

"Do what?" Patrick asked.

She made a two-hundred-and-seventy-degree gesture around her. "Wyoming. It's like the Wild West out here."

Before Patrick could defend his chosen home state, Max Alexandrov approached. The county attorney looked nervous. Patrick hadn't noticed him leaving the prosecutor's table. "Excuse me, Flints. A word?"

The defense attorney was with him, a young, earnest-faced guy named Stu Ryan. The two attorneys bid each other goodbye. Then Ryan turned to the Flints, his gaze direct. "I'm sorry for what your family had to endure. Congratulations on the sentence."

Patrick nodded, but his brows drew up. A defense attorney showing empathy for the victims. Would wonders never cease?

Ryan walked away.

Max bowed slightly to Patricia. "Ms. Sand."

Patricia looked like she was sucking a lemon. "Mr. Alexandrov."

"Please. Call me Max."

Patricia nodded but didn't respond in kind.

Patrick shook the prosecutor's hand. "No bad news, I hope?"

"Oh, no, no. I just wanted to tell you again how sorry we all are that Barbara escaped custody."

"And knew how to get into your house and take your truck," Patricia said, under her breath, but loud enough that the group all heard her.

Max's cheeks colored. "Yes. And that, too. We dated briefly, but it was a long time ago. She hoodwinked me."

"She hoodwinked a lot of us," Susanne said. "Me included."

A strangled sound escaped Trish's throat, but she kept her eyes down.

"And I'm sorry for what she put you all through as a result. Susanne, you have the county's undying gratitude."

Patrick put his arm around Susanne. He still shuddered when he thought about his unarmed wife going after Lamkin and the baby. And all the while suffering through a blinding migraine, no less. She was amazing. Always had been. The county was almost as lucky to have her as he was. He hated that she'd put herself at risk, but he wasn't the one to cast stones when it came to that.

"Thank you," she said.

Max rolled his lips. "Anyway, I thought I'd also let you know that Eddie will be charged with enough federal crimes to keep him behind bars the rest of his life."

"No surprise there," Patrick said. "The others got off too easy."

Orion, Luke, and Juice, whose real name, it turned out, was Giuseppe, had escaped punishment. Luke, dead from the shot George had taken in self-defense. Orion and Juice, buried in the rock-slide. Patrick hadn't, for once, put his own life on the line to try to dig them out. The Search & Rescue team had pinpointed their location later, but recovery of their bodies was deemed futile. Fragments of the plane and even paper scraps and a few intact bills of the money were recovered, however, in exactly the location Patrick had identified.

And, according to Elvin—who, minus one amputated foot, had been singing like a canary in exchange for a reduced sentence—it had been a lot of money. The second of two equal loads. One delivered the day before, successfully, and this one, which had ended so badly.

Nearly a million in cash per load, which jived with Patrick's estimate. More than enough to motivate the mobsters to hire George to lead their desperate attempt to get it and to try to silence the witnesses. Far more than Patrick would have ever believed could be generated from illegal activities on the reservation. *Goes to show what I know.*

Elvin had implicated Eddie in multiple crimes, like their money laundering agreement for the mob on the reservation. But instead of running the cash through legitimate enterprises, the two had expanded their illegal activities, milking wealthy clients they booked out of Jackson for high stakes poker games, poaching, drugs, and prostitution. Elvin was naming names, too. He pointed authorities to a secret ledger of clients to back up his claims. Indictments were being issued up and down the coast of California, as well as in Utah, Arizona, Nevada, Montana, and at home in Wyoming.

He also pointed the finger at Eddie for several murders, including Jimmy Beartusk, who'd ratted Eddie and Elvin out to the feds under threat of prosecution for a burglary he'd committed years before. Based on his information, the feds had set up roadblocks along the north, south, and east borders of the reservation, hoping to intercept the money and not knowing that Beartusk had broken down and admitted everything to his partners. Eddie and Elvin had hired a reservation pilot to transport the first load out of Dubois to the northwest, in order to avoid the dragnet the feds had set up. Beartusk met his end on takeoff. After the murder, the pilot had backed out and not been seen since. An investigation into his disappearance was pending, based on Elvin's claim that Eddie had killed him and hidden the body in a remote part of the reservation.

Cardinale had hired Bruce for the second load, and the rest was history that Patrick was all too painfully and personally familiar with.

Max's cheeks colored. "Also, I was hoping that Ms. Sand would allow me to take her to lunch."

Patricia looked as startled as if Max had just told her she'd won the Publisher's Clearinghouse Sweepstakes. "Why would I want to go to lunch with you?"

Patrick covered a smile with his fist.

Max laughed, an embarrassed sound. He looked at Patrick. "She doesn't pull any punches, does she?"

"Never," Patrick said, his voice dry.

Max straightened his shoulders. Patrick had never known him to be a man who faltered under pressure. "I didn't make a good first impression, but I promise, I'll try really hard to change it, if I could have the pleasure of your company."

Now it was Patricia's turn to blush. "I leave tomorrow."

"It's just lunch."

"Oh."

"But if it goes well, there's always dinner."

"Oooooh."

"Yes?"

She bit her lip, and the seconds ticked by. Then she nodded.

Max smiled. "Is it too soon to steal you away now?"

Patricia turned to Susanne and mouthed *oh my gosh* behind Max's back.

Susanne said, "Go on. We'll see you later."

"If you're sure," Patricia said.

"Go," Patrick and Susanne said at the same time.

The county attorney and his sister walked away together, and Patrick laughed. "Well, what do you know?"

"I know lunch sounds good," Susanne said. "I'm hungry, too."

Ronnie Harcourt was suddenly in their midst, little Will cradled against her shoulder. "Not to eavesdrop, but let Jeff and me take you to The Busy Bee. As a thank you for getting Will back for us."

Susanne put her hands to her cheeks. "Oh, Ronnie, I'm the one who lost him."

"Nonsense. He'd be in Canada now if it wasn't for you. I hear rumors that my boss is going to try to deputize you."

Perish the thought! Patrick said, "How about we meet you there in a few minutes?"

"Perfect. Jeff is out in the hall holding court with well-wishers. I'll let him know you said yes. We'll get a table." She sashayed away, cooing in Will's ear and smiling as people congratulated her. The adoption wouldn't be final for some time yet, but there was nothing standing in its way now.

Patrick couldn't be happier for the Harcourts, or for Will. *Barb Lamkin versus Ronnie and Jeff Harcourt?* The boy might never understand how lucky he was, but Patrick did.

"I don't want to go to lunch." Perry's tone and expression were flat.

Patrick hoped his son's recovery would be sooner rather than later. He knew Perry would never forget his friend or what had happened—Trish wouldn't either—but he was a strong kid, and he was loved. Patrick had seen that combination work miracles before in the wake of tragedy.

Trish crossed her arms. "Let me take the Suburban, and I'll drive him home."

Susanne and Patrick exchanged a look. *Can we trust her?* Susanne shrugged.

Patrick said, "I guess we could ask Jeff and Ronnie for a lift."

Susanne added, "And there's leftover fried chicken in the refrigerator."

She didn't mention the refrigerator lightly. She had given George another chance. How could she not after he'd saved the kids? He'd shown up early Monday morning and finished the job. Then he'd refused to accept payment for the work, but Patrick had slipped five twenties into the glove compartment of his truck. They'd owe that young man and Henry for the rest of their lives.

And Ben. They owed Ben. *But we don't owe him our daughter.*

"Thanks," Perry said.

Trish held out her hand.

"Straight home." Patrick tried to keep his voice light as he dropped the keys in her palm.

She closed her fingers in a fist, then nodded and wheeled away from him, Perry in her wake. The space they left felt hollow inside Patrick's chest.

Patrick and Susanne exited the courthouse onto the Main Street sidewalk. The mid-day sunlight shone brilliant and rich, like autumn instead of summer. He reached for Susanne's hand and held it across his chest to his heart. Patricia wasn't completely wrong with her wild west comment. Wyoming shouldn't bear the blame, but it was undisputed that they hadn't faced mayhem like this in Texas. This last year —in some ways it had been the best of times. Their beautiful surroundings, new friends, and dream house. In others, it had been the worst. But everyone's bad luck had to run out sometime. He felt sure theirs had run its course.

They strolled toward the restaurant hand in hand. It was a short walk. Through the front window, he saw Ronnie lift little Will's hand and wave it at them.

"Oh, thank God. We found you." Vangie's Tennessee drawl was unmistakable.

Patrick and Susanne turned toward their friend. Her face was drawn. She was clutching baby Hank to her with a death grip. He wriggled and looked disgruntled. Henry was a hundred feet away, back toward the courthouse, jogging to catch up.

"Vangie? Are you okay?" Susanne asked.

Patrick girded himself. Vangie was definitely not all right.

Henry arrived, slightly out of breath. "Vangie. Honey."

"I think you're making a mistake," Vangie said.

"About what?" Susanne asked.

But Patrick knew. He stiffened.

Vangie twisted back and forth, rocking Hank. "Ben. He's a good boy. He just needs people to give him a chance."

"I . . ." Susanne looked at Patrick, her eyes panicked. She had always hated confrontation.

Patrick stepped in. "He's a nice kid. He was great up on the mountain." He knew he sounded wishy-washy. He *felt* wishy-washy.

"Then why are you forbidding Trish from having anything to do with him?" Tears leaked from Vangie's eyes. She didn't bother to wipe them away.

"Their history . . . and she's so young . . . he's two years older." He felt strangled, like he had a golf ball jammed in his throat.

Vangie sputtered, her eyes angry and her lips unable to find words.

Henry said, "Now that we have Hank and Ben, we understand why parents have to be protective. But we've also learned that parents want the best for their kids. Ben has become like a son to us. He's proven himself to us. And he's talked to us. Told us things. What that boy has been through . . ." Tears came to his eyes, matching his wife's. Henry Sibley—tough cowboy, flinty rancher, the epitome of Wyoming manhood—crying. "And, well, he's broken up right now. This is a big setback for him. So, we wanted to look you in the eyes and tell you that we're vouching for him."

Patrick held up a hand. "This is nothing against you guys. This is about Trish making good choices."

"She's a smart girl."

"Thank you."

Vangie said, "She made some good choices with respect to Brandon Lewis, from what Susanne told me. Not letting him pressure her into a mistake. Staying away from him when he came back around after their break-up. We trust Hank in her care."

"About that." Susanne's voice shook. "With Ben out at the ranch, we don't think it's—"

Patrick took her hand again. "Give us a minute. This is a lot to think about, and we should talk as parents for a moment."

Susanne glared at him. Vangie shrugged. Henry nodded. Hank started squalling.

Patrick led his wife a few steps away toward Clear Creek. He gazed into her flashing eyes. He didn't blame her for being angry. He'd interrupted her. But something important had occurred to him.

"If your parents had forbid you to see me when you were sixteen, what would you have done?"

Susanne crossed her arms. It reminded him of their daughter. "This isn't about me."

"But, still."

She sighed. "I would have done it anyway. And I probably would have been more reckless."

"They didn't think much of me, back then." Patrick smiled.

"You weren't a kidnapper!"

"Let's assume for a moment that Ben was a victim of his father and uncle, too. Can you imagine that's possible?"

Lines appeared between her brows. "It's possible, but—"

"What if we allow them to see each other, but only when supervised until we get to know him ourselves? Henry and Vangie could help us keep them between the lines."

Suddenly, she smiled at him. "Patrick Flint, what has gotten into you? Have you forgotten she's your baby girl?"

A pang of sadness hit him. "She was. She's growing up fast."

Susanne slid her arms around his waist. "She still is, and she always will be."

Patrick felt a vibration in his lower lip. He bit down on it.

"It would be on a trial basis only, right?"

He lay his head against her hair as Main Street seemed to spin around them like a carousel, with the two of them riding double on a purple elephant, reaching for the brass ring that was just beyond their fingertips. Being a parent wasn't for wimps. This, all of this, was hard stuff. John's death and Perry's grief. Loosening the reins on their daughter to let her continue a relationship with a boy with a rocky past.

He said, "That's what I'm thinking. They might earn their way into more trust, but they might also blow it."

Susanne drew in a deep breath and pushed back from him. She nodded slowly. "I guess that would work."

"Let's go talk to the Sibleys, then."

"Wait." She caught his hand. "Everything's going to be okay, isn't it, Patrick?"

He willed his voice to convey confidence, even though their life in Wyoming had taught him that nothing was ever certain. "Of course it will be."

And it would. Because he believed in them. Together, they could do anything. She smiled at him, and they turned to face their friends.

***

Next up: There's more **Patrick Flint** and family coming in *Stag Party*. Get yours at https://www.amazon.com/dp/B08VD4G5H2. When a man who isn't who he claims to be befriends Patrick Flint and his son during a wilderness excursion with movers and shakers from across the globe, it puts the father-son duo dead in the bullseye of a murder target. To stop a gang of ruthless killers, the Flints must unriddle the mystery man's identity before the killers put a stop to them all.

Or you can adventure on in the *What Doesn't Kill You* mystery world:

Want to stay in **Wyoming**? Rock on with Maggie in ***Live Wire* on Amazon** (free in Kindle Unlimited) at https://www.amazon.com/dp/B07L5RYGHZ.

Prefer the **beginning** of it all? Start with Katie in *Saving Grace* on **Amazon** (free to Kindle Unlimited subscribers), here: https://www.amazon.com/Saving-Grace-Doesnt-Romantic-Mystery-ebook/dp/B009FZPMFO.

Or **get the complete WDKY series** here: https://www.amazon.com/gp/product/B07QQVNSPN.

***

And don't forget to snag the **free** *What Doesn't Kill You* **ebook starter library—including a Patrick Flint short story**—by joining Pamela's mailing list at https://www.subscribepage.com/PFHSuperstars.

For my aunts and uncles—Margaret, Bill, Paul, Susie, Patrice, James, Frank, and Janice—who have gone along with these books without complaint, even when their alter egos aren't always shown in their truest and best light. I keep reminding them their literary jobs are to push Patrick's and Susanne's buttons, which they do brilliantly! And don't worry, Frank and Janice, your turn will come soon. As always, for my true love and parenting partner, Eric. Our offspring seem to follow a three-fifths rule. Only three of the five can be happy at once. If at any time one moves from bad to good, it throws our familial world out of balance and requires another to slide toward the abyss. As Patrick would say, parenting ain't for sissies!

ACKNOWLEDGMENTS

When I got the call from my father that he had metastatic prostate cancer spread into his bones in nine locations, I was with a houseful of retreat guests in Wyoming while my parents (who normally summer in Wyoming) were in Texas. The guests were so kind and comforting to me, as was Eric, but there was only one place I wanted to be, and that was home. Not home where I grew up, because I lived in twelve places by the time I was twelve, and many thereafter. No, home is truly where the heart is. And that meant home for Eric and me would be with my parents.

I was in the middle of writing two novels at the time: *Blue Streak*, the first Laura mystery in the What Doesn't Kill You series, and *Polarity*, a series spin-off contemporary romance based on my love story with Eric. I put them both down. I needed to write, but not those books. They could wait. I needed to write through my emotions —because that's what writers do—with books spelling out the ending we were seeking for my dad's story. Allegorically and biographically, while fictionally.

So that is what I did, and Dr. Patrick Flint (aka Dr. Peter Fagan— my pops—in real life) and family were hatched, using actual stories from our lives in late 1970s Buffalo, Wyoming as the depth and backdrop to a new series of mysteries, starting with *Switchback* and moving on to *Snake Oil, Sawbones, Scapegoat,* and *Snaggle Tooth,* with more to come. I hope the real life versions of Patrick, Susanne, and Perry will forgive me for taking liberties in creating their fictional alter egos. I took care to make Trish the most annoying character since she's based on me, to soften the blow for the others. I am so hopeful that my loyal readers will enjoy them, too, even though in some ways the novels are a departure from my usual stories. But in many ways they are the same. Character-driven, edge-of-your-seat mysteries steeped in setting/culture, with a strong nod to the everyday magic around us, and filled with complex, authentic characters (including some AWESOME females).

I had a wonderful time writing these books, and it kept me going when it was tempting to fold in on myself and let stress eat me alive. For more stories behind the actual stories, visit my blog on my website: http://pamelafaganhutchins.com. And let me know if you liked the novels.

Thanks to my dad for advice on all things medical, wilderness, hunting, 1970s, aeronautical, and animal. I hope you had fun using your medical knowledge for murder!

Thanks to my mom for printing the manuscripts (over and over, in their entireties) as she and dad followed along daily on the progress.

Thanks to my husband, Eric, for brainstorming with and encouraging me and beta reading the *Patrick Flint* stories despite his busy work, travel, and workout schedule. And for moving in to my parents's barn apartment with me so I could be closer to them during this time.

Thanks to our five offspring. I love you guys more than anything, and each time I write a parent/child (birth, adopted, foster, or step), I channel you. I am so touched by how supportive you have been with Poppy, Gigi, Eric, and me.

To each and every blessed reader, I appreciate you more than I can say. It is the readers who move mountains for me, and for other authors, and I humbly ask for the honor of your honest reviews and recommendations.

Thanks mucho to Bobbye Marrs for the fantastic *Patrick Flint* covers.

Patrick Flint editing credits go to Rhonda Erb, Whitney Cox, and Karen Goodwin. The proofreaders who enthusiastically devote their time—gratis—to help us rid my books of flaws blow me away. Thank you all!

SkipJack Publishing now includes fantastic books by a cherry-picked bushel basket of mystery/thriller/suspense writers. If you write in this genre, visit http://SkipJackPublishing.com for submission guidelines. To check out our other authors and snag a bargain at the same time, download *Murder, They Wrote: Four SkipJack Mysteries*.

p.s. My dad is defying his diagnosis and doing fantastic now. It's my prayer we'll be collaborating on this series for many years to come.

BOOKS BY THE AUTHOR

Fiction from SkipJack Publishing

The *What Doesn't Kill You* Series

Act One (WDKY Ensemble Prequel Novella): Exclusive to Subscribers

Saving Grace (Katie #1)

Leaving Annalise (Katie #2)

Finding Harmony (Katie #3)

Heaven to Betsy (Emily #1)

Earth to Emily (Emily #2)

Hell to Pay (Emily #3)

Going for Kona (Michele #1)

Fighting for Anna (Michele #2)

Searching for Dime Box (Michele #3)

Buckle Bunny (Maggie Prequel Novella)

Shock Jock (Maggie Prequel Short Story)

Live Wire (Maggie #1)

Sick Puppy (Maggie #2)

Dead Pile (Maggie #3)

The Essential Guide to the What Doesn't Kill You Series

The *Ava Butler Trilogy*: A Sexy Spin-off From *What Doesn't Kill You*

Bombshell (Ava #1)

Stunner (Ava #2)

Knockout (Ava #3)

The Patrick Flint Series

Switchback (Patrick Flint #1)

Snake Oil (Patrick Flint #2)

Sawbones (Patrick Flint #3)

Scapegoat (Patrick Flint #4)

Snaggle Tooth (Patrick Flint #5)

Stag Party (Patrick Flint #6)

Spark (Patrick Flint 1.5): Exclusive to subscribers

The What Doesn't Kill You Box Sets Series (50% off individual title retail)

The Complete Katie Connell Trilogy

The Complete Emily Bernal Trilogy

The Complete Michele Lopez Hanson Trilogy

The Complete Maggie Killian Trilogy

The Complete Ava Butler Trilogy

The Patrick Flint Box Set Series

The Patrick Flint Series Books #1-3

Juvenile Fiction

Poppy Needs a Puppy (Poppy & Petey #1)

Nonfiction from SkipJack Publishing

The Clark Kent Chronicles

Hot Flashes and Half Ironmans

How to Screw Up Your Kids

How to Screw Up Your Marriage

Puppalicious and Beyond

What Kind of Loser Indie Publishes,

and How Can I Be One, Too?

Audio, e-book, and paperback versions of most titles available.

ABOUT THE AUTHOR

Pamela Fagan Hutchins is a *USA Today* best selling author. She writes award-winning romantic mystery/thriller/suspense from way up in the frozen north of Snowheresville, Wyoming, where she lives in an off-the-grid cabin on the face of the Bighorn Mountains. She is passionate about hiking/snow shoeing/cross country skiing with her hunky husband and pack of rescue dogs (and occasional rescue cat) and riding their gigantic horses.

If you'd like Pamela to speak to your book club, women's club, class, or writers group by streaming video or in person, shoot her an email. She's very likely to say yes.

You can connect with Pamela via her website
(http://pamelafaganhutchins.com)
or email (pamela@pamelafaganhutchins.com).

PRAISE FOR PAMELA FAGAN HUTCHINS

2018 USA Today Best Seller
2017 Silver Falchion Award, Best Mystery
2016 USA Best Book Award, Cross-Genre Fiction
2015 USA Best Book Award, Cross-Genre Fiction
2014 Amazon Breakthrough Novel Award Quarter-finalist,
Romance

The Patrick Flint Mysteries

"Best book I've read in a long time!" — Kiersten Marquet, author of
Reluctant Promises
"*Switchback* transports the reader deep into the mountains of
Wyoming for a thriller that has it all--wild animals, criminals, and one
family willing to do whatever is necessary to protect its own. Pamela
Fagan Hutchins writes with the authority of a woman who knows
this world. She weaves the story with both nail-biting suspense and a
healthy dose of humor. You won't want to miss *Switchback*." -
- Danielle Girard, *Wall Street Journal*-bestselling author of
White Out.
"*Switchback* by Pamela Fagan Hutchins has as many twists and turns
as a high-country trail. Every parent's nightmare is the loss or injury
of a child, and this powerful novel taps into that primal fear." -- Reavis
Z. Wortham, two time winner of The Spur and author of *Hawke's
Prey*
"*Switchback* starts at a gallop and had me holding on with both hands
until the riveting finish. This book is highly atmospheric and nearly
crackling with suspense. Highly recommend!" -- Libby Kirsch, Emmy
awardwinning reporter and author of the *Janet Black Mystery Series*

"A Bob Ross painting with Alfred Hitchcock hidden among the trees."
"Edge-of-your seat nail biter."
"Unexpected twists!"
"Wow! Wow! Highly entertaining!"
"A very exciting book (um... actually a nail-biter), soooo beautifully descriptive, with an underlying story of human connection and family. It's full of action. I was so scared and so mad and so relieved... sometimes all at once!"
"Well drawn characters, great scenery, and a kept-me-on-the-edge-of-my-seat story!"
"Absolutely unputdownable wonder of a story."
"Must read!"
"Gripping story. Looking for book two!"
"Intense!"
"Amazing and well-written read."
"Read it in one fell swoop. I could not put it down."

What Doesn't Kill You: Katie Connell Romantic Mysteries

"An exciting tale . . . twisting investigative and legal subplots . . . a character seeking redemption . . . an exhilarating mystery with a touch of voodoo." — *Midwest Book Review Bookwatch*
"A lively romantic mystery." — *Kirkus Reviews*
"A riveting drama . . . exciting read, highly recommended." — *Small Press Bookwatch*
"Katie is the first character I have absolutely fallen in love with since Stephanie Plum!" — *Stephanie Swindell, Bookstore Owner*
"Engaging storyline . . . taut suspense." — *MBR Bookwatch*

What Doesn't Kill You: Emily Bernal Romantic Mysteries

"Fair warning: clear your calendar before you pick it up because you won't be able to put it down." — *Ken Oder, author of* Old Wounds to the Heart

"Full of heart, humor, vivid characters, and suspense. Hutchins has done it again!" — *Gay Yellen, author of* The Body Business

"Hutchins is a master of tension." — *R.L. Nolen, author of* Deadly Thyme

"Intriguing mystery . . . captivating romance." — *Patricia Flaherty Pagan, author of* Trail Ways Pilgrims

"Everything about it shines: the plot, the characters and the writing. Readers are in for a real treat with this story." — *Marcy McKay, author of* Pennies from Burger Heaven

What Doesn't Kill You: Michele Lopez Hanson Romantic Mysteries

"Immediately hooked." — *Terry Sykes-Bradshaw, author of* Sibling Revelry

"Spellbinding." — *Jo Bryan, Dry Creek Book Club*

"Fast-paced mystery." — *Deb Krenzer, Book Reviewer*

"Can't put it down." — *Cathy Bader, Reader*

What Doesn't Kill You: Ava Butler Romantic Mysteries

"Just when I think I couldn't love another Pamela Fagan Hutchins novel more, along comes Ava." — *Marcy McKay, author of* Stars Among the Dead

"Ava personifies bombshell in every sense of word. — *Tara Scheyer, Grammy-nominated musician, Long-Distance Sisters Book Club*

"Entertaining, complex, and thought-provoking." — *Ginger Copeland, power reader*

What Doesn't Kill You: Maggie Killian Romantic Mysteries

"Maggie's gonna break your heart–one way or another." *Tara Scheyer, Grammy-nominated musician, Long-Distance Sisters Book Club*
"Pamela Fagan Hutchins nails that Wyoming scenery and captures the atmosphere of the people there." *— Ken Oder, author of* Old Wounds to the Heart
"I thought I had it all figured out a time or two, but she kept me wondering right to the end." *— Ginger Copeland, power reader*

OTHER BOOKS FROM
SKIPJACK PUBLISHING

Murder, They Wrote: Four SkipJack Mysteries,
by Ken Oder, R.L. Nolen, Marcy McKay, and Gay Yellen

The Closing, by Ken Oder
Old Wounds to the Heart, by Ken Oder
The Judas Murders, by Ken Oder
The Princess of Sugar Valley, by Ken Oder
Keeping the Promise, by Ken Oder

Pennies from Burger Heaven, by Marcy McKay
Stars Among the Dead, by Marcy McKay
The Moon Rises at Dawn, by Marcy McKay
Bones and Lies Between Us, by Marcy McKay
When Life Feels Like a House Fire, by Marcy McKay

Deadly Thyme, by R. L. Nolen
The Dry, by Rebecca Nolen

Tides of Possibility, edited by K.J. Russell
Tides of Impossibility, edited by K.J. Russell and C. Stuart Hardwick

My Dream of Freedom: From Holocaust to My Beloved America,
by Helen Colin

FOREWORD

Snaggle Tooth is a work of fiction. Period. Any resemblance to actual persons, places, things, or events is just a lucky coincidence. And I reserve the right to forego accuracy in favor of a good story, any time I get the chance.

Made in the USA
Las Vegas, NV
07 July 2021

26071443R00174